Heartbeats

Salty Dog Press acknowledges the traditional owners of the country in which we live and work. We pay our respects to all Aboriginal and Torres Strait Islander Elders, past and present.

First published 2025 by Salty Dog Press
Copyright © Paulene Turner 2025
Text Design by Karen V. Scott

ISBN: 978-0-6457309-2-0

Heartbeats

PAULENE TURNER

Salty Dog Press

ALSO BY PAULENE TURNER

THE TIME TRAVEL CHRONICLES
Secrets of the Nile
Revenge of the Black Knight
Shoot-out at Death Canyon
Black Tides
Samurai Steal
Point of Origin

For those who believe in love, an ungovernable force
for which we yearn from our first breath to our last.

Author's Forward

Heartbeats is a collection of short stories in a variety of genres, linked by sub-plots of love. I'm not a big fan of romance stories *per se*. But when a tale is about something else and romance is an extra, I'm all in. Most stories are more compelling with a little bit of love, don't you think?

This volume includes science fiction, fantasy, hard-boiled detective, historical fiction, fairytale, spy, ghost, time travel, rom-com and drama stories. Most were written as competition entries for NYC Midnight writing challenges, which pit writers from all over the world against each other in heats of about 25-35. At midnight, New York time, we all receive an email containing a genre the piece must be written in and two prompts to be included. Plus, a hard deadline for submitting the story for judging. Being forced to write stories in many of these genres pushed me outside my comfort zone. And there was always one prompt that was impossible to include without some kind of major story switchback. However, I was often pleasantly surprised by what I ended up with.

I entered both the NYC Midnight short story (2,500 words) and flash fiction (1,000 words) challenges. The former is more my style as I'm a sprawling storyteller. Trying to fit all my thoughts into 1,000 words feels a bit like the ugly sister in *Cinderella* trying to squeeze her big foot into a tiny glass slipper.

The first round of the NYC Midnight Short Story Challenge gives you eight days to complete your piece. It's eight days of grimacing each time you remember what you signed up for, waking with a knot of dread in your gut and—at least several times a day—declaring loudly to anyone who'll listen, that you've run out of ideas and *can't write anymore*!!! The last few days I scramble to write something—*anything*. Along with 4,000 other writers, I usually submit a few minutes before the deadline.

And, yes, every minute in the challenge is torture. Like holding a blow-torch to your creativity and ego.

But if you end up with something you love—and I think I speak for all writers here—the feeling is *unbelievable*. Creating something from nothing is a major high. It's why we write! We're all addicts, junkies, going after that feeling. Like Gollum with his ring, we love and hate the creative process. It makes you doubt every part of yourself. You immerse yourself in another character's skin and try to imagine, in a visceral way, how they feel, what they would do. You struggle to come up with all the story details and make it mean something.

The best thing about the competition is that it forces you to create material you can polish and expand upon later.

I started both *The Bodyguard* and *Soul Mate* for the short story challenge but abandoned them when I realised they wouldn't fit the word length. Once the deadline had passed, I went to work on them, giving them whatever space they needed.

The novella *The Woman Who Fell to Earth* came out of a discussion in my Spanish language class. We were learning conditional tense and the teacher posed a question: "If you had your time again, is there anything you would do differently?" As a time travel writer (I have written a six-book series called *The Time Travel Chronicles*), my mind flew to regret and time travel as I imagined someone going back in time to attempt to change something in their life—but it not working out quite as they'd planned.

The Mysterious Smile sprang from something I had long wondered about: how did Leonardo da Vinci come up with those brilliant ahead-of-his-time ideas?

And I wrote my novella *Too Many Sherlocks* as a submission for an Australian publisher who wanted "a Sherlock Holmes story where the great detective is missing."

In this volume, I have listed the genre and prompts I had to use in case you're interested, though in some rewrites (such as in *I, Spy*), I dropped a prompt that didn't fit the new, expanded version.

Here's the thing you need to know about writers. If you give us no boundaries—"Write whatever you want at any length!"—most of us will struggle to produce anything at all. It's only when those parameters are narrowed with a hard deadline—like a dare to our writer's ego—that our lizard brains get to work.

I hope you enjoy these varied tales which have one thing in common—thrumming heartbeats of love. Some are about the first sparks of a new love. Some about lost connections, hearts broken.

Love evokes images of soft, sweet things—heart-shaped chocolates, fields of flowers, hazy summer light—but there's nothing soft about it. It's an ungovernable force of nature which bestows boundless energy and drive upon those in its grip. The object of your love colonises your mind, floods your heart with a tsunami of feeling. It's a kind of divine madness. Utterly awesome when it works out.

But when it doesn't…?

Love is not for the faint-hearted; it takes courage. After all, isn't it the ultimate risk? You lay your soul bare to someone, hoping they'll love you back, handing them the power to break your heart.

Still…without love, what's the point of anything?

Contents

Soul Mate

GENRE: GHOST

PROMPTS: A COMMUNITY, A LANDLADY

♡

When death arrives, most souls go straight up or down to their final destination. But some linger in between until those who love them, still among the living, are ready to let them go.

Death was not quite how I imagined it would be.

As a life-long atheist, I'd pictured instant oblivion—a never-ending sleep with no consciousness of anything on earth or in Heaven. Not this.

"Breakfast!" My landlady's shouts rocket me awake. "Come and get it! And don't come moanin' and hauntin' me with your grumbling belly if you miss out!"

I climb out of bed in my private room in this two-storey mint-green house full of old-world charm and ghosts. Located in a northern suburb of Sydney, Australia, the house looks like any other on the street. Only the uncut grass (ghosts don't do lawns!), surfeit of spiders' webs and strange percussive sounds emanating from the upper rooms at night give any clue that the house is haunted. We never stay too long in one place. Last month, we haunted an abandoned house near Reykjavik, Iceland, with views of blue ice and grey whales.

1

My room is simple—bed, mirror, sink, old-fashioned trunk and use of a shared bathroom (which cleans itself—a heavenly touch). It's for short stays. Longer-term guests have bigger spaces, sumptuous sofas, waterfall taps. How do we all fit into an ordinary suburban house? It seems ghosts take up whatever space they need in some kind of Tardis-like afterlife magic, as far as I can figure.

All the guests here are In-betweeners—souls suspended somewhere between life and the afterlife. In our backyard are two wooden doors—one dark-toned, one light. We'll all pass through one of these before our journey is done. Which door and when? That is the question.

But we can't go through either until those who love us, still among the living, are prepared to let us go.

"Mornin' Emma!" says the landlady, Maz—short for Marilyn. "A great day to be not-quite-dead, ain't it."

"Sure is."

The sky is blue. There's a hint of jasmine on the breeze. Rainbow lorikeets flit around the branches of a tree outside my window. *Not so bad.*

I arrived in this realm one night after a long week of work when I fell asleep at the wheel of my car and ploughed head-on into a truck.

Emma Boyd. Loving daughter of Charles and Lena Boyd. Treasured fiancée to Harrison Gallagher. Taken too soon, the headstone said.

Time is fuzzy here, but I'd guess that was around six months ago. Since then, I've become part of this community of souls in a halfway house between life and death, awaiting eternal placement through one door...or the other.

"You look a little pale today, Hon." Maz peers at my face. "You feelin' okay?"

"Fine!" I say.

"Well, enjoy the day as if it was your last. Because one day..."

We say it together: "...it will be!"

Maz winks and clicks her tongue, tucking a strand of wavy blonde hair beneath her sailor's cap.

Breakfast is the usual crazy buffet. The rock stars—and there's a lot of them here—start with vodka and orange, followed by rocky road chocolate smothered with marshmallows and Turkish delight. Elvis breakfasts on lobster thermidor and chips the size of doorstops. David Bowie has cappuccino and Italian donuts.

Movie stars generally eat leaner. Humphrey Bogart has ham and eggs; Lauren Bacall, watercress soup. Many of the starlets I recognise from old films stick with black coffee—more from habit than concern about their weight. Everyone in this place stays looking the way they did at their best during the living years.

Shakespeare nibbles an apple as he works on a new play, his quill tucked behind his ear. He calls Maz over to read lines whenever he wants to hear how they flow.

It's a lively, loud community with music, monologues and mania. New people come and go all the time. Few politicians or lawyers spend much time here—some people are easier to let go of than others. But famous actors and musicians, still held close in many living hearts, stick around much longer. Some may never leave.

"Saved you a seat!" Franklin Kent, my halfway house friend, sits at the quieter end of the table. A rock star in the sixties, with twilight blue eyes, and dark hair, shiny as a shampoo ad, Franklin had one song that was a *very* big hit. After that he slipped into obscurity and eventually died, penniless, in a condemned building in his fifties. He played his hit song for me once…*meh!* Still, someone obviously liked it enough to keep him here all this time.

"So, what shall we do today?" Franky asks. "Feel like spooking a few churches, give the old pastors a thrill? Or shall we visit our enemies, whisper sour nothings in their ears and make them spill their cappuccinos?"

He grins and a dimple appears in his right cheek, giving me a hint of why teenage girls and guys used to weep and faint at his concerts.

"Any of your enemies still above ground must surely be in nursing homes," I say, "and we ought to leave the poor blighters alone. Anyway, shouldn't we be thinking of good deeds to raise our profile with—" I point upwards "—and move us closer to the right door?"

"Ah, but which door is the right one?" Franky whispers. "Not sure any of these rock stars will think an eternity of harp music such a great prospect."

"You two behave now, won't you?" Maz winks as we get up to go. "Never know who's watching!"

"Marilyn dear! I nee-eed you!" Shakespeare trills.

"Coming, Will!" Maz shrugs. "For my sins!" She heads over to confer with the Bard.

As I raise my hand in farewell, Franky grabs my arm and holds it up to the light, his expression grim. He doesn't need to say it. My arm, my whole body, is more transparent today than it was yesterday. We both know what that means.

My fiancé, Harrison, is preparing to move on.

"I really thought he loved me," I shout to Franky as we float above the high-rise buildings and stunning harbour of Sydney.

"He did. He does," Franky insists. "This doesn't mean he's forgotten you. You're still in his heart."

"It's that woman he met at the client party. I knew it! Cheating bastard."

"Shhhh!" Franky points upwards in warning.

"I don't care who hears!" I shout as I dive head-first between the office buildings and begin swooping in and out of the city traffic. The cool wind feels good on my face. A car's brakes screech behind me; one of the more ghost-aware drivers has detected my presence. I look back and see Franky shaking his head in disapproval.

"I would never have let him go so quickly," I yell over the traffic noise.

"And that would be good, how?" Franky demands, catching up. "Do you want to stay in the halfway house forever?"

Franky grips my hand and drags me through the maze of city streets to a park overlooking Sydney Harbour and the Opera House, where he deposits me on the grass.

"It's all right for you," I say. "You sing one song in your twenties and people love you eternally. You get heaps of time to build up your good-will points."

"Maybe." Franky leans back, head on his hands. "But I was a rock star. Lots of drugs and meaningless sex. I have a lot of catching up to do."

I huff and lop off the head of a purple agapanthus flower nearby.

Because I can. Franky taught me how to "contact" earthly things. And I'm getting quite good at it. Though, strictly speaking, we're not supposed to touch anything outside the house.

"And the fans don't 'love' me the way Harrison loves you," he says. "They don't know me. If they did know the *real* me…well, I would have shot through the doorway to the dark place decades ago."

Unable to stay still, I levitate and drift about, eavesdropping on earthly conversations. A mum playing *I Spy* with her kid. A man getting heated on a business call. I catch a snippet of romance by the pond.

"I adore you," a chunky man in his twenties tells a woman, stroking her dark hair. They drift forward to kiss but I zoom between them, screeching: "He says that now! But as soon as another hot girl or guy comes along, he'll forget all about you!"

The lovers rear back in confusion. "Your lips are ice cold," the woman says, touching her mouth.

"Oh, for Heaven's sake!!" Franky seizes my arm and hauls me into the clouds, so fast, I think I might throw up. Given I don't have any stomach contents, that would be quite an achievement.

"Don't throw away points like that, Emma! You're acting like a spoilt child!"

I pout and try to pull away, but he keeps hold of me as we float back to the ground, to an empty bus stop I know well—because it was the one nearest the apartment where I lived with Harrison.

"Why don't we go see your fiancé," Franky says. "Find out what's happening."

"Good idea."

"But you have to stay calm. Promise?"

"Promise."

Moonlight spills through partly open blinds revealing a modern apartment with a plethora of framed pictures of Harrison and me. One picture, I note, is slightly askew. I use my "contact" skills to fix it.

"What are you doing?" Franky whispers.

"Just tidying up. Why are we whispering?"

A male voice echoes along the hallway. Like seaweed on a stream, we drift through the air into Harrison's bedroom. He's on his usual side of the bed, in a circle of lamplight as he talks on the phone.

"All right, just a couple of drinks then. Marble Bar, six o'clock? Okay. I'm looking forward to it, too."

As he hangs up, he has this self-satisfied look on his face. I catch a glimpse of a woman's picture on the phone screen. Too smiley. Too pretty. *Too alive.*

"CHEATER!" I hurl at him.

Harrison gasps and looks around, holding his breath as his eyeballs swivel in their sockets.

"Did he hear me?" I whisper.

Franky signals that I should follow him out and back to the living room.

"He can sense you," he says. "When you've had a strong connection during life, there is sometimes a lingering intra-dimensional awareness."

"Did you see his face when he was talking to *her*?" I study my arm in the darkness. "I feel more like the invisible woman every second."

"Don't you want him to move on, Emma? Have a life, some happiness, while he's still among the living?"

"Yes, of course, but—" I sigh as I try to order my thoughts "—I just thought it would last longer…the love we had. I still feel it. Why doesn't he?"

Franky presses his lips together but stays quiet.

"I guess I'm not ready to let him go," I admit.

Franky nods, sadly, before exiting through the brick wall—*which still freaks me out.* I do the same and we drift through the air, like two clouds, surfing the breeze.

"They're meeting at the Marble Bar," I say. "I know where that is."

Franky's dark brows form a tight line. "Not a good idea, Emm."

"Neither was driving home when I was so tired after that monster week at work. But I did it anyway. Because I wanted to see Him. Harrison. The love of my life."

I died for him. I figure he owes me a smidge more than six months of grieving.

The next night, Franky accompanies me to witness Harrison's first date since my death. Despite my strong suggestions that "I'll be fine on my own!" and attempts to give him the slip on the way there, Franky's hell-bent on keeping watch over me.

It's Friday evening and the Marble Bar is buzzing with city workers celebrating the end of the business week. Men in suits and women in skirts and high heels slurp down alcohol in the dazzling rococo room—all marble and gold with leadlights in the ceiling. I double take when I get my first glimpse in a mirror behind the bar and see everything in the room perfectly reflected back, except Franky and me.

"Yeah, a bit weird, that," Franky says, noting my expression. "Not sure I'll ever get used to it."

Harrison's already perched on a barstool. It was always his habit to arrive early; he never wanted anyone to be uncomfortable, wondering if he'd show. He's nervous, slurping his beer and trying to read the news on his phone as his gaze ricochets back to the entry. Looking for *Her.*

And, suddenly, she's right there, in front of him. He gives her a way too big smile—revealing, at least to me, that he's nervous. His uneasiness doesn't recede when she sits down.

"Well, this is awkward," Franky says, watching the pair make stilted small talk. Harrison's hands can't settle. He's probably craving a cigarette to make himself appear more at ease, though he gave up smoking years ago.

"I can't watch this," Franky says. "I think I'll give them some space. Over there. Wanna join?"

"No, I'm good."

Floating through the crowd—and I do mean *through* the crowd—Franky leans on the bar next to a stunning redhead sitting alone. She's not young—late thirties or early forties is my guess. But she definitely has something. Guts to come on her own, for one. And a style born of confidence. *Is that Franky's type?*

He moves behind her and gently blows on her neck. The few strands of hair that have escaped her stylish chignon dance about. Patting them down, the woman glances around suspiciously.

Franky leans on his elbow, making gooey eyes at her. "Where have you been all my life? And Death," he says.

"Wow, that line is so old...almost as old as you," I call out.

Franky scratches his cheek, middle finger up, for my benefit.

"Okay, then," he begins again. "How about, what's a nice girl like you doing in a—" he stops, looks around, frowns "—what am I saying? This is a nice place. You definitely fit in here."

"But who let you in?" I shout. From this angle, Franky's eyes are full of reflected light. They seem so alive, it's hard to believe he's not.

"I'm glad you came out tonight." Words from Harrison's date—*Brittany*—call me back to the reason I'm here.

"I'm glad I came, too," Harrison replies. *Lame, lame.* I almost want to coach him to a better response.

"I didn't think you would." Brittany sips her Kir Royale, a sparkling red concoction in a champagne glass.

"Well, it's just a couple of drinks."

From the tight smile Brittany gives, I see she's disappointed. She was hoping for more. I smell her perfume—too much—and note her perfect nails and makeup. I'm betting she's wearing shapewear to hold her stomach flat, too. She's gone all out tonight. Like a fisherman who preps his boat and supplies carefully before going after a big catch. She's a predator, I decide. *Not right for him.*

Harrison keeps looking around, brow creased, as if he senses me here.

"Are you expecting someone?" Brittany asks.

"No."

"Step back," Franky shouts. "Give him some room."

I take a small step away and give my friend my innocent-not innocent smile in response. He shakes his head slowly in warning.

After the first glass, things loosen up between Harrison and Brittany. They manage to have an animated conversation about holidays. When she says she'd like to go to Croatia, he freezes.

"Have you been there?" she asks.

"Yeah," he says. *With me.* "It's lovely." *We had one of our best holidays there.* Brittany waits for him to say more, but the conversation stops cold.

Meanwhile, Franky is reading the phone screen over the redhead's shoulder, his hand resting on her arm. Almost as if she detects something, she puts her hand over his. The two of them look quite cosy together.

"Back off, Romeo!" I call out.

He winks and continues to read. *Which I find unaccountably irritating.*

My ghostly hackles rise further as Brittany raises the subject of Harrison "losing someone close." He stares fixedly into his glass, a muscle twitching along on his jawline as he clenches his teeth.

"I'd rather not talk about it, if that's okay?" he says.

"Sure, no worries."

I almost feel sorry for her. Until I realise that I've now been dispensed with as a topic. Forgotten. The mood eases between them, their unspoken agreement that there'll be no more talk of the dead; time to focus on the living.

"What do you say, we leave them to it?" Franky is back at my shoulder.

"Not yet."

I watch Brittany laughing, with her perfect teeth, and wonder how many sets of braces it took to get them looking that good.

"You thirsty?" I ask Franky. "Because I am."

Brittany has a fresh glass and I really fancy a taste. (For some reason, we only have beer and whisky at the halfway house.) I position my face over her glass and look up at Franky, who watches darkly. Then I use all my ghostly focus and contact powers to slurp up a huge sip. I drain a third of the glass in one sip, too fast—some of it goes up my nose. I giggle and wipe it away.

"That's funny," Brittany says, looking at her drink. "I could have sworn I had a full glass."

That makes me laugh even harder. Franky doesn't seem amused. Not then. Nor when I wave my arm, the way he taught me, and knock her drink all over her.

"What the—?" Brittany looks around for someone to blame, but no-one's there. "I'm not sure how that happened..." She wipes drink from her clothes. "I'll be back." She hurries to the bathroom.

"What did that achieve?" Franky folds his arms, annoyed.

"It made me feel good."

"What about Harrison? Does he feel good?"

My fiancé appears less than relaxed as he takes up his phone and looks at a picture of the two us together.

"Yes!" I fist-pump the air. "He still wants me!"

He looks at a few more pics, then puts the phone down and glances towards the bathroom.

"Don't stop! There's more!" I shout at him. "What about the Croatian pics? Why don't you check them out?"

I hold my arm up to the light. It's fainter than before.

"I guess the date's going better than I thought," I say. "What do I do?"

"I could boost up his memories of you," Franky says. "That will give you a little more time to get your head around this."

"Really?" I nod, giving him permission.

Franky stands in front of Harrison, closes his eyes, takes a breath and gently exhales. Eventually, he's expelling grey smoke, which envelops Harrison completely. When the mist clears, Harrison rubs his eyes and picks up the phone, scrolling in earnest through pictures of the two of us. But they don't make him happy. He seems more disturbed than ever. Breathing heavily, he glances towards the restrooms and leaves.

I'm shocked. *He'd never leave anyone hanging like that!* I'm not sure how I feel about it.

When Brittany returns, she finds his empty seat and a fifty-dollar bill on the bar for drinks.

"Fuck!" she says. Which makes me smile.

"Our work here is done."

The next morning, I'm whole again. As solid as the rock stars howling into their mugs and drumming on the breakfast setting.

"Morning, Honey," says Maz. "Another beautiful day to be halfway."

"Sure is!"

Hungrier than usual, I order eggs and toast. It's delicious. Even the usual morning racket today seems amusing when I'm usually tearing my hair out by now.

Franky seems quiet. "Good to have you back," he whispers.

"Good to be back," I say. "She wasn't right for him."

"Probably not," Franky agrees. "But I guess we'll never know now, will we?"

I ask him what he did last night to boost up Harrison's memories of me. At first, he doesn't want to tell me, but I keep on at him. I'm no quitter.

"I just shared some images of you with him," he says. "The way your hair looks with a backdrop of stars. How your eyes swirl like the Milky Way when you're happy. How your laughter sounds like the cascade of coins into a poker machine tray when you've had a big win."

"Oh, right."

I'm a ghost, but I still feel kind of chilly at the moment.

"You know," he adds, "soppy stuff to stimulate the romantic memories."

Soppy stuff? I nod.

"Franky, Emm, want a part in a play?" Maz calls out. Shakespeare is coaching Maz in a monologue from his new work (with a woman in the lead).

"We don't want to show you up," Franky says.

"In your dreams." Maz winks.

"Marilyn, focus," says Shakespeare. "Now, in this scene, the woman is fighting the whole patriarchy. But does she back down? No. She's prepared to die for the principles she believes in."

Wow! I have goosebumps…which, for a ghost, is really something!

"You know in the time when I was popular—" Franky begins.

"For five minutes—" I clarify.

"Well, in those *five minutes,* a famous director asked me to play Romeo in a film."

"You? Romeo?"

"Yeah. But I was such an arrogant prat, I didn't even show up for the audition."

Franky as Romeo? He certainly had the look, or so his fans would say.

"Shall we look in on Harrison, this evening?" he asks.

"Yeah."

As night descends, we return to the flat. Harrison's sitting up at the breakfast bar, scrolling through pictures of us. He must have started straight after work because he's still in his suit, though he's thrown his tie on the floor. *I hated him doing that.*

He looks perturbed as he scrolls but stops and smiles at an image of us swimming in the clear Adriatic Sea. I bet he's remembering the funny little man who insisted on taking our photo that day. The guy was so old and quirky, it was hard to believe he'd ever seen a mobile phone, much less knew how to use one. But he took heaps of shots and they turned out to be some of the best of the holiday. Harrison and I both chuckle at the same time.

"I'll wait outside," says Franky, "give you two some privacy."

My fiancé tenses and looks around the room, as if he's heard something.

"Why did you leave me?" he whispers.

"I didn't want to," I say. "I still don't."

He gulps down the rest of his wine and refills the glass with the little that's left in the bottle. "Why?" he says more loudly. Demanding an answer.

For a moment the barrier between our worlds feels gossamer thin. He fixes his intense gaze on me, as if he sees me there.

"There's no answer! There's no reason. It just happened," I say.

"There has to be an answer!" he shouts.

The *ting* of an incoming phone message breaks the spell. He snaps the phone up. It's from Brittany.

-Just checking you're okay?

-Sorry about last night, he types.

-Was it something I said?

-No. I had an emergency.

-What emergency?

He flings the phone onto the sofa and gulps down more wine. Then starts to open another bottle.

"Haven't you had enough?" I say.

He turns to me. "Don't you start! I'm just getting started!"

There's no talking to him when he's like this. His sweet, easy-going nature turns sour and incendiary.

I can't watch this.

I head back out through the wall and find Franky waiting at the edge of the bay. The water is still tonight. And really dark. *Is it that dark behind the second door?*

"Thought you'd be a while longer," he says.

"I'll go back when he's run out of wine."

Franky raises his eyebrow and nods.

"She texted him," I say.

"Really? Few choice words, I imagine, for standing her up?"

"No, she seemed quite calm." *Calmer than I would have been.*

"We might need to boost up his memories of you again," says Franky. "But it works best if he's asleep, so…shall we come back later?"

"Okay."

Will we have to do this every night? I wonder. To stop me winking out like a burnt-out star.

"And in the meantime…!" Franky grins mischievously and shoots off, a silver streak against the liquorice sky. I follow.

He heads towards the city at speed, making his way to the busy bars around Circular Quay.

"What are we—?"

Diving down to ground level, he zooms right through a group of drunken men in suits, before flying up again, clutching a wallet.

"You picked someone's pocket?"

Franky grabs a wad of cash, then drops the wallet. The guys below snatch it up. "Steve, found your wallet!"

"What do you want money for? We can't spend it!" I say.

"We can't, but…"

Franky's off again. I follow him to a city park where a homeless woman is bunking down on a bench, surrounded by plastic bags.

"Hey!" he calls, letting a couple of large notes flutter down like snowflakes to land at her feet. She picks up the money, looks up and smiles.

"Can she see us?"

He just keeps flying. I try to keep up.

It's a wild night. We make more "magic" money drops at several places. When he sees a man sitting alone on a bench, he swoops down and sits beside him. Just sits, sharing the silence. It's weird, but, somehow, I can sense the guy's sadness ebbing. "Is that you, Evelyn?" The man strains to see through the air.

We fly over the city, observing life beneath us. A small girl points upwards. "Look, Mummy, those people are flying."

"Kids and dogs can sense things others don't," Franky says. "Want an ice cream?"

At a late-night stall, a buyer reaches for a pink cone, but Franky whips it out of his grasp. The man and the seller look up. "Wow! Did you see that! The wind just took it!"

"Must be some strong updraft!"

Franky lets some cash drop. The seller catches it. "The wind taketh and it giveth too!"

I can't stop laughing. This is the most fun I've had since ...*ever*.

"Isn't haunting meant to be scary?" I splutter.

"Depends on the ghost."

We fly down to a party on a boat on Sydney Harbour and bop away to some wild music. As Franky sings along with a song, I wince. "And you used to be a pop star?" I shake my head. "I guess it was the sixties!"

"Come here, you!"

He chases me around the deck. I laugh and whoop and somehow manage to knock a pink cocktail off a tray. The waiter looks around, spooked, as he tries to figure out how that happened.

"Oops!" I say.

"Wanna have some real fun?" Franky asks, darting off before I answer. We head out to the Sydney casino, making straight for a busy roulette table.

Franky goes round the table, studying each player. "Who do you like?"

"What do you mean? Who do I think will win?"

"No, who do you like?"

I pick a middle-aged guy, down on his luck. He places his last chip on the number seven.

"Watch this," says Franky. The silver ball rolls around and stops and Franky snatches it up and moves it to number seven.

"Yes!" The man goes wild as chips pile up in front of him. "Let it ride! I'm feeling lucky tonight!"

We both shake our heads but don't wait to see what happens.

"Not sure you did that guy a favour," I say as we fly back over the harbour.

"Harrison's probably sleeping now," Franky says. "We can do the smoke if you like."

Harrison? I'd almost forgotten about him.

"Let's go."

We fly across the Sydney Harbour Bridge. From up above, the rows of cars resemble a motherboard, with colourful pieces fitted together on a metal grid. Then we head west.

Passing through the warm brick walls of Harrison's flat, we find my fiancé face down on the floor, whimpering. His glass of red wine has spilt and soaked into the pale carpet. Images of us are playing on a slideshow on his TV screen.

Franky and I sit on the sofa and watch the moments of our lives scroll by. Of Harrison and me on holidays. At my birthday party with friends. Celebrating after he'd won a big case. On a weekend in the Hunter Valley vineyards where we first said the "L" word to each other.

"You had fun together," says Franky. "I never had anyone special like that. I was too cool for just one person. Had to spread the love." The words don't go with his tone of self-loathing.

"Yeah, we were lucky," I say.

"But at least I never had to say goodbye to anyone I loved."

I squat down and look at Harrison, red in the face, teeth wine stained, murmuring "Why?" over and over.

Concentrating, I manage to gently stroke his hair. It seems to comfort him. "There's no reason. Just bad luck."

"Something tells me he won't need any more reminders of you tonight," Franky says.

Near Harrison's hand on the floor is his mobile phone, and the last text he typed. Still waiting to go.

Franky squats down to read it. "It's to Brittany."

-Sorry, can't meet you. Too soon. Please don't call again.

My ghost friend's expression is serious. "Shall I press Send?"

Yes. "No."

Seeing Harrison like this makes me feel so ashamed. Of myself. For choosing this for him. For someone I loved. *Love. Will always love.* But no matter how much I still feel it, and want it to continue, it can't.

Franky's distracted by the pictures on the screen. He smiles at a couple of me and Harrison with his sister's French bulldog. Then turns his watery eyes to me, more earnest than I've ever seen him: "I'm so sorry for your loss."

"Me too."

We had fun tonight, Franky and me. It doesn't mean I love Harrison any less. It's just adjusting to a new reality. Moving on. He needs to move on. So do I.

"Is there any way to undo the smoke thing you did?" I ask. "Reverse it. Make him forget me more quickly?"

"I can dim his memories of you—" Franky grasps my hand "—but I could never make him forget you, Emm. No matter what else happens, who he's with, part of you will always be with him. Here." He touches his chest. "Just as he'll always be with you."

I kneel down over the phone and focus my ghostly powers on the keyboard—deleting his message to Brittany and composing a different one.

-Let's try again. Promise I won't run away.

Franky is unusually still as he watches me. "Are you sure?"

I nod. Then lean down and whisper in Harrison's ear: "Goodbye, my love." I manage to graze his cheek with my ghost lips.

Before I hit Send.

I'm almost invisible now. More a suggestion of a spook than an actual spectre. I watch Will Shakespeare rehearse the new play with Maz. The two of them get pretty fired up and shout a lot over artistic differences, but it's worth it for Maz's performance, which is transcendent. I always knew she had it in her.

Meanwhile, Frank Sinatra is giving my Franky singing lessons—which, in my opinion, he needs. Though, as I watch him sing a Sinatra song, *I've Got You Under My Skin*, I feel ghostly tears cooling my cheeks.

"Can we fly around a bit more?" I ask. *One last time.*

He takes me to the top of the Sydney Harbour Bridge where we sit on the highest platform and take in the sweep of the sparkling harbour. I inhale the cool air, a potpourri of sea and car fumes in the deep twilight of the evening. Around us, city lights wink on like fairy fires in the tall buildings. We look down at a super-long staircase, where a new group of bridge climbers is just getting started.

"And we didn't have to walk up all those steps to get here," he says.

"Thank God!" I say with feeling, then slap my hand over my mouth, looking heaven-wards. And we giggle like naughty children.

"Did you enjoy the halfway house?" Franky asks.

"Yea-ah. But you can have too much of a good thing."

"The morning jazz jams?" he asks.

"The swearing."

"Afternoon rock jams?"

"The swearing."

"The all-night no-idea-what-I'm-playing jams?"

"And how bad will it be when Mick Jagger and Keith Richards show up?" I ask.

Franky mimes lifting himself up by an invisible noose, tongue out. It makes me smile. He's learnt a few ghostly tricks in his long stay in between worlds.

"You know, now that I really look at you, I think I remember my mum had a crush on you when she was young."

He shrugs. "What's not to love?"

And then there's this silence, filled up by a ghostly howl as the wind swirls around us and random voices drift up from the street.

"How long will it be, do you think, before your fans let you go through the door?" I ask.

"My fan," he corrects me. "Singular. There's only one left. Betty. She's seventy-four, lives alone. Has a shrine to my memory. Though it's really her own memory of happier times she can't let go of."

"So why don't you work the forgetting smoke on her? Then you can move on—" I pause, before adding "—with me."

I'll feel a lot braver going through the door if he's beside me.

And now I discover that, yes, ghosts can blush.

Franky takes my hand and ghost-kisses it. He's pretty good at it, so it feels like a normal kiss. "I'd go through any doorway with you. Dark, light. Whichever one you pass through is the one for me."

"So come with me, then."

He shakes his head sadly. "I can't take that memory away from Betty. Life's been no picnic for her. I'm all she has."

By the time we get back to the house, I'm barely an outline.

And Maz is waiting for me. "It's time," she says.

As I head into the garden, I look up at the faces of rock stars and famous movie stars at the windows, gazing down at me with fear and longing in their eyes. Some of them may never get to this point.

Waiting before the two doors, I take a last glance back at Franky's window. He waves and winks from above, then opens his window and blows me a kiss. *Which I feel.*

I touch my cheek. "See you soon," I whisper.

He might look like the same vain selfish pop star he was back in his time. But he's long past that.

"Whatever door opens, that's the one you have to go through," Maz says.

My mouth is suddenly dry. *This is it.*

"Don't worry if the pale door doesn't open. It's not the end of the world," she whispers.

"Really?"

And Marilyn Monroe gives me the incandescent smile which made her so famous and winks. "Some like it hot."

Coffee Lovers

GENRE: ROM-COM

PROMPTS: A COFFEE HOUSE, A RIVER

An artist working in a coffee shop in New Orleans discovers that true beauty lies beneath the froth.

Close up on a cappuccino. In a brown ceramic cup. The topping is bridal white, flecked with chocolate sprinkles. It smells like heaven. Tastes almost as good. A work of art for all the senses.

"Which table?"

"Err, eleven," I say.

Helena, the coffee house manager, carries the cup through the busy tables to a dark-haired woman working on a laptop. Phoebe, mid-twenties, is one of our regulars. She takes a sip and gets a white froth moustache.

I heat the milk again. The *shoosh*ing sound, like the distant roar of the ocean, is the soundtrack to my life these days. I'm an artist with paint and pencils mostly but until I earn enough money from that, I make coffee art in my job as a barista at *Aromas*, a coffee house in the French Quarter of New Orleans.

Through the haze of the steaming milk, I take in the scene. The buzzy vibe, the laughter. And Fleur. Early twenties with dark wavy hair to her waist, and eyes like artisan chocolates. I'd like to paint her. Draped in faux leopard skin—a jungle goddess. But first, I'd have to get to know her.

The milk screams—a protest at my inattention—and scorches my thumb. I run it under cold water. The pain ebbs.

"There's some aloe vera in the fridge," says Helena. "Looks like green slime but works wonders."

Helena is Australian and *Aromas* is her baby. Built in a converted warehouse with high ceilings, two blocks from the Mississippi River, it's filled with interesting lights, coffee-themed art, and old espresso machines in glass cases. Hessian sacks around the room spill out fragrant coffee beans from all over the world. There's an air of devotion about the place—to the coffee bean. Cappuccino cathedral.

"In Australia, we take cappuccino seriously," says Helena. "But not much else." She's tall and pale with wispy blonde hair and smiley blue eyes.

Aromas has only been here a few months but everyone already knows it's The Best. The young and the old, the deprived and the depraved of New Orleans pass through. On cold nights, Helena even takes a van out to deliver cappuccino to the homeless. Everyone is addicted to her coffee.

She's fussy about her staff and interviewed widely for a handful of positions. "I only want people who understand coffee," she says, "who appreciate its sensuality, its art." I must have said the right thing because she took me on even though I'd never made a cappuccino before.

"The only thing I ask of my baristas," she said before my first shift, "apart from making each cup a drop of heaven, is that you don't hit on the customers. Don't date them, not while you work for me."

"Fine," I said. "Can I ask why?"

"Santiago, you're a good-looking guy," she said. "In this job, you'll meet a lot of women—or men, if you prefer…" She pauses for confirmation. I grin but give her none. "If you date someone and the romance sours, they might feel uncomfortable coming back. Then I lose a customer and they lose their coffee house—which is even worse."

"No dating customers," I said. "Got it."

"Let me guess. Skinny cappuccino? No choc sprinkles?" Fleur, the Goddess, is right in front of me.

She turns to me, eyes glazed, thoughts elsewhere. "What? Oh yeah, thanks."

"And how's your day been?"

My question hangs, unanswered, as she picks up her cup and weaves through the tables to her group at the back. Her skin glows, her teeth are perfect. *Maybe I should paint her lolling on a bed with rose petals all around.*

"How many coffees do you think you make a day?" Phoebe is back for another caffeine hit.

"Hundreds. And that's just for you."

"And what's the secret ingredient for a good coffee?"

"You know I could tell you, but then I'd have to kill you."

Phoebe is like an unmade bed—always messy, but comfortable. Her default expression is wry.

I pour cold milk into the silver jug, sinking the heat nozzle just below the surface briefly before plunging it deeper into the creamy liquid.

"How come you don't heat the milk up for as long as other cafes?"

"You ask a lot of questions."

"I am a journalist."

"Investigative?"

"Music."

"Well, if you must know..."

"I must..."

"We put hot water in the cups to warm them so we don't need to heat the milk for as long."

"And heating up the milk is bad because ..?"

"You lose a lot of the natural sugars. Satisfied?"

"For now."

As she walks back to her table, I call: "If you have any more questions, just shout 'em out." She grins.

A lull in customers gives me a chance to catch up on orders. First, hot water to warm the cups. Grind the beans. Put the fluffy granules into the portafilter—levelling it with my finger, then compressing it with the metal tamper. Lock filter into place, place cups to catch the waterfall of liquid gold—not too fast or too slow or the coffee becomes bitter.

I heat the milk, swirl it round and bang the jug down three times on the table to polish it to a shine, like beaten egg whites. Pour the coffee into the cup, add milk, then begin the jerky movements necessary to create cappuccino art on the foam. A plastic stirrer and tube of chocolate sauce are the tools to finesse my designs.

I've done flowers, stars and a half-decent swan. I tried other animals too, but they need work. I've mastered the heart shape, but I want something extra for Fleur. So, with the chocolate sauce, I write 4 U inside the heart. Less subtly, I scribble on a paper napkin: *Meet me at the Cat's Pyjamas in Frenchmen Street at 10pm.* I fold it, put it on the saucer with the usual hand-made chocolate. Impulsively, I snatch a second chocolate from the bowl—heart-shaped—and put that on too.

I watch Helena take the coffee to Fleur. Nerves bubble inside me like over-frothed milk.

It's frosty on Frenchmen Street—the heart of jazz in this town. People keep warm by dancing to a street band. A block down is the *Cat's Pyjamas*. Jazz-lovers crowd the doorways, spill onto the pavement.

I squeeze inside. Tonight, there's a trio of guys over sixty. They're really good; jazz is in their genes.

I scan for Fleur, catching my reflection in a mirror behind the bar. My wavy black hair is wilder than usual. I run my fingers through it, but it defies order. I have the pale skin of my American father, the shiny beetle eyes of my Chilean mother. I'm usually confident about my appearance, but not tonight.

I make it to the back of the bar without seeing her. *She's not here.* Disappointment, like water from a cracked levee, rushes over me. She's not coming. Well, of course she's not. *Why would she? What was I thinking?*

"Santiago!"

My view is blocked by a huge man in a New Orleans voodoo T-shirt.

Like a large cruise ship, he moves off slowly to reveal ...Phoebe, sitting at the bar. Is this a coincidence? On the bench beside her, I spy the napkin with my handwriting on it. *Oh no!* I see what happened. The coffees got mixed up and she got Fleur's by mistake. *This is embarrassing.*

"Hey?" she shouts.

I nod and stretch my mouth into a smile, which I hope looks natural.

Worming my way through the warm bodies to her side, we listen, in silence, to a couple of songs—it's too loud to speak anyway, but louder inside my head as I figure out what to say. Clearly, the girl has the wrong idea here. I have to set her right. But gently. The song ends abruptly. I open my mouth to speak but a drum solo starts up, making communication impossible. So, I point to the door. Phoebe nods, slugs down the rest of her drink and gets up.

Outside, the street party is still going strong. The road is thick with dancers; some look like they're in a voodoo trance. The cars inch through them, drivers tapping the beat on the steering wheel.

We walk along the street. The noise recedes till we can hear the *clip-clop* of our shoes on the sidewalk. It's cold but refreshing after the crowded bar. On the corner, we listen to a solo saxophone player for a while, dropping coins into his music case.

"So, you're an artist?" says Phoebe.

"How do you know?"

"I can tell by the coffee designs. Plus, I might have asked Helena about you."

She gives a shy grin, a tad flirty. *Awkward.*

"My cappuccino art has a fair way to go."

"I like the monkey," she says.

"Monkey?" I frown. "You mean koala bear. I tried that to remind Helena of home."

"Oh," says Phoebe. "Well, maybe it does need work. What can we expect next? Picassos, Monets, Van Gogh, all out of froth."

"Don't let Helena hear you call it froth. Other cafes make froth. We make dream cream."

I love the French Quarter with its narrow Parisian-style streets, wrought iron balconies and great musicians on every corner. And of course, the reason I moved to this city—the vibrant art in shop windows.

We pass a painting of a red dog, taller than me, and a stylised superhero cartoon, in high gloss. "One day, my paintings will be in those shops."

"Maybe I'll buy one with the first cheque from my multi-book publishing deal."

"Really? You've got a publishing deal?"

"Not yet. But one day..."

We stroll along the Mississippi, which is silvery in the moonlight, no hint of the usual mud brown. A large paddle steamer docks. On the upper deck, a pair of lovers cling to each other.

I've been in town for two months from sunny LA. Phoebe's been here a few months longer.

"I understand why it's called the Big Easy now," she says. "I had to get the rush of New York out of my system before I could appreciate the N'Orlins rhythm."

She's easy to talk to, and funny, but I'm really tired. It's been a long day and I'm crashing after my earlier adrenalin rush. I sneak a look at my watch. Phoebe catches me and pretends not to.

We arrive at Jackson Square, lined with fortune tellers at fold-up tables, predicting futures by candlelight.

"Would you like to know what your future holds?" a skinny woman with a magenta headscarf asks. Phoebe shakes her head.

"Go on," I say. "It'll be fun."

She sits opposite the woman who stares into a glass ball and begins murmuring. In the candlelight, Phoebe's face looks soft and vulnerable.

When she's done, she says: "I'm going to meet a dark handsome man, who'll steal my heart away." She twirls coyly.

"That's not so farfetched," I say. "I'm sure there are plenty of men out there—dark and fair—who would wish to steal your heart."

She gives a tight smile, no light in her eyes.

I can't hold back a yawn.

"I'd better get home," I say. "I've got an early shift."

I pull my jacket tightly around me against the cold and start to move off.

"Santiago," she calls. "Can I ask you something?"

I turn back.

"Did you mean to send that note to me? It's just, I've had this feeling all night, you were expecting someone else."

"No, of course not," I say, too quickly. "I don't know many people in town. I thought we could be friends."

"Friends? Well, we all need those."

She draws her lips up in a smile, but it doesn't take an artist's eye to see it's a poor imitation of the real thing.

The next day, I experiment with coffee art. I have to discard several cups (I pay for the spoils) as I try a special design—Fleur's profile.

"Hey, I saw you walking with Phoebe last night," says Helena, refilling the chocolate bowl. "I hope that wasn't a date?"

"We're just friends."

"She does the cappuccino run for the homeless with me sometimes, you know. She's a great girl."

"No argument there."

Around lunchtime, a government inspector called Simon Milton comes in, asking to see Helena. When she offers him coffee, he declines. "I only drink tea."

He's in a grey suit and black shirt, with clear green eyes and a serious mouth. About forty. "People say you have a secret ingredient in your product," he says. "Something highly addictive. Can you tell me what that is, Ms Braithwaite?"

Helena smiles. "Well, there's caffeine."

"And?"

"Freshly ground beans, good coffee craft, and..."

"And...?"

"Love. In every cup," says Helena.

"Love?" he says, left eyebrow pinging up. "Are you certain it's not something more potent? Like cocaine?"

Half a dozen inspectors storm into the building, clear everyone out for about two hours while they do tests on our coffee beans. They find nothing, but Helena loses the morning's income. All her customers have to go elsewhere for their coffee.

"Tell me, Mr Milton, did someone phone you with a tipoff about this alleged cocaine?" says Helena.

"I'm afraid I'm not at liberty to say."

"Did you consider it could be someone with a grievance, like one of my competitors?"

"We're sorry to have inconvenienced you, Miss Powers. We'll be on our way."

"No, you will not. Sit down. I'm making you a coffee."

"I don't drink—"

"You're going to have a coffee and that's that," says Helena. "Now sit."

He could say no, but he doesn't. Eyes downcast, lips pouty, he looks like a puppy who's done his business in the house.

He sips tentatively at first, but then I see something in his face— wonder. He's taken in by the magic that is coffee and this place. By the time he leaves, he's a convert, I can see. Helena sends him off with a list of her chief competitors to visit for a "chat".

"Do you think he had nice eyes?" says Helena.

"No dating the customers, remember?" I reply.

By the next evening, my design is good enough to show. I take the coffee to Fleur myself. On the saucer is a serviette with an invitation to meet me for a sunset stroll along the Mississippi.

She's deep in conversation as I place the cup down. I linger for a moment, hopeful. She sees the design, looks up at me and smiles.

"Did you do this? It looks like me."

I grin.

"I'm putting this on Instagram." She snaps a photo. "Are you an artist?"

I nod. "I'd like to paint you."

I can't control my grin as I walk back to the cappuccino machine.

"Is this from you too?" she shouts. "An invite to walk along the river at six?"

Helena, stops, coffees in hand. "Well, answer the girl, Santiago. Did you invite her for a walk after your shift?"

"I, ahh…"

She lowers her voice. "You can go out with her. You just can't work here too. You have to choose."

I love this job; I don't want to lose it. But I know, if it comes down to it, I've made my choice. I open my mouth to speak when a voice chimes in from behind.

"It wasn't him. That note was from me."

We turn to see Phoebe behind us.

"You?" says Fleur, coming over. "You want me to go for a walk with you?"

Phoebe nods.

"Well, you're hot and all," says Fleur. "But I'm more into guys than girls. Sorry."

"Just thought I'd ask," says Phoebe.

I slink back to the counter, beyond mortified.

"That was a turn-up," says Helena. "I had no idea Phoebe was that way inclined. I thought she had a thing for you, actually. Still, whatever rocks her socks. Everyone is welcome here. Except tea drinkers."

I make a special cappuccino for Phoebe, pay for it myself, load the saucer with extra chocolates, adding a note: "You are a good friend." I push through the crowd to her table, but she's gone.

Fast forward a month. Mr Milton—or Simon, as we call him now—is a regular. He loves cappuccino. Helena makes all his drinks personally.

Fleur and I have been out a few times without the boss knowing. One night she took me to a bar to hear her grandma sing. The woman is Dee Dee Porter—famous in jazz circles. She was amazing.

Fleur is sweet and lovely, but like the steam off the hot milk—difficult to hold and a little insubstantial. She was keen on me painting her, though, and I did think about it. I even bought the paints (I had settled on a cat woman theme.). In the end, I painted her grandma instead.

During that month, Phoebe didn't come into *Aromas* once. I found myself looking for her, missing her easy humour.

"I wonder what happened to Phoebe," says Helena. "Perhaps she's gone back to New York. I wish her well. Though, I'd like to have said goodbye."

At the end of my shift, I wander the streets, mulling over how badly things ended with her. I was so focused on Fleur's physical form, I'd missed something potentially better. I'm not quite sure what. Now I'll never know.

Then I think, what if she is still in New Orleans, just avoiding *Aromas* because of me? Where would she be? I make a list of the three next best cafes and keep a watch on them.

On day two, I see her sitting in the window in Corelli's cafe.

When Phoebe's cappuccino is delivered, she looks down and freezes. Atop the white polished cream is a weird monkey. Her eyes drop to the serviette on the saucer. She reads it. "Can you forgive me? Monkey man."

Slowly she turns and sees me, peering from behind Corelli's cappuccino machine (they did me a favour!). She takes a sip and smiles, with a little froth moustache.

No Place Like Home

GENRE: SPY

PROMPTS: A SHIP'S CARGO HOLD, A BOX OF RAISINS

♡

When Tash's husband fails to return home from work one evening, she struggles to make the police take his disappearance seriously. Now, more than three years later, a stranger knocks on her door.

The white SUV pulled up outside my house just on sunset and a dark-suited man got out, merging with the shadows as he approached my front door. I thought spies drove black cars. *Bit disappointing really.*

He introduced himself as Jeff from "the agency". What agency? He didn't say. I suppose that was on a need-to-know basis. And I didn't need to know.

Ushering me into the back seat, he climbed in after me.

"How are you feeling, Mrs Montague?" His tone bordered on patronising.

"Bit nervous. And it's Ms Delaney. I kept my name." He nods, not surprised. It would take a lot to surprise him, I reckon. "You can call me Tash."

"So, Tash, I believe the office explained that tonight we'll be doing a spy swap. Which means we release a Russian agent in our custody.

And the Russians return your husband to us."

"Just one agent?" I'd seen films where some agents were worth several on the other side. Jeff ignored the question.

"We need you to observe your husband, closely," he said. "There's some chance—only a slight one—they'll try to substitute one of their own agents, with his face surgically altered."

What the—?

"You mean plastic surgery?" *Have I stepped into a Bond film?*

"We expect that you, Tash, will be able to tell the difference."

I nodded, as if that wasn't the strangest sentence I'd ever heard.

Driving in silence through Sydney's streets, we turned onto a peninsula and headed towards the water. The driver parked in a side street. Jeff led me along a bush track, through a security gate, to an out-of-the-way cargo terminal where an enormous red cargo ship—like a gash of blood against the dark water—stood anchored.

"This is so weird," I said.

Jeff smiled tightly.

And it was weird. Over three years ago, my husband kissed me goodbye as he left for work. He never returned. After weeks pestering the police to take his disappearance seriously, a grim gentleman appeared at my door, claiming he was from a government agency and that Matt had been working for them when he went missing.

"We think the Russians took him."

The Russians took *my Matt*? I remembered thinking. What could they want with him? *He doesn't even speak Russian!*

Now, Matt was back and somewhere in the cargo hold of this giant, rusty ship.

"This way," said Jeff.

We climbed the gangway to the deck, which smelt strongly of petrol and cheap detergent. The engines thrummed beneath my feet, my heartbeat twice as fast. Dead-eyed boatmen smoked as they watched us moving about.

My high heels echoed on the metal stairs (definitely not spy footwear). The temperature rose with each step down. My face felt clammy; I wished I'd worn waterproof makeup.

We entered a low-ceilinged space crammed with crates, with narrow corridors between them, like rat runs. A ruddy-faced man, his shirt soaked with sweat, stood at the end of the row. Seeing us, he made a "get-on-with-it" gesture in the air.

Jeff nodded to an agent behind us who brought the Russian prisoner forward. I expected he'd be cowed and broken. He looked anything but. His almost translucent gaze, settling on me, made me shudder.

"Right," said Jeff. "It's happening."

For an interminable moment, I struggled to get enough air into my lungs.

Then... Matt came around the corner.

"Natasha!" He ran forward and wrapped his arms around me, lifting me off the ground.

"Matt! It's good to see you."

We looked each other over, smiling shyly.

"How have you been?" he asked.

"Getting by."

"Still writing those lovely kids' stories?"

Even in this dull place, his eyes seemed filled with light. I felt my cheeks heating up and wished Jeff wasn't watching and smiling-not-smiling.

"What have you been doing?" I asked. A ridiculous question. We laughed nervously, releasing some of the tension.

Matt looked good. Still handsome, with that strong jaw and dark eyes like chocolate Tim Tams that melted all my defences.

At least that's how it had been at first. Ten years of marriage had changed things. His job at the agency didn't help. He always seemed preoccupied, evasive.

In the end, we barely spoke. The clocks ticked loudly in our lifeless living room. He'd say things like: "You still writing stories about batty bats and dragons named Norbert? Most people would have given up after so much rejection."

It wasn't a compliment. Nothing much was by then. "You wear a lot of blue." "You're so like your mother." "Don't ask about my work; you won't understand!" "Shepherd's pie again?"

If he hadn't disappeared when he had, I'd have asked him to go. I'd begun looking into new living arrangements.

But now, he was different. His time in a Russian gulag had shaken things up. For the better.

"I brought some raisins," I said, offering the box. "Your favourite."

"How thoughtful! I could do with the antioxidants."

I shook some into his hands. He popped them into his mouth, chewing happily. And the way he looked at me...like I was land, and he'd been at sea a long, long time.

"Can I have a word with your wife?" Jeff asked. "I won't keep her."

"Better not!" Matt winked.

"Is this your husband?" Jeff whispered.

I nodded.

"You're sure?"

"Yeah."

On the way back, Jeff rode in the front. Matt and I held hands like high-school sweethearts in the back. At home, he didn't comment on all the new blooms in the garden. ("Too many colours is commonplace!")

I guessed he'd be happy with shepherd's pie now too. Anything would taste good after prison food.

Especially when he'd never had it before.

"Raisins?" I said.

He took some more, beaming at me. I smiled back.

Matt always hated raisins. Years of torture wouldn't have changed that.

Oh well. Naslazhdaytes', poka mozhno. An old Russian saying. *Enjoy it while you can.*

And I intended to.

The Mysterious Smile

GENRE: TIME TRAVEL

♡

They say you should never meet your heroes.
Sometimes, you should listen to them.

In a home-made laboratory, in the backyard of my parents' house, I stare at an empty bench and hold my breath. My dark hair is dishevelled, I know, and my eyes have a wild, watery look about them which goes well with the stubble breaking through my pale skin. But I don't care.

"How much longer do we have to wait?" Sasha is impatient.

"Shhhh," I say, my gaze fixed on the bench.

She huffs but keeps the video recording as we focus on the empty space, awaiting a miracle.

And then, with no fanfare, nor rippling of the air, not even a techno-logical "ting", a honey-coloured teddy bear is sitting where nothing was before.

"So, it's 6.29 on the fifteenth of April, in the year 2035. I'm Milo De Luca, twenty-seven years old, from Sydney, Australia. This is Eddie—" I hold up the toy "—and he's the first bear to travel through time."

Sasha pops her blonde head in front of the camera, joy swimming in her sea-blue eyes. "You did it, Milo! And I witnessed it. Sasha Lockhart, also from Sydney, Australia. Should I give my tax file number or something?"

As I press the OFF button on the video, Sasha launches herself at me and we hug and bounce around, wild with excitement. I break free to retrieve a bottle of champagne from the lab fridge—Moet et Chandon, purchased especially for this moment. Popping the cork, a tide of golden liquid fizzes over my hand as I fill two champagne flutes.

"To how many years of research paying off?" Sasha asks, seizing a glass.

"Too many." I sigh.

In truth, I've worked tirelessly since I was seventeen, facing setback after setback in my quest to conquer the mysteries of Time. Other scientists laughed at my ideas, calling me "a dreamer" and a "weekend Bunsen burner". I may not have PhDs like them and I'm not a member of any top science institutes; I'm self-taught, self-funded and motivated. But now, I'll have the last laugh because I've proved them all wrong.

Sasha holds the Time and Space Machine, which resembles a mobile phone with colourful lights pulsing on a screen, considering its weight. "Weird to think *this* can transport you through time."

"And space," I add. The most important part, so I can explore time zones outside of Sydney, or even Australia.

I take a minute to look around the laboratory in quiet tribute. The test tubes are lined up like scholars. Scribbled calculations and clock doodles cover the walls and the papers around my work bench. Library shelves sag with well-thumbed scientific volumes.

Have I really done it? It hardly seems real. I feel light-headed and dizzy.

"I'm not sure I should drink too much of this—" I hold up the glass "—after no sleep for forty-eight hours."

"Seventy-two," Sasha corrects me. "But who's counting?"

We take our drinks out to the backyard, edged by colourful flowers. Sinking onto the grass, we sip as we watch a glorious suburban sunset.

"To my friend, and the cleverest man who ever lived," says Sasha.

"I can't claim to be the cleverest. There was—" and here, she joins in: "—da Vinci."

"Or Leo, the God, as we call him," she says, jumping up and gesturing theatrically. "Not just a painter, but an inventor, a visionary. He invented the helicopter, the parachute, the tank. And a multi-coloured cocktail at my local bar, for which I am truly grateful. How did a man from the Middle Ages dream up all these things? How? How?"

I can't help laughing. "Am I so very boring?"

"On some subjects. Not all." She moves closer, as if about to whisper a secret, and her lips graze my cheek. "Not to me." Backlit by the sun, her expression infused with a tiredness beyond exhaustion, she's never looked more beautiful to me.

"I couldn't have done it without my brilliant assistant," I say.

"Is that all?"

"And friend?"

She raises an eyebrow, inviting more.

"My sweet love."

Sasha has worked for me for the past nine months, but the latest development in our relationship is still quite new. Neither of us know where it's going. I just know I want it to keep on going.

As she leans her head on my shoulder, we savour the sour beverage and the sweet moment of triumph.

"The question now," she says, "is are you going to call the Science Society, or shall I? Or we could go and tell them in person, so I can film the smiles slipping off their smug bastard faces."

"Not yet," I say. "They won't believe us. They'll say we doctored that video."

"Well, you can do it again. Send Teddy off and back once more."

I shake my head. "No. Now we need a human trial. If I achieve that, they'll have to see the possibilities."

"Which human? You?" Sasha is aghast. "That would be dangerous."

"Which is why I can't ask anyone else to do it."

"Can I come with you?" she asks.

"Out of the question. Calibrating the journey for one will be difficult enough. And I can't risk you. You're too important to me."

Sasha runs her index finger around the rim of the glass, watching the golden bubbles slowly rise to the surface and burst. "And what about us?" she says. Her gaze dissects me like a scalpel. "You said we had to press pause until you achieved this. But after that, you'd take time out."

"And I will," I reply. "As soon as I return from this trip…and I've written up my research." *And made this year's science grant applications.*

I reach for her hand, but she pulls away, draining her glass. "So where will you go for the first trip through time?"

I feel my cheeks stretch into a grin. *Is that even a question?* I know exactly where I'll go. I've always known. I'll visit *Him*. My hero.

Leonardo da Vinci.

A few days later, I'm ready to leave. Chugging down a half-glass of sauvignon blanc for courage, I take some deep breaths and press *INITIATE TRAVEL*.

Instantly, I'm in a tube of light, ringed by swirling white mist stretching to infinity. Inside, it's cold and everything shudders, like a plane in rough skies. Crashes and bangs beyond the walls unnerve me. But it's the voices, haunting and troubled, crying out through the fog that almost make me press *RETURN TO TIME AND PLACE OF ORIGIN*. The machine lurches and begins to spin, for so long, so fast, I black out.

Florence, 1477

Returning to consciousness, a scent of cheap spirits and turpentine fills my nostrils. Voices, muffled at first, shape themselves into words.

"Have you got ants wriggling in your pants?" A man's voice, croaky and deep. "Sit still, woman. Unless you want me to paint you a nose the size of the Duomo."

"You try sitting still for a few minutes," a woman replies, nasal and whiny. "It's impossible. Like lice are crawling over your skin. In this dump, they probably are. I don't know why I agreed to do this."

"Because I paid you, Love." The man is speaking in Italian, I realise, which I'm fluent in. "It's more than you'd get serving plonk at your father's tavern."

I'm still a tad dizzy as I stand up and see. . .a dark-haired woman on a sofa, posing for a portrait, painted by a long-haired man with his back to me. The man stabs his brush at the canvas like he's trying to hurt it.

Spotting me, the woman's sullen expression morphs to a grin. And she throws her head back in a kookaburra cackle.

"What is so funny?" the painter asks, hands on hips. "Have you been at your father's spirits again?"

"And what if I have?" the woman snaps back. "If I'm to spend time in this drafty den, I need a little warmth in my belly."

"As long as that's all you've got in there."

She doesn't hear the last part; she's tipping sideways to see me. "There's a man behind you."

The painter spins around, his dark eyes sweeping up and down me. "You're not due for another hour."

It's around now I notice two things. One, that I'm completely naked. Time travel evidently preserves the body, but not the clothes you travel in. And two, the painter looks familiar. He's younger, more unkempt, and smellier than I imagined, but he's uncannily like...

"Leonardo! When can I see the painting?" the woman whines.

Leonardo?

"Patience, Lisa. When I'm done, not before."

"That's not fair."

"Stop your moaning!"

Moaning...Lisa? What?

And now I study the part-finished canvas upon the easel, the work is *really* familiar in dimension and outline. Though not in detail. It portrays a dark-haired woman with a lascivious grin in a gaudily coloured hat.

Ohmigod! This is Leonardo da Vinci. And he's painting the *Mona Lisa*. But not as we know it.

"Anyway, I'm done for today." Lisa, stands up, readjusting her clothes. "You can stay, sir." She winks at me. "Don't burden yourself with garments on my account."

"I paid for an hour, Lisa! You owe me a drink. Several!" Leonardo shouts as she descends the wooden stairs.

He hurries to a desk, scribbles something on a scrap of paper, wraps it round a rock—one of many he keeps in a bowl—and hurls it out of the window.

"Oh, that's very mature!" Lisa screeches from the street below. "And by the way, you missed!"

Leonardo paces, muttering: "I need something to more accurately knock sense into empty heads." His lips twist to the side as he withdraws a notebook from his artist's gown and scrawls something within.

"I suppose you're an artist too?" he says, joining me at the easel. "You can't trip over a drunk in the street these days without him being a practitioner of fine arts."

"I paint a little," I reply. Then, recalling who I'm talking to: "But I wouldn't call myself an artist. Not like you, Mr da Vinci."

Leonardo's bottom lip curls as he examines the painting. "Perhaps I could use a novice's eye to tell me what's wrong with this painting."

What's wrong with it? Everything. To start with, he wasn't meant to paint it for another thirty years.

"Have you something I can..." I gesture to my naked form.

Leonardo points to a cupboard in the corner, containing a pile of soiled clothing. I reel back at the smell as I pull on some dark brown leggings and a loose green tunic, sleeves puffed to the elbow, before returning to the artwork. "Well, the model's smile is a bit..." *clown-like and obscene* "...too much," I venture.

"Too much?" Leonardo's right eyebrow pings up in artistic pique but, as he assesses the painting, the pair realign. "You may have a point."

"And the colours are very bright. I wonder how it might look if it was a little more...smoky and mysterious."

"Smoky and mysterious?" Leonardo scratches his chin, then pulls out the notebook and scrawls something in it. I try to see what, but he whips the book back with a furtive air.

"What's your name, sir?"

"Milo. De Luca." My gaze strays to the paintings on the walls. Religious paintings with mother and baby in vibrant colours. Angels, with bird-like wings, birds with human faces. Renderings of the human form with words painted over them: *Boring; Bring Me Something New; Not another nude.*

"Don't look at those," says Leonardo. "Rubbish. I keep them to reuse the canvases."

At the side is a triptych of a debauched-looking dinner party. Again, the form is familiar though the details so strange, it's like I haven't just travelled through time, but to a parallel universe.

"Oh, that was a dinner I attended—" Leonardo waves it away "—where some fellow artists and I resolved to get out of the art business and take real jobs. It was supposed to be our last night in the profession."

"Like a last supper?" My voice cracks.

"Yes."

"And by a real job, you mean…?"

"Tanner, cobblestone-maker, gongfermor?"

Gongfermor? Who empties barrels in castle privies? Leonardo da Vinci? For a moment, I forget how to breathe and clutch the wall to stop from falling.

"But painting's not all I do," Leonardo says. "I'm an inventor too."

I exhale as Leonardo points to some designs sketched on board and loose paper piled up on the floor. My hands shake with anticipation as I hold them. *To think I'm about to see da Vinci's first models for his genius creations!*

And then I see his first page. It takes a moment to make sense of the lines. Again, the drawings are weirdly familiar, yet utterly foreign. The first, I'm guessing, is his prototype for a helicopter.

"Well, what do you think?" Leonardo asks.

I want to say something—anything—but I have no words. This flying vehicle has a cabin, but instead of propellers, Leonardo has sketched large bird feathers on top.

"It's a flying machine," says Leonardo impatiently, as though anyone with eyes could see that.

"But how would the feathers lift the machine off the ground?"

"You may well ask the birds that same question!" Leonardo says.

I lick my lips and move to the next design. I hold it one way, then the other, then sideways.

"It's a device to transport one from the top of a mountain to the bottom without bodily harm," Leonardo offers.

A parachute? An early version. Very, *very* early. I draw my cheeks into a smile, like curtains opening in a theatre. The design includes a harness for a human to lie horizontally, with giant fairy wings on their back.

"How do the wings work?"

"The wind," Leonardo says.

I wait for more explanation but there is none, though I catch him squinting at the drawing as if searching for further clues himself.

"I see," I say. Though I've never felt more like a blind man stumbling in a dark cave.

"These days, you can't just be an artist," Leonardo adds. "You need to have a second talent. I'm trying out 'inventor'. If that doesn't succeed, I could become a 'court scoundrel'. That works for some."

I'm taut with trepidation as I prepare to look at the third design. One of his more forward-thinking inventions was the army tank. This is a version of that, I believe. (Though it's not certain.)

It's a giant metal horse.

"Those Greeks had a lot of luck with the Trojan horse. Why not us?" he says.

I can't see wheels on the device, but rather a long string at the back, as if it's meant to be pulled by someone. *A giant, perhaps?*

"Hmmm. Interesting."

"I've heard that said before. 'Interesting!'" Leonardo folds his arms, pouting. "You think I'm crazy."

"No, no, no, no, nooooo. Not at all."

I just can't understand how someone with no practical sense of, well, anything, could become the brilliant inventor hailed across the centuries.

As Leonardo prepares his next canvas, I take the opportunity to look around me. The apartment is small and cramped, overlooking a cobbled street. Rough wooden floor, candles on the wall, a wooden bench with a soiled blanket for his models. And canvases everywhere, piled up, hung up, side by side, end to end. Two bowls sit on his artist's desk: the one filled with rocks and another with jewellery—gold rings, earrings, bracelets.

Then I notice, beside his paints, unattended... Leonardo's notebook. I lick my lips. His notebooks are legend. He never went anywhere without one. He sketched everything that interested him and jotted down all his thoughts and ideas. While he's preparing the next canvas, I snatch up the book and flick through, hoping to glimpse the spark that will fire up the foremost mind of science and art.

What do I see? Doodles of birds, like children's cartoons. Lots of expletives, in artistic lettering. And sketches of men and women's private parts, captioned crudely. *A dangly delight for a duchess. What is this thing called, Love? Madam, put that thing down; you know where it's been!* Once again, I feel like I've tripped over my expectations and landed in a bucket of vomit.

I flick to the back page of the notebook and see a list of items. *1 X ring, Signor de Vetchi, 2 X earring Signora Malvolio, 1 X bracelet, Signora Collette Luteci,* and so on. Glancing over at the jewellery bowl, I see a ring with *MV* engraved upon it. Is this an inventory of items received in payment for portraits? *Or something else?*

Leonardo snatches the book from me.

"Sorry. I, err..."

"Well, then...bring out Signor di Giovanni." He gestures to my trousers.

I hesitate, unsure of his meaning. Leonardo leans in. "Lose the leggings, Luigi. Time to show the world what you're made of."

"Oh, I'm not a model." I laugh nervously.

"Then who the hell are you? Turning up here without a stitch on? Were you and I...?" Leonardo tilts his head, eyebrows raised in question.

"No." My face warms. "I'm an admirer. Of your *work.*" I add the last part quickly.

"You admire *my* work?" Leonardo regards me with suspicion. "You're a spy, aren't you? That Michelangelo is always trying to find out what I'm up to."

"No!"

"How did you get in here without me hearing you?"

"I don't know. I think I had too much—" *what would they drink here?* "—wine? And woke up over there."

Leonardo glances at the space where I first appeared and back at me, his eyes narrowing. "On your way, then."

"Nice to meet you," I say. I take a last look around, then head down the stairs.

"Wait," Leonardo calls as I'm halfway down. He draws the curtain of hair out of his eyes. "I would like to paint you sometime. You have something about you, Milo De Luca."

I flush with satisfaction, from my crown to my big toe. *Leonardo* remembers *my* name.

Out on the street, the cool air hits me like a bucket of ice. Which I need. I feel muzzy and over-heated with shock and disbelief.

Was that *the* Leonardo da Vinci? Or could it be another artist with the same name? And if it was *Him*, how did he go from *that* misguided, uninspired Leonardo to the one I knew—the Visionary, a household name even hundreds of years hence?

The cobbled street is narrow between the rickety two-storey wooden buildings. The only light comes from candlelight spilling from first-floor windows and starlight reflecting on the (suspiciously wet) cobbles. My gaze snags on something white in the darkness, a piece of paper— the one Leo threw out of the window.

My breath hitches as I snap it up. I try to read the writing. HCNEW. There are some letters I recognise—W and H—but the others seem like some strange language, or…they're written backwards. *Of course!* Leonardo was famous for backwards writing—mirror language— to protect his ideas. My overtaxed brain is slow to process the letters. *WENCH.* I presume it's intended as derision. An insult from Leonardo to Lisa. *The* Mona Lisa.

I look up at the window to find Leonardo watching me, half in, half out of the shadows, before he withdraws once more into the darkness.

"Hey! You with the nice legs!"

I look around to find Lisa in the doorway of a bar, *The Rose and Thistle*, waving me in. "Come have a glass of wine."

"I don't have any money to pay," I say.

"Leo didn't pay you?" She tuts and shakes her head. "Never mind, we'll do what I do whenever he tries to cheat me. We'll put it on his bill."

I follow her into the bar. And to be clear, I'm following "the moaner, Lisa", into Leonardo da Vinci's local drinking establishment. Where *he* is going to pay for *my* drink. Lisa goes behind the bar and pours me a cup of red wine from a ceramic cask.

"Saluti!" she says.

It's crowded tonight, with men in long tunics over leggings. Sawdust is sprinkled around the floor, casks of wine sit on the wooden service counter. A pig runs after a chicken. Just your average Renaissance bar.

Lisa, serving the all-male clientele, is something to behold. She chides this one, laughs loudly, lewdly, with that one, and turns another out, with a take-no-prisoners air. She's a vibrant woman of many colourful moods, but none of them—at least while I'm watching—are contemplative or understated. I witness big broad smiles, dark thunderous brows, but not a single half-smile to drive a world crazy for hundreds of years. *So where did that come from?*

I rub Leonardo's note between my fingers, feeling its solidity to assure myself that this is real; I really am here. Maybe I could present it to the Science Society as proof of my journey. They'd test it, find the paper was made in the 1400s. I could get Sasha to film the shock and awe on their faces.

Sasha. I sip my wine and take a moment to think about my "girlfriend". Well, not officially mine, yet—I couldn't make a commitment like that until I'd completed my work. But hopefully, she soon will be.

I call up a memory of her dancing on the lawn, her intelligent eyes, her perfect teeth. Her blonde, wavy hair catching the sunlight, like it was on fire, like a painting. A Botticelli. *The Birth of Venus*. Sasha has been patient, taking a back seat to my work, my obsession. But she deserves more, and when I get back, I'll give her my full attention. We could even take a holiday somewhere? Florence, perhaps?

"You're a thief!" An old man leaps to his feet, fists raised at Lisa. "One minute I had a full glass and the next it's half empty."

"Sit down, Marco," Lisa commands, laughing indulgently. "It's just the way with drink. There's not a man in this room who will disagree. Nor a woman, for that matter. We ladies keep hoping you men have a full vessel, but it usually runs dry well before our thirst is quenched."

Everyone dissolves into bawdy chuckling, including the complainer. Lisa looks over at me and winks.

I spot something at the end of the bar, a strange-looking broom, with a leather belt strapped to the top. "Excuse me, what's that?" I ask as Lisa passes by.

"That's Leo's latest invention," she says. "He says if I strap the broom around my waist, it can sweep up behind me as I go."

That was one of Leonardo's inventions? My face must have betrayed my thoughts, because she raises her eyebrows and nods. "Loony Leo comes up with something new every week."

"L..l..loony Leo?" I can hardly get the words out.

She points to another of his inventions. A wooden sculpture dangling from the ceiling, likes a child's mobile, with three fish: big fish, mouth agape, medium fish, and little fish. As you twirl it around, the big fish eats the medium fish, who devours the smaller one.

"Clever," I say.

Lisa nods and leans in conspiratorially. "After a few drinks, we draw our patrons' attention to it. And while they're gawping, we pour half their drink back into the barrel. So they have to buy more."

What the—? Could Leonardo da Vinci have made that cute sculpture for such a grubby, mercantile purpose?

"He's devious, that one." Lisa taps her nose. "Watch yourself around him. He's not called Light-fingered Leo for nothing. Your coin and jewels are not safe when he's nearby. The man's been known to pay his bill with rings and gold from his rich, foolish clients and not-so-rich local inebriates."

My mind flashes to his desk and the bowl filled with jewellery. Were those pieces *stolen? Surely not!*

They say you should never meet your heroes. I'm not sorry I met Leo, but certain aspects have been . . .disappointing. He's definitely slipped from god to mere mortal status for me, with the emphasis on *mere.*

And then…I have a sense, for the second time today, of freefalling through space. I gasp and pat myself down as I realise, with horror, I don't have the time machine on me. I'm not even sure where it is. Presumably I had it in my hands when I arrived. I must have dropped it while I slept, somewhere in Leonardo's studio.

I take off, at speed, stumbling over the uneven cobbles in the dark, splashing through a puddle reeking of urine. I take the stairs to

Leonardo's loft two at a time. A naked man is bent over, head in the cupboard. When he turns to look at me, his face is trenched with confusion.

"Where's Leonardo?" I ask.

"I wondered the same thing." He scratches his head volubly. "He was sketching me in an Atlas pose, you know, holding up the world. And then, he squatted down over there behind the canvases. I heard him make a few 'Ahhh' sounds and he was gone. Just. Disappeared. I thought he might have slipped downstairs, but I don't see how. I was just checking the cupboard, in case it was some kind of trick. But he's not there."

His voice is a background drone, drowned out by my ragged breathing as I search the floor in and around the pile of canvases and sketches of ridiculous inventions to find...nothing at all. I check and recheck every inch of Leo's loft, even places I haven't been (like the privy! Ooh! Don't get me started!). But it's nowhere. The time machine is gone.

And I know who has it. *Light-fingered Leo.*

I sink to the ground, head in my hands, reeling with the desperation of my situation.

"Are you all right?" the model asks.

No, I'm pretty far from all right. I'm stuck here, in this time. Possibly for the rest of my life. I know no-one except Lisa. I have no idea how to live here. I think of my lab, the familiar smell of burnt chemicals, the colourful spines of books in the library. I'll never see them again. Or my family.

Or Sasha. The thought of losing her, and her smile, and her laughter like wind chimes, before we've really even begun, stabs my chest so hard I find myself clawing at my collar.

"Of course, he's okay," a familiar voice answers. "Aren't you, Milo?"

A hand appears before me to help me to my feet. Leonardo's. He looks neater and smells of aftershave—Dior, if I'm not mistaken. His hair is still long but shiny and groomed, like it's been washed and blow-dried. He's wearing the same shirt he had on earlier, but it's paired with black denim jeans. *My jeans.*

As our eyes meet, I know. His smug grin confirms it.

"You can go," he tells the model. "I don't feel like drawing right now."

The protest on the boy's lips dies as Leonardo holds up some coins. The boy grabs them, pulls on some clothes and gallops downstairs. All the while, Leo and I hold the eye lock.

"Where's my time machine?" I demand.

"It's here. Unharmed."

He holds it up and I snatch it. "You had no right to take it."

"Many apologies," he says, and bows. "You are, truly, a genius, sir."

That appeases me a tad. *Leonardo* thinks *I'm* a genius. "What did you think of the future?"

"I saw creatures in strange clothes, and cities of such impressive scale and design. And some Netflix series. One about me."

"How long were you there?" I ask.

"A month," he says. "I did consider staying longer. Permanently, even. But this is my home. And I have a lot of work to do."

He looks with distaste around the room. "Though I'm not staying in this chicken coop for much longer. There's a nice little estate in the Tuscan hills I have my eye on."

So, he's returned richer than when he departed?

"Steal anything while you were there?" I ask, my voice acid.

He chuckles. "I did acquire a few keepsakes."

Acquire? "And some ideas, I suppose? Inspiration for your inventions? Your art?"

"Well, we'll see," Leonardo says, cryptically. "Time will tell."

From his self-satisfied air, I can tell he's taken all he needs to become the person he will be. I'm not sure why it annoys me as much as it does, as he's only stealing from himself. Or is he?

"But I would advise you to get going soon, my friend," Leo says. "The power source on the machine is dangerously low. I wasn't sure how to boost it up. Nor was your assistant."

"My assistant? You mean Sasha?"

"I call her Alexandra, but yes..." The way he says her name, in this oily, pretentious fashion, incenses me.

"You didn't do anything to her, did you?"

"Well, I know things are more 'open' in the future, but in this time, a gentleman does not kiss and tell."

He tips his head and a broad, over-confident smile breaks out, like the plague, on his face, which I really *really* want to hit just now.

"To return, you just have to press RETURN TO—"

"*I* know how to operate *my* machine, thank you." My tone is flinty enough to set the room alight. I glance down then and notice Leo's boots. They're mine, too. My favourite pair. I imagine I might see them in Leo's self-portraits in future.

One thing confuses me. "How did you arrive back here with your clothes intact?" My garments had evaporated during the journey.

"Alexandra helped me make a minor adjustment to the time-spin ratio. That seemed to work."

He has a dreamy look as he mentions Sasha again. *How dare you!* I want to say. And a lot more besides. But I'm keen to get going on the journey home, to fix anything that needs fixing. I satisfy myself with a final glare, before I press RETURN TO PLACE AND TIME OF ORIGIN.

As I blast off, I hear him shout: "Thank you! So much! What a month! Arrivederci, mio amico!" He laughs. A resonant and sinister laugh that seems to echo through the mist all the way home.

Eventually, the spinning begins, and, though I try to resist, I fall unconscious.

When I awake, I'm back in my laboratory. It's a month after my departure.

I give a cry of excitement, checking everything is as I left it. Some science equipment is gone, a few books are missing—one of my favourite works on da Vinci, among them. Plus, a ring of onyx and gold my parents gave me for my 21st birthday. I know where that will be now—in a bowl, in a Florentine loft, with the rest of the stolen loot. I know, too, that when I inspect my wardrobe, a pair of my jeans will be missing and some boots. I wonder what else Leo took while he was here.

On my lab bench is a note in a strange hand. The letters are half backwards. das ooT, daB ooT. *Mirror writing.*

I'm about to check it in the glass when I hear behind me: "Leonardo, do you fancy a break? We could have an aperitif—"

Seeing me, Sasha stops, open-mouthed. She looks me up and down, taking in the dank tunic and leggings, before launching herself into my arms. I embrace her too but can't help thinking about that flicker of disappointment in her eyes when she saw it was me. Not *Him*.

"So, the time machine really works?" she says.

"Yes, it does. And I'm guessing you met Leonardo?"

"Leo the God? Yes, I did."

"God no more. Just a person, and a flawed one like the rest of us," I say.

"He won't be back then?"

"Not if I can help it."

She nods and smiles but a tautness around the jaw hints at disappointment.

"What's that?" She points to the note in my hand.

"It's from Leonardo." She snatches it from me, squinting at it. "Where's a mirror?"

I point to a small glass near the sink. We bump heads as we clamour to inspect it. "Too bad, Too sad," I read.

What does he mean by that?

"Was Leonardo everything you hoped he'd be?" Sasha asks.

"No." I sigh. "He didn't really live up to expectations."

She twirls her hair and smiles. "In some ways, maybe not. In others…"

For a moment, she seems lost in her own secret musings. And when she looks up at me again, she has this look—a half-smile that is mysterious and smoky and way too familiar.

And I know…what else he took from me.

The Golden Lasso

GENRE: FANTASY

PROMPTS: A GOLDEN LASSO, A FUNERAL PROCESSION

♡

Jewel ran away to the mountains to escape a sticky romance and learn to become a dragon wrangler. But now she's back, and the heat is on.

I wasn't sure how I'd feel seeing Opal again.

Last time I saw him, I was headed for the mountains to learn the skills of a wrangler and join the dragon rangers—guardians of the borders of the High Plains kingdom. Opal was the deputy sheriff. I was a farm girl, good with critters, not so much with people. Not right for the partner of a future sheriff of the kingdom, as the chief wizard liked to point out. Opal and I knew we should call it quits.

But then there was the goodbye kiss.

I'd intended to be away a year or more and fly home, triumphant, on my dragon partner, a golden lasso at my hip, and show the wizard I was worth more'n two bits. But here I was, recalled six months early, for Sheriff Amber's funeral.

I thought I was over Opal. But a single glance at his crinkly dark head in the crowd below and my blood was running hotter than dragon's breath once more.

"Now hold on, Jewel." My dragon partner, Bluefire, turned his aquamarine gaze upon me as we rode through the skies. "A dragon's breath ain't that hot! You're in a bonfire league o' your own there, girl!"

"And what about the little emerald dragon at Shieldvale?" I said, patting his ridged hide. "As I recall, your blue wings turned green when you saw her, the blood was pumpin' so hot through your veins."

"I had a touch of dragon flu that day, I believe," he said.

Yeah, right! Love flu, more like.

Bluefire gave me a cheeky dragon grin. He was small for a dragon and hadn't yet attained his maximum shine. But he had a full dragon measure of twisting the truth.

"Your human lives are so short, you really should tell Deputy Sheriff Opal how you feel and mate with him to attain your heart's desire."

And he was direct to the point of embarrassment.

"Let's just do our job today, shall we?" I said. "Take a pass over the funeral procession, check all is as it should be."

"Copy that, pardner."

As Blue flew over the line of mourners, I leaned sideways to see the critters of the kingdom that had turned out to farewell Sheriff Amber. The sheriff had a reputation for being hard but fair and not pandering to any one species but treating 'em all equal. It earned her respect from most, though, naturally, not from the wizards who thought they deserved special treatment always. The sheriff had been fixing to put all that down in black and white, too, for those that could read, in a constitution for the High Plains kingdom. But she never did get to sign off on that document before a strange fever overcame her and she slipped into her final sleep.

Now here we were peering down on her body, supine upon a feather bed, carried by her close friends, looking just as if she'd dozed off in the sun.

Next up was the chief wizard in his high-top sombrero and dragon skin boots. Wizards and witches followed at his heels, magic fizzing around them like a heat haze. The elves came next, marching in symmetry. Then the trolls in lockstep. Then goblins, dwarves, fae, spirit animals, foreign dignitaries. Even sirens in nearby Silver River sang sad songs for the sheriff.

Overhead, four dragon wranglers guarded the mourners—me and Bluefire among 'em. The lead rider, Sienna, rode a magnificent desert dragon in shades of orange and gold. There was a crimson and a shimmering silver. Bluefire was a mix of sea greens and sky blues.

Dragons had keen vision and sense of smell so they could give warning of any threats from nearby lands—from the northerners, who hankered after our gold, and the easterners, who desired our trolls and dragons for heavy lifting.

And, speaking of enemies, I spotted, below in the crowd, the familiar blonde head of Nettle, my old rival, stickin' so close to Deputy Sheriff Opal you couldn't fit a fairy breath betwixt 'em. Nettle was pretty enough, I suppose, if you liked sunshine-wrapped prickly pears.

"You really don't like her, do you?" said Blue.

"She ain't right for Opal."

"And when did you become the county matchmaker? How often have you told yourself it'd be better if Opal forgot about you?"

It was annoying enough that Blue read my thoughts. Did he have to have opinions on them too?

Nettle caught my eye and smiled like she had the last canteen o' water for a hundred miles. She whispered something to Opal and he looked up. And they both sniggered.

What the—?

"They're laughing about your lasso," Blue said. "Because it's made of troll hair, not gold and magic like the other wranglers carry."

Nettle laughing at me wasn't surprising. The woman was sour as a grove of lemon trees. But Opal joining in? *That hurt.*

It'd be three more months till Blue and I earned our golden lasso. Till then, we trained with an ordinary rope. The golden lasso didn't just loop and tie things up, it could dampen magic, which would come in mighty handy if ever our enemies crossed into High Plains with a cohort of ornery wizards at their back. Or...if our chief wizard got to thinking a tin star might look pretty on his wizard's cape.

"C'mon, Blue, let's take a spin," I said. I needed to clear my head. "We'll do a southern sweep! Back soon!" I called to Sienna.

We flew fast over the countryside, which looked like a patchwork quilt in shades of green and brown. The farmhouses below seemed so tiny. Even the sheriff's sprawling homestead looked like a child's toy. The cool wind blasting my face felt good. Blowing away the hurt. And the embarrassment. *How could Opal laugh at me like that?*

"Tell me what was it brought down the sheriff," Blue asked. "Age? Snakebite?"

"I heard it was a fever o' some kind." Must have been a potent one. The woman had looked hale and hearty enough when I left.

"The deputy sheriff's eyes, when he looked up at us just now . . .were strange."

"Cruel, you mean?"

"His pupils were unnaturally dilated. Either he's deeply in love or under some kind of spell."

Yes! That explains it. And to my satisfaction. Nettle had tricked him, spiked his morning coffee or somesuch; now he was helpless to resist her. Only...

"Much as I don't like Nettle, she ain't stupid," I said. "She knows love potions only work for a short time. You can't really spell someone into loving you."

"What if real love ain't the aim?" Blue said. "What if it's more a case of getting hitched quick-smart to a shiny new sheriff."

What the—? Could that be right?

"That schemin' skunk!" I said.

We dipped low to follow Silver River meandering through the fields. Sirens undulated gracefully through the water. A couple touched their lips with their human fingers to blow kisses to us.

Passing Mermaid Rock—so named as folks thought it was shaped like a fish tail, though I couldn't see it—I recalled a time Opal and I had picnicked there. We had fae cakes and seaweed rolls and the sirens serenaded us with love songs. Oh, we blushed so hard that day. I remember we had to cut things short as Opal needed to sort out some strife at the *Drunken Dragon* saloon. But the way he looked at me as he was leavin'...was nothing like the look he gave me just now.

"Yep, Opal's in trouble," I said, suddenly sure of it.

Was Nettle really fixin' to marry him? And soon?

"You think Nettle loves him? Or is she jes' social climbing?" I asked. The girl was nothing if not a suck-up to those who could keep her movin' in an upwards trajectory on the hierarchy. Leastways, that was the impression she gave, all high and mighty, lookin' down on everyone like she'd already been crowned Queen of the Plains.

"Or is something else going on here?" Blue asked. When it came to devious thinking, no-one could match dragons.

"Like what?"

"Well, the timing does seem…serendipitous."

"That there's a big word, Bluefire. Sounds a lot like suspicious to me?"

For Opal to be so far gone, Nettle must have hurried over, lickety-split, to slip the potion into his drink as soon as she heard the sad news about the sheriff.

"Perhaps." Blue answered my thoughts. "Unless, of course, she had prior knowledge of the death?"

"When you say 'prior knowledge'…?"

"Maybe someone had an inkling Sheriff Amber would be passin' on soon and let her know beforehand," Blue said.

Someone…like the wizard? *That snake in my boots.*

Blue's sparkly dragon eyebrows rose to the edge of his ridged brow as he nodded.

"Diabolical!" I said. "If it's true."

Nettle wed to Opal would be the perfect spy for the wizard. Like a spider, sittin' in a golden web catchin' flies and passing the juiciest to him, she could give him advance knowledge of all the sheriff's plans. And she'd be well-placed to turn Opal round to the wizard's way of thinking on most things.

We continued low over the Enchanted Forest, Blue's tail skimming the treetops, making the leaves dance in our wake. Through the foliage I glimpsed the colourful lights of fairies playing in the branches. A couple of young elves popped their heads above the canopy, their mouths forming an "O" on seeing Blue.

"Howdy!" he called.

Screaming with delight, they ducked down, then popped up again, laughing.

We cruised over the rainbow-coloured crops and grapevines that were the speciality of High Plains country. The farmers in the field and trolls pushing heavy equipment waved to us.

"But this is all just speculation," I said. "Could be Sheriff Amber died of natural causes, and Opal really is in love with Nettle." *And it's all just wishful thinking on my part.*

"But there was something else wrong with that procession we saw," Blue said. "I can't quite smoke it out of my mind." Blue narrowed his eyes, and the golden centres swirled hypnotically from intense concentration.

I cast my mind back too. The funeral had moved slowly by the river. The death bed was prettily adorned, with hand-made quilts from a dozen families. The wizards were up front. The humans, grim-faced. The elves, graceful. The trolls, co-ordinated... *Co-ordinated?*

"Since when do trolls move in such orderly fashion?" I said. They were usually more like a rockslide, the air around them peppered with expletives as they rammed into each other and trod on other trolls' toes.

"That's it!" Blue said. "That's what was amiss. But why would that be?"

While I was in an examining frame of mind, my memory caught on something else, like a fishing line snaggin' on a rock. I'd seen it at the time but hadn't really *seen* it.

It was Sheriff Amber, lying on that bed, looking as if she'd just dozed off in the sun. *Because her cheeks were still pink.*

"Does blood pump through dead cheeks?" I asked.

"No, it does not."

"Is it possible the sheriff ain't actually dead?" I said. "Just enchanted to seem that way."

"Yes, it's a definite possibility."

"And the trolls?"

"Nothing short of powerful magic could give them anything like grace."

This plot was bigger than Nettle and her domestic scheming.

Blue sniffed twice. "And they've lit the funeral pyre."

"If the sheriff wasn't dead before, she sure as heck will be when they've done. Come on!"

Blue flew fast into the wind, flattening himself to minimise air resistance. I pulled my elbows in and put my head down, clinging on with every muscle and nail.

"The wizard is aimin' to remove the sheriff," I said, "and replace her with Opal. With Nettle by his side, steerin' him to do the wizard's bidding."

"And the new sheriff's first order of business will be to tear up the constitution for the High Plains," Blue said. "I'd bet my dragon treasure on it."

"If we're wrong, it won't be good," I said. "Messin' with the sheriff's burial on this auspicious day? There'd be a bounty on our head, which every scorpion and cave-troll will be lookin' to claim."

"Better be right then." Blue sounded nervous.

We swooped low, advancing like an arrow aimed at the sheriff's deathbed. The flames licked higher as the feather-stuffed quilts caught fire.

"She's not dead!" I screamed on approach. "The sheriff's alive!"

All heads turned my way, but no-one made a move to do anything.

Blue hovered over the bed and inhaled deeply, his blue scales turning bright green as he sucked up the flame, bit by bit, till only a swirl of smoke remained. Then he belched loudly.

"Well, pardon me, folks." He blushed.

No-one reacted. Not the opinionated humans, the fair-minded elves, the fun-loving trolls. Hollow-eyed, they gawped back at us.

"What a bunch o' scarecrows live on these plains." Blue shook his head in disgust.

"That's not their normal aspect," I said.

"Glad to hear it."

Sheriff Amber lay still on the death bed. *Wake up, Sheriff! Please, please don't be dead!*

"How do we wake her?" I said.

"The wizard's doing this," Blue said. "Look!"

The chief wizard's eyes were dark with fury as he watched us, his lips moving constantly like he was talking to himself.

He's enchanted everyone.

I looked up, hoping to find our fellow dragon wranglers aiming their lassos at the wizard. Instead, three golden circles came at us.

"Oh no!" The ropes zizzed past, almost catching Blue's tail. Just in time, he zig-zagged out of the lassos' path.

"The wizard enchanted the wranglers too!" I said. "And their ropes."

"And, look, he's coming for us now."

A wall of rippling air moved toward us, almost invisible, but for an occasional silver gleam catching the light.

"Hold on." Blue shot straight up, till the wave had passed, then loop-the-looped back down.

"Look at the wizard's fingers!" I said. "They're twitching magic! Can you blast some flame at him!"

"It'll burn everyone around him. You'll have to use your lasso."

Right. But, as mine didn't have special powers, I'd have to do this old school.

Snatching the rope from the saddle, I twirled it three times in the air. As Blue angled down towards the wizard, I let fly. The loop dropped onto the wizard's shoulders, breaking his concentration. The crowd jerked slightly. I yanked the rope down over his hands and pulled it tight, as if he was a colt straying from the herd. So tight, I heard a finger snap.

"Ahhhh!" the wizard yowled.

Below us, everyone in the procession shook their heads and looked about, as if just woken from a dream.

Sheriff Amber sat up on the funeral bed, rubbing her head. "What in a troll's toenails am I doing here?"

Three golden lassos snapped the wizard's way, tying him and his evil magic down.

Now Opal looked up and gave me his slow-burn smile. "Well, howdy, Jewel! Mighty pleased to see you."

"Howdy, deputy sheriff."

"Hold onto your hats, folks," said Blue, "here comes the bonfire! Yee-haa!"

Off the Menu

GENRE: ROMANCE

PROMPTS: FROGS' LEGS, A PASTURE

♡

When a German soldier goes searching for lunch in occupied France,
he gets more on his plate than frogs' legs.

Dinan, France, 1944

He's back again. At table eight.

Earlier than usual; the morning sun turns his hair a rusty gold, like the toffee crust on a crème brûlée. As he smiles, a dimple appears in his right cheek. I feel my lips relax and hope I'm not smiling back. It wouldn't look good.

Rainer is a German soldier, in the force occupying my hometown of Dinan, in northern France.

"Bonjour Simone," he says with a heavy German accent.

"What do you want, Herr?" I'm snappish as usual.

"A word?"

We are in *Le Paturage du Ciel* (Heaven's Pasture), a bistro where I work, just outside town. Jean-Claude, the owner and chef, runs it from his home—four tables in the front room, six more in the gravel garden, with upturned crates for furniture. Behind the house is a pasture where he grows vegetables and herbs for our house specialty: crepes.

Until recently, all our customers were French. Then some German soldiers found us and spread the word. Now, at lunchtime, the place swarms with them, like an infestation of cockroaches we can't stomp on or shoo away.

The first time he came to the bistro, Rainer sat at table eight, a sunny spot in the middle of the garden.

"What do you want, Herr?" I said, my standard opening to our German customers, cold as a Russian winter.

He turned to me, blue eyes curious, mouth ready to smile. "I'd like to know your name," he said.

"Are you ordering me to tell you?"

"I give no orders here, I only make requests."

"Well, I have a request," I said. "That you place your order for food. Or leave. So, someone else may take your seat."

His expression deflated like a soufflé when the oven door was opened too soon. I left him studying the menu while I served another table—some French neighbours. As we exchanged news about people we knew who'd been hurt or killed "by the Germans" (I said loudly), I felt his attention on us. A sneaky glance revealed a muscle clenching on his jaw. Good, let it stay clenched.

I took my time with the French people, then went back to him. "Okay, what's good here?" he said, still pleasant, though I could see it took more effort.

"If you're asking about the food, it's all good here. If you mean the people, I'd say everyone not wearing a uniform is good."

I thought he might lose it at that point. Part of me wanted him to.

I was just so angry about the Germans in our town, about everything to do with the war. It felt as if, not blood, but hot fury and hate flowed through my veins.

Jean-Claude and I looked on it as a patriotic duty to be as rude as possible to the Germans who came here, without being shot. Things were touch and go sometimes.

Like now, with Rainer. I watched his chest expand within his green-grey German coat, but then slowly deflate as he exhaled. After that, he chewed through his food silently and left.

France one, Germany zero.

I was surprised to see him back the next day.

"My name is Rainer," he began. "And you are...?"

A beat. "Simone."

He smiled as if it was some kind of victory, making me regret answering.

"I've always wanted to come to France," he went on. "Now I'm here, it's everything I imagined it would be."

"Join the army," I said. "See the world, meet people from other countries, then shoot them."

His mouth went slack. I think he was genuinely hurt. "I wish the circumstances were different," he stammered, "but are all French women as...forthright...as you?"

"What do you expect, Herr? You are not on holiday here. Tell me, in Germany, do you barge into your neighbours' homes without invitation, leave your muddy bootprints on their floors, then expect cake?"

"No, of course not. I'm sorry."

I should have felt triumphant; I had struck a blow for national pride. But I didn't.

"There was an especially annoying German in here today," I said as Jean-Claude and I washed up that afternoon. "I hope he doesn't come here again."

"It's good not to let the Germans get too comfortable," said Jean-Claude. "But be careful you don't go too far, Simone. These men are not clowns. They are killers. Never forget that."

He was back the next day, like a cold you couldn't shake off.

"Can I have a plate of frogs' legs?" he asked.

"Sorry, frogs' legs are off the menu."

Most Germans wanted to try frogs' legs—a French delicacy. Denying them the chance—though we had a plentiful supply—was our form of French resistance. That, and spitting on their food.

"No frogs' legs?" said Rainer. "Okay, then I'll have the—" He broke off to watch Jean-Claude carry a plate of fried legs to the French people at the next table. He raised his eyebrows at me. I raised my chin. "I'll have the spring crepe," he said, "if you still have any of those?"

A couple of days later, we got some tragic news. Daniel, our goat's cheese supplier, had been shot in town. He was a big, hairy guy with a quick smile. I'd known him since I was a girl. He was also an active member of the French Resistance. His loss hit me—hit us all—hard.

As soon as Rainer came in, I think he could tell something was up. He sat at table eight, but didn't make himself comfortable as usual. He took one look at my eyes, red and puffy from tears, and stood up again. "Perhaps I should eat elsewhere today?"

"Yes, why don't you," I said. "You could try München, or Hanover, or some place in Germany!"

Head bowed, he crunched his way across the gravel towards the street.

"Herr! Wait!" I called out. He turned back.

"You might as well stay. The money you spend, we'll give to Daniel's widow to help pay for his burial."

He sat down. "I am very sorry," he said, removing his hat.

Bitter words swam on my tongue. What right did he have to be sorry when Daniel's murderer was one of his own countrymen? Who knew? Maybe it was Rainer himself who had pulled the trigger. But I held the words back.

"Thank you," I murmured instead.

We were extra busy that day. The lunch tables turned over three times. Towards the end of our service, three Germans sat at one of the indoor tables. They spat as they spoke and filled the room with their braying laugh and ugly consonants.

The worst of the three was a tall man with a long face, like a horse, and cruel eyes. They wanted frogs' legs.

"Frogs' legs are off the menu," I said, no hint of apology.

"But I just saw you take a plate to that French woman there."

"They were our last legs."

"I don't believe you, Fräulein," said the man.

"Pfff, I don't care what you believe, Monsieur."

The sizzling in the kitchen seemed loud as all went quiet around us. Then it stopped altogether, as Jean-Claude's bulky frame filled the doorway.

"This is the third time you have given me this...lie," said the man. "It is an insult to me. It is an insult to Germany."

"You are an insult to me and France," I said. "Get out of the restaurant. And do not try to come back again, or next time I will put poison in your food!"

Horseface drew his gun. The shiny barrel of the weapon was a long dark tunnel of death thrust in my face. But I stuck my chin out at him—unwilling, unable, to back down.

And then the back of a grey-green uniform blocked my view of the man. Rainer stood between me and his fellow soldier, hands up in a gesture of surrender.

"The lady is not lying," he said. (One of my French patrons translated the German conversation for me later.) "I have eaten frogs' legs in this restaurant before. They're not as flavoursome as I'd hoped. They taste like fish."

Jean-Claude came out too. "Monsieur, regrettably frogs' legs are in erratic supply these days. If you wish to try a plate, perhaps we can place a special order for you and your friends for the next time you grace us with your presence here."

A deadly silence. I heard the click of a gun primed to shoot. But Rainer stayed put. "The crepes here are very good," he said. "Much better than fishy frogs' legs."

The man put his gun away but shot death stares at me. I sent mine right back.

Jean-Claude's face was slimy with sweat as he removed his grubby chef's apron and handed it to me. "Why don't you take over in the kitchen for a while, Simone? I'll serve the customers."

As Rainer was leaving, I caught up with him. "I did not ask for your help, Herr. I do not need help from a German."

It took him a minute to process my words, the smile lines on his face rearranging themselves into confusion. His jaw tightened and I noticed how well-defined it was—like one of Jean-Claude's cutting boards. "I apologise, Simone. For my actions and for those of my fellow soldiers."

"And for your information," I said, "frogs' legs do not taste like fish. They're more like chicken. Everyone knows that."

Jean-Claude and I were a little worried for the next few days that Horseface and his friends might come back for retribution. But we didn't see them again. Presumably, they'd moved on to bully some other poor French restaurateur.

On his next visit, I didn't spit in Rainer's food. And as he gave me his crepe order, I said: "If you'd like the frogs' legs, we have some today."

He gave me such a warm smile in response, I almost cancelled the order.

There were a few days when he didn't come in and I felt unaccountably anxious and tetchy. Whether I was worried something bad had happened to him, or he was doing bad things to others, I couldn't say.

Whenever he turned up after an absence, I gave him an extra serve of French pride. "Thank you, I enjoyed that," he said when he'd finished his crepe.

"You did? What a pity!"

Over the next two weeks, he sought opportunities to tell me about himself or ask questions about me. He was a bookkeeper, who liked to paint landscapes in the Impressionistic style, "which I like very much, though I am not convinced it is true art". He said he loved the spontaneity of France. "It's so different to Germany. Not as efficient, but exhilarating."

He got a few things out of me, too, like how I'd lost my mother when I was four and I dreamt of having my own bistro by the water some day.

"The war won't last forever," he said. "One day, you will have your restaurant."

"But what will be left then?" I said. "Will the whole world be German? Will I have to put bratwurst and sauerkraut on the menu?"

"I certainly hope not," he said.

A grin stole onto my face then. I banished it quickly.

Now, here we are again, and it frightens me how glad I am about that.

"Simone, come for a walk with me?" he says.

"No!" I hiss.

"I need to talk to you."

I send him off to wait for me at the oak tree at the bottom of the pasture where we won't be seen. Ten minutes later, I hurry down the road to join him. The air is scented with warm earth and herbs. The field is a vibrant green and tall stalks sway in the breeze, like spies trying to sneak a peek.

"I can't believe you asked me for a walk," I say, storming over. "What would people think if they saw me strolling with a German, who, for all I know, killed their brothers or sons."

"It's not personal. I fight to defend the people around me," he says. "No more, no less."

"That is just words, *blah-blah-blah*, that tell me nothing."

"We are both creatures of our times, Simone," he said. "Floating with the current, no real control over where we go."

"You say that, but you can control how far you go in fulfilling your duties to your country. You are responsible for that. And for how much you enjoy it."

He takes a very slow breath and puffs out loudly. "You are right," he says. "We will all have to account for our actions one day."

His blue eyes have a faraway quality, like he's in a dark tunnel looking towards the light.

I wonder what he wants from me here. Romance? Am I another French delicacy he wants to try before he goes home? That's not going to happen. Though standing here, I feel intensely vulnerable as I realise just how much I like him. His patience, his strength, his humility.

"I must say goodbye," he says. "I'll be leaving soon."

"When?"

"Imminently."

"You don't expect me to kiss you?"

"No! I mean, I cannot say I haven't imagined what it might be like.

But, no, I would not ask it of you."

"Good, because I would rather cut off my lips than kiss an enemy soldier."

He smiles and shakes his head. "Simone, so much fire in you. It is admirable, but very dangerous. Please, I urge you, have the feeling but don't show so much."

"Don't tell me what to do. I will show as much as I wish. For you Germans deserve it and I am not afraid."

"You should be afraid. I have seen people killed, and brutally, with far less provocation. I do not want you to be among them. Be smart and live to spread your fire another day."

I wasn't sure what to say to that.

"Why did you ask me to come here?" I said. "To tell me to be good and behave like a German girl would?"

"No." He tells me he overheard Horseface and his friends talking about getting revenge for the frogs' legs incident before they leave Dinan. "You should tell Jean-Claude to close the restaurant for a while and stay away from the house. I do not want anything bad to happen to either of you."

As furious as I am at this news—and I am, ranting and raging so fast Rainer can't keep up—I cannot be angry with him. I know he's taken a risk coming here to warn us. And I am grateful for that.

"You know, you're not what I expected a German soldier to be," I say.

"You are everything and more than I hoped for in a French woman."

Five years later

I've just finished setting for dinner in my restaurant, *Neptune's Pasture*, on the water. It's a warm evening and the breeze carries a scent of seawater and freshly turned fields. I take a minute to pull apart a baguette left from the morning to throw to the ducks on the water.

As I turn back, I see an early customer sitting at an outside table. It's a man in a dark suit, reading the menu.

"Are you ready to order, sir?"

"Yes, I am," he says. He has a heavy German accent, which still makes me bristle. I try to glimpse his face, but the menu covers it.

"May I have the frogs' legs please?"

"I'm sorry, Herr, but frogs' legs are off."

Rainer lowers his menu, a broad smile on his tanned face. "Why doesn't that surprise me?"

Princess for a Day

GENRE: FAIRYTALE

PROMPTS: A TURTLE, AN ISLAND

♡

Claire thinks she has found her Prince Charming and is ready to sail off into the sunset. But in real life, the ending is just the beginning.

"Now, Claire, you get to live happily ever after," says one wedding guest. "While we all turn green with envy."

My reply sticks in my throat, like a fish bone. I smile and wave as the last of the guests board the *No Regrets*, a sleek cruiser straight out of a Bond film. The sky is pink, the water silvery as they shrink into the distance. Leaving me and my new husband alone on our private island.

"Hey, wifey." Jack slings his arm over my shoulder. "I'll open some champagne." He tears off across sand so white it hurts your eyes, sprinkled with rainbow-coloured confetti.

"No more, please," I call. The first glass tastes divine, the tenth more like last night's bed pan.

Jack doesn't hear me. He's haring towards our beach mansion—designed by a famous architect, decorated by an Oscar-nominated art director.

I kneel in the powder-soft sand and pick up a pink confetti disk. Anyone finding these years from now will assume a wedding happened here and it was the happiest day of someone's life.

They'd be wrong.

Yes, today was my wedding day. But, in my twenty-eight years, I've never felt more alone.

I met Jack eighteen months ago in LA. I was a would-be actress, waiting tables till my big break came. After months of auditioning, I grew weary of rejection. And the effort it took for friends and family to continue sounding optimistic about my future.

So, when the company I worked for was hired to cater a party for a well-known Hollywood producer, I wanted to go. I wasn't rostered on; I had to pay another waitress double my salary to take her shift. But it would be worth it for the contacts, I figured. My last shot at realising a dream.

The week before the party, I spent every spare moment at the gym. I visited the tanning salon, beautician and hairdresser to the rich and famous (which cost more than a year's styling elsewhere). And bought a pair of shoes with the highest heels I'd ever owned for that long-legged look.

As I entered Mr Newbridge's beachfront home, I gasped. The light-filled rooms, art objects to die for, the calming sound of the sea were like something out of a fairytale. I expected Cinderella to sweep in at any moment.

But if she did, I didn't see it. Carmen, the shift manager, took one look at me and gave me kitchen duty. "Stay there. Don't bother the stars, or you'll never work for me again!"

What a cow!

Still, I snuck onto the floor a few times, carrying trays, my heart fluttering as I spotted actors I recognised from TV and film.

The biggest star was Jack Heathcliff, star of *The Prince of Hearts*, the most in-demand film actor on Earth. Our eyes grazed each other's briefly and I thought I detected the beginnings of a smile when Killjoy Carmen intervened.

"Nice try, Claire. Get back to the kitchen."

Annoyed, I slugged down the half-empty glasses of champagne I'd collected—"Shame to waste good booze!"—until Carmen caught me and sent me packing.

The clock struck twelve as I was ejected from the premises.

Oh, great! Walking home in these shoes would give me blisters the size of golf balls, if I didn't twist my ankle first. *Something to take home with me, a symbol of my utter failure.*

"Leaving so soon?" A producer I recognised was leaning against a tree, smoking.

I sucked my stomach in, pulled my shoulders back. "I've finished my shift."

He whistled and held up an arm and a black limousine, shiny as an oil spill, cruised up. A uniformed driver opened the door.

"Can I give you a lift somewhere?" he asked.

"Yes, thank you."

"Call me Marvin."

But before we'd even left the driveway, his hand was on my knee, then thigh and climbing rapidly. I slapped it away.

"I thought you wanted to be an actress," he said.

"Not that kind of actress."

"Stop!" He opened the limo door and shoved me out. I tumbled out, grazing my knee and hearing my heel snap as the tyres churned gravel, spitting some in my eye, as he took off.

In the dark, I couldn't find my second shoe. Cursing, I took the other one off and began the long walk home barefoot. As stones bit into the pads of my feet, I felt so foolish, so ashamed. So done with this stupid Hollywood dream.

"Excuse me, ma'am?" A car pulled up, Jack Heathcliff at the wheel. "You were a waitress at the party, weren't you? Can I drop you somewhere?"

"No, thanks." I walked grimly on. *What's the point?*

"Is this yours?" Jack dangled my lost shoe. "I found it on the driveway." He stopped and handed it to me.

"Thanks."

I took it and kept going.

"If you don't want a lift, perhaps I can walk you home?" he said, catching me up. "You never know what predators are about."

And then the Prince of Hollywood locked his car and fell into step beside me.

Three months later, we were engaged. He was sweet and funny and said I smelled like cotton candy. Like home.

But the movie business is fickle. It loves you one minute, abandons you the next. You drink to celebrate the triumphs and even more to forget the flops. Jack needed to forget. So, he took something stronger. A lot of somethings.

On our first anniversary, we celebrated at one of Hollywood's finest restaurants. I spent a lot of time at the table alone while he was in the bathroom. He dozed off in his dessert.

Two glasses of champagne sit on the benchtop, bubbles rising to the surface and bursting.

I look around my beach house. It's filled with original artworks. Very beautiful. I have a French chef and a view of sunset over the Caribbean—which I usually watch alone.

An aquarium glitters with pirate treasure—real jewels, in our case—and exotic fish. I peer inside at our latest acquisition, a yellow-bellied slider turtle, beautifully patterned. It claws at the glass, a sound which grates on the ear, as it struggles to free itself.

"Darling," I call out to Jack in the bathroom. "Come drink your champagne!"

There's no reply. *Not unusual.* I wait for the familiar *thump* from the bathroom. My new husband spent a lot of time "indisposed" during our wedding. I told guests it was nuptial nerves.

"Here's to the happy couple." I raise the glass and down the wine before heading in to pick my prince off the floor.

The fairy tale has ended.

Now the real love story begins.

Too Many Sherlocks

BRIEF: WRITE A SHERLOCK HOLMES STORY IN THE STYLE OF SIR ARTHUR CONAN DOYLE IN WHICH THE GREAT DETECTIVE DOES NOT APPEAR.

♡

When Sherlock Holmes goes missing, Dr Watson asks theatre doyen Irene Adler for help locating him. The search takes him to the highest and lowest parts of Victorian London.

CHAPTER ONE

As the sometime-chronicler of the exploits of the great detective, Sherlock Holmes, I have been fortunate to witness the workings of his extraordinary mind on many occasions. Sometimes, when considering a case, he would go as still as a corpse as he turned facts over in his mind. At others, he was a whirlwind, running here and there with no need for rest or sustenance in pursuit of answers that had eluded the police. However, one of his most intriguing adventures began while he was mysteriously absent and I was called upon to start the investigation without him.

During the course of this baffling case—which took us to the heights and depths of London society—I became better acquainted with a most singular individual, among whose achievements I count the stirring of tender feelings within the great detective himself. Holmes loudly declaimed any connection with feelings or matters relating to the human heart. Except when it involved her. The individual I speak of is known in London circles as Irene Adler. Though Sherlock refers to her, simply, as The Woman.

I had met Ms Adler a few times when she called upon Holmes at our shared residence at 221B Baker Street. Although those encounters were brief, I was struck by the brightness of her eye, the elegance of her carriage, and a general air of astuteness about her. Often, I imagined I saw a smile hiding at the corner of her mouth, as if she were enjoying some secret amusement, the details of which she alone knew.

But on this evening, a deeper and more personal acquaintance between us was about to begin.

At the time, Sherlock was nowhere to be found and, as the hour grew late, our tickets for the evening's performance of *Moll Flanders* at the Theatre Royal lay unclaimed on the dining table.

"Mrs Hudson, have you any idea where Sherlock is?" I enquired as our landlady entered carrying the mail and the evening newspaper. "I've not seen him in two days and we have a theatre engagement tonight."

"He's a bit large to be mislaid, Doctor," Mrs Hudson said, "so I can only assume he's been detained on some business or other and has thoughtlessly forgotten your engagement."

Holmes could be thoughtless in many ways, I knew. He thought little or not at all of the comfort of those around him when practising his violin late at night or conducting science experiments in our shared living room. Often, in the midst of a problem, he was thoughtless of his own need for food, drink and sleep. But never before had he forgotten a social arrangement with me, one which offered the possibility of observing London's glittering society at close quarters—of benefit in his role as consulting detective—while providing him an opportunity to bask in the warmth of an admiring public, sating his deep need to show off.

It was especially odd he would forget a performance which starred Irene Adler, whom he considered the queen of her sex.

"Should we be worried, Doctor?" Mrs Hudson asked.

"I shouldn't think so," said I, more blithely than I felt.

"Come to think of it," Mrs Hudson continued, her forehead trenched with concern, "I haven't seen him since he went out looking very spiffy two nights ago. Had his hair combed and all. And there was a sweetness in the air around him. If it had been spring, I'd have thought it was the scent of a flower drifting on the breeze. Only no flowers worth their stalks are blooming in this freezing weather. So, I wondered, could he have sprinkled floral water upon himself?"

"Highly improbable!" I assured her before wishing her a good night and asking her to send Sherlock to the theatre if he returned home presently.

Night was closing in, its icy fingers taunting exposed wrists, ankles and aching joints. Grey clouds scuttled across the inky sky like vermin in a drain as the cacophony of street life rose—the clatter of carriage wheels on the rutted road, the squeals of children and the deep-throated cries of newspaper-sellers spruiking their wares.

A man in a top hat dashing between carriages flinched as a hansom driver cracked his whip over a horse's flank. A high-pitched woman's scream told of a cut purse plying his trade nearby.

Just an ordinary night in London town.

I hunched beneath my lapels. Smoke from charcoal burning in a brazier almost covered the scent of waste—horse and human—pervading the streets as I made my way on foot to the theatre.

Before I'd gone far, a small boy appeared on the footpath before me. His legs were like matchsticks with dirt so ingrained upon his face as to resemble a birthmark.

"Please, Doctor, sir," he pleaded, wringing his bony hands. "Have you got any jobs for me? Only Mr Holmes is nowhere about and I've the devil of a hunger gnawin' at me belly."

I recognised the boy. He was one of Sherlock's young hounds, a group of street children, marked by no-one, observing everyone. He paid them regularly for information and, I suspected, for benevolent reasons to which he would never own.

"I am wondering where Mr Holmes might be myself," I said, crouching to the child's level. "If you would be so kind as to make enquiries on my behalf?" I handed him a clutch of coins.

The boy's brown eyes were as round as buttons upon a winter coat. "Don't worry, Doc, I'll find him!" He turned to go.

"Wait! Boy! What's your name?"

"My mother, who laid down for her final rest when I was but crawlin', called me Dante."

"Dante!" I repeated, amazed one as humble as he would possess such an august appellation. "Well, Dante, I trust we'll meet again."

"You can count your coin on it, Doc!"

He grinned and darted off along the street, to shouts of, "Oi, watch it, you little runt!"

On my way to the theatre, I detoured via Scotland Yard and made enquiries after Inspector Lestrade. I'd encountered the officer several times during my adventures with Holmes and had come to regard him as a friend. I wanted to invite him to the show to make use of Holmes's unclaimed ticket. But Lestrade had been called away on urgent detective business, the desk sergeant said. I left him a note and continued to the theatre.

Squeezing past theatregoers spilling out onto the pavement, I moved into the reception room, where men in dress coats and women with rich velvet gowns shaped over corsets of whalebone chatted excitedly before curtain's rise. Light from wall sconces flickered on their faces, glancing off shiny buttons and adornments.

I took a moment to scan the foyer for Holmes—to no avail. As I cast about, though, several pairs of eyes met mine with the spark of recognition. An older woman in a silver shawl mouthed "Dr Watson" to her companion; I read it as clearly as a headline in the *Times*. Some of Holmes's fame was, regrettably, flowing onto me. Eager to escape further glances, I moved along the hall and into the theatre.

The three dress circles rose up like layers of a wedding cake in gold and cream. I was seated in the stalls, which were full but for Holmes's empty place beside me.

All my troubles receded as the lights came up and Irene Adler took the stage in the story of Moll Flanders, a woman making her way through life on nothing but cunning and beauty. Though Moll committed wicked acts along the way, Ms Adler's performance evoked sympathy for her character, highlighting how few choices were permitted to a woman alone in a heartless society. Indeed, she was so convincing in her role, I forgot at times I was watching a play. It made me wonder about Irene Adler's personal history—how it compared with the eponymous Moll's, struggling through life with no man's protection.

I fancied I saw Ms Adler glance over, once or twice, at the empty seat beside me, and a shadow of disappointment cross her face.

After the show, I made my way backstage to see Irene Adler.

The dressing room corridor boomed with the laughter of performers now at ease. I passed rooms where actors who had played heinous villains onstage had changed into street wear and appeared as harmless and likeable as the next person. I marvelled at the artifice of the theatre.

Halfway along the corridor, a dozen casts of heads stood upon shelves, bearing wigs, facial hair, and all manner of facial augmentations—noses, chins and cheeks. I touched a false chin. It was warm and spongy in texture but looked so like skin, I was in awe.

"Dr Watson!" Ms Adler's voice summoned me from a doorway further along. "What a pleasure to see you!" She gestured me into her dressing room.

Hers was larger than most others I'd seen, with a mirror at the centre and lights dotted around it. Pots of makeup and brushes lay upon a table nearby. Bunches of flowers and impressive floral arrangements occupied a portion of the room. Cards peeking out of the bunches revealed they were from Count So-and-so and Lord Such-and-such. Unsurprisingly, this striking and talented woman had a host of admirers, many from the highest tiers of society.

A bottle of French champagne sat unopened in a silver ice bucket. Most of the ice had turned to water but for one recalcitrant cube, like an iceberg floating in northern seas.

"Are you alone, then?" Ms Adler asked. "I thought I saw an empty seat where Mr Holmes was meant to be?"

"He was unable to attend, I'm afraid."

"Cad!" she declared, still smiling. She'd changed out of her stage costume into a beige and navy dress. Her long dark hair flowed freely; her emerald eyes were as piercing as a cat's and as mysterious. "I'm so glad you, at least, could come, Doctor," she effused.

"I wouldn't miss it. And the pleasure was all mine."

"What excuse does the great detective offer for his absence?" Nothing about her delivery conveyed even the slightest annoyance.

"I can only assume he is engaged on very important business," I said. "Nothing less would keep him from attending."

"Assume?" she said. "Do you not know where he is?"

"No. He has disappeared before without sending word but—"

"You're worried about him." She reached for the champagne. Deftly, she worked the cork open and filled two glasses, handing one to me. As the golden liquid fizzed in the glass, I explained that Holmes had not been seen for two days. Recalling Mrs Hudson's observations about the floral scent in the air at the time, I paused. "You were not engaged to meet him, were you? Our housekeeper noted he had been quite particular about his toilet, which was not his habit."

Ms Adler sipped her drink slowly. "We had arranged to meet for supper in the *Cafe Royale*. I am sorry to say, Mr Holmes did not keep the appointment."

"You mean...he stood you up?"

She nodded, all humour gone. "At the time, I thought he was just being Sherlock. Rude, careless of my feelings."

"Holmes is careless of the feelings of most people, regardless of rank," I said, "but never of yours, Ms Adler. If he did not keep his engagement with you, and did not send word to explain his absence...?"

She shook her head.

"That is cause for concern." As I spoke the words, I felt them to be true.

Her smooth brow creased. She opened her mouth to reply, but a young woman, barely more than sixteen, with rosy cheeks in a pale face, burst into the room, erupting with a jumble of words delivered so quickly they all ran together.

"Slow down, Rachel. And try again," Ms Adler coaxed.

"There's a gentleman says you're expectin' him and begs to know what's keepin' you," said Rachel. "He also says he can get any actress he wants in London and doesn't have to wait for a tardy one." The girl looked steadfastly at her hands as she spoke the last. "Beggin' your pardon, Miss."

"Nothing to pardon, Rachel."

I popped up like a jack-in-the box. "I will happily send this rude gentleman packing. And explain he does not need to speak to you, or any woman, like that."

"No need, Doctor," Ms Adler said, barely ruffled. "I can handle him."

I took that as my cue to leave. "Then I won't keep you any longer. I just wanted to thank you for the ticket and congratulate you on a wonderful show."

"We will speak about this business with Sherlock further," she said. "I will call at 221B Baker Street at ten tomorrow morning, if that suits."

I could have told her not to trouble herself. Instead, I nodded agreement. Something was afoot with Sherlock, I could feel it. Speaking to this intelligent woman might shed some light on the situation or, at the least, quell the fear rising within me like a river in flood. And, if by some chance he was back home by the morning, well, he could explain the empty seat to her himself.

"And, Doctor?" she called me back. "Please call me Irene."

CHAPTER TWO

My dreams were filled with shadowy figures pursuing me, and Sherlock calling my name from somewhere I could not find him. I awoke to Mrs Hudson shouting outside my door. "Sorry to wake you, Doctor, but Inspector Lestrade is here!"

I dressed quickly and headed downstairs to find Lestrade pacing, thumbs in his belt hooks, his habitual frown accentuating his ferret-like features. "Ah, Watson, there you are," he exclaimed. "I heard you'd called into the station last night. How was the show? From all reports, Miss Adler is as pretty as a plum pudding with custard."

"Indeed she is. And talented too."

We conversed for a few minutes about the theatre before he interjected.

"I had the shock of me life last night!" He clapped his hand to his chest. "We pulled a cadaver out of an opium den in town and I swear it looked just like Holmes. Tall, beaky, thinning on top."

"And?" My heart stopped beating as I awaited the answer.

"Wasn't him."

"Are you sure? Sometimes, a stint of indulgence can leave one's features in a flaccid state."

"Gave him a good going over myself," said the detective. "It wasn't pretty. But, rest assured, it wasn't our mutual friend."

That was a great relief. "Was the man's death due to an overdose?"

"That's the strange part," Lestrade said, his eyebrows meeting in a caterpillar line of concern. "His throat had been crushed. There were red marks around here." He indicated the front of his neck. "Some powerful hands had a really good squeeze, and the poor devil was too drugged up to resist. I tell you, I wouldn't want to meet the man on the ends of those hands." He made a whistling noise.

Mrs Hudson, mounting the stairs with tea and toast for me, offered her own opinion. "Well, you know what they say. Big hands, big..." She raised her eyebrows and cackled like a crone.

The Inspector and I shook our heads at the woman and I was about to respond when Irene Adler ascended the stairs, in dark attire wearing a hat with a veil over her face.

"Good morning, Doctor. Inspector."

"A pleasure, Miss Adler," said Lestrade.

"I was hoping Sherlock might have returned overnight. Have we any word from him?"

I shook my head.

"Well, I wonder if we can discover something about his movements from an inspection of his living room," she said.

As her eyes roamed the room, Lestrade raised his eyebrows at me. The pair of us had tried this before on a different case and had failed quite spectacularly.

"I'll start with the obvious," said Ms Adler, removing her hat. "The place has been turned over by an intruder."

I frowned. "What? No, Holmes is just not a tidy man."

Irene looked askance at me. "But the leavings of his pipe are scattered over the seat and floor in such a random pattern as to suggest it was cast aside carelessly." She knelt and looked under the sofa, emerging with Sherlock's pipe.

"By Jove, you're right!" I asserted. As slovenly as my friend's habits were, he would never discard his instrument in such a cavalier fashion.

"I didn't do a thorough examination of the scene when I arrived," Lestrade mumbled, "or I might have concluded the same."

Someone had been here. But when? Was it last night while I was at the theatre? Or while I slept in the next room?

She moved to a study of Sherlock's mail, stacked neatly on the table.

"You can't tell me an intruder's been through them," Lestrade said. "That pile of letters is neater than my wife's recipe cards. And no-one dares touch those, especially not the recipe for Grandma's eel pie."

"Indeed," said Irene. "The pile is neat. Which in itself is interesting, considering Dr Watson's assertion that Sherlock is an untidy man.

"See how all the letters are open and face down on the desk, with the oldest on top?" she said. "Usually, the most recent piece of mail sits on top, face upwards. Which would imply someone has been through these letters methodically, starting from the most recent, turning each one over as they read it, before moving to the next. In so doing, they inverted the order and reversed the documents."

I could see she was right. It was obvious when you thought about it.

"Did they find anything, do you think?" I asked.

Irene shook her head. "If they had, they would have ceased looking; the rest of the pile would have been left as it was. As the entire pile has been sifted, we can assume they searched the lot and found nothing. Oh, and they're left-handed."

Lestrade looked quizzically at me.

"Because the pile is sitting so far to the left of the desk," she added.

I imagined a left-hander's action as they perused the pile and realised she was correct again. Meanwhile, Lestrade nodded sagely as if Blind Freddy and all his sightless siblings could have seen that.

Her attention moved to a bulletin board by the bookcase, on which several letters and papers were pinned. Examining each paper in turn, she stopped on an empty space in the middle. "What was there before? I see the mark of a drawing pin, recently removed. Something has been taken, Dr Watson. Do you know what it was?"

"I think it was a likeness of Holmes, drawn by a grateful client," I said.

"So, whoever came here went away with Holmes's likeness. Clearly, they're looking for him and they've never met him before," Irene concluded.

As she trawled through the test tubes on Sherlock's work bench, raising each one to the light, the better to assess it, Lestrade scratched his head. "Madam, can I ask, are you related to Holmes? His long-lost sister, an aunt twice removed on his father's side?"

Ignoring the Inspector's question, Ms Adler focused on a collection of magnification devices in the top drawer. "Holmes has a loupe here," she said matter-of-factly. Picking up a handful of stones from a bowl on the desktop, she placed a small tubular glass to her eye and squinted closely at them. "The most powerful one I've ever seen."

"A loupe?" Lestrade pressed it to his face and, as he looked around the room, his magnified bloodshot eyeball was disturbing to behold.

"It's an instrument to determine the quality of a gemstone, such as a ruby or diamond," Irene explained. "Mr Holmes seems to be acquiring knowledge in the lead-up to inspecting a gem."

Pacing back and forth, her lips twisted to the side in thought. "As it is Sherlock we are talking about, it will be no ordinary gem, but one quite extraordinary. Gentlemen, I'm thinking he could be involved with the recently discovered Callaghan diamond. Have you heard of it?"

Lestrade and I shook our heads in unison.

"It is said to be the world's most valuable diamond. Soon to be added to the Queen's Crown Jewel collection."

The Inspector lowered the glass now, but his eye—both eyes— remained enlarged with awe as Irene explained that her contacts in high places had spoken of a diamond from South Africa which was to be re-set into the royal sceptre the next day.

"Not only is the jewel valuable in monetary terms," she expounded, "but the prestige that would go to Britain as the caretaker of this prize would be significant. Mr Holmes's possession of the loupe and the timing of his mysterious absence would suggest the two are related. Though, of course, I'm just speculating."

The officer and I stood dumbstruck at this astonishing news and the ease at which she'd arrived at it.

"I'm sure, Inspector, if you'd had the information as I had," Irene said, "you would have reached the same conclusion and more quickly." Again, I saw a suggestion of humour about her lips.

"Indeed," Lestrade agreed. "So that's what Sherlock's up to then? Very good."

But was it good? I wasn't so sure.

"Won't there be people from foreign powers across the water keen to get hold of such a prestigious jewel and symbol of power for their own elevation?" I asked.

"Indeed, Doctor Watson, I believe you're right," Irene replied. "Possession of the jewel will draw considerable jeopardy to its custodian. Perhaps that's why our friend has disappeared without word. I suspect he's in hiding. And there may well be much to hide from."

"Holmes in hiding?" said Lestrade, his right eyebrow askew. "Pish and nonsense. The man is not one to hide from anything."

I was pleased with Lestrade in that moment. "He's right," I said.

"Well, perhaps in this, his consideration for England has overridden his ego," she offered.

"That, indeed, is hard to believe," I said.

"So, let's assume the intruder was looking for the diamond, or some clue as to Holmes's whereabouts," Ms Adler said. "Did he find it, I wonder? The action with the pipe would suggest otherwise. It has been my observation that some men, when thwarted in their aims, throw or smash something to relieve their anger. Usually something belonging to the person they view as responsible for frustrating their ambitions."

A tightness around Irene's mouth led me to believe she'd had personal experience of such petulance.

"In this case," she continued, "the intruder flung the pipe in a gesture of pique. Which is good news for us. For it suggests Holmes is still at large. And if he is, and he's in hiding for the reasons we have surmised, you'll have no need to fear for him, Doctor. Rest assured, he will have the protection of Her Majesty's best agents."

It was reassuring to hear her conclusions. "But can they protect him from himself," I said, "and his need to outsmart his protectors and make fools of them?"

"We can only hope."

She set about examining the rest of the room as Lestrade and I watched. After a fifteen-minute surveillance of our shared apartments, she concluded: "The man you are looking for is large—head and shoulders above the rest—with red hair, a limp on his left side and a scar on his right cheek. He is German by nationality, with a habit of gambling...and he likes gardening in his spare time."

If Lestrade and I were wide-eyed before, our eyes were now moons resting upon our cheeks.

"How on earth have you arrived at that conclusion?" the officer burst forth.

"Firstly, footprints in the fallen ash from Sherlock's pipe allow me to determine the length of our intruder's stride—here one step, there another—which permits a guess at his height. See how the footstep on one side is more pronounced than on the other, suggesting a limp."

Lestrade followed the tobacco trail with his magnifying glass.

"The pattern of the ash suggests the pipe was thrown in the fashion of a dice, like so, under-arm, rather than over-arm like a cricket ball. Perhaps from a habit of gambling.

"And the red hair—" we watched her move to the sofa cushion and carefully lift off a single hair, which she passed to Lestrade "—was a stroke of luck."

"You said he was German, and a gardener?" I prompted, feeling like a dog awaiting scraps at a banquet table.

"A footprint found in the hallway is from a particular style of a German brogue. Although a popular import among English gentlemen some years ago, it has since fallen from the Must-Have fashion list. I conclude, therefore, it was likely worn by a native of that country, one not so well-off that he could change his shoes each season according to fashion's dictates."

The long list of assumptions she'd arrived at so easily gave the detective a gloomy aspect. "And the gardening hobby?" he enquired dispiritedly.

Irene produced a jagged thumbnail, the colour of ear wax with dirt lining its edge. "I found this behind the sofa cushions, where it must have torn off during his search. The crescent pattern of dirt beneath the nail is suggestive of someone who, habitually, has their hands in the soil."

"Could he be a grave digger?" Lestrade offered, momentarily brightening. "Or a grave robber, perhaps?"

"Clever, Inspector." She smiled broadly. "He might well have been. However, as those activities usually involve a spade rather than clawing at the earth with fingernails, he was probably also an avid planter."

"And the scar?" I enquired.

"On his right cheek, shaped like a sickle."

"How could you possibly deduce that?" I asked.

"It's so large, I can see it from here. Right across the road from where he's standing."

Lestrade lurched towards the window, and I grasped his arm to pull him back behind the curtains so we wouldn't be seen and give the game away. Sure enough, a man stood across the road, pretending to read a paper—I could just make out its German header—with a noticeable scar upon his cheek.

"In my circles, I've heard whispers of a man," Irene said, "a redhaired German who does secret work for his government or anyone who has the funds to pay."

"So, this German monster was in our house last night?" I enquired. As an ex-army doctor, I was not given to flutters of fear over golems and suchlike. But the look of this man, the size of him, and the sense of malevolence emanating from him, even from afar, made me shudder. Especially as I pictured him roaming around the house freely while both Mrs Hudson and I lay asleep in our beds.

"Don't worry, Doctor Watson," Irene said. "While you're unaware of his presence, he has good reason to preserve your life. Because he's hoping to follow you. He wants you to lead him to his quarry, Sherlock Holmes."

A search of the rest of the apartment confirmed items missing from Holmes's wardrobe—some shirts and trousers, spare socks. It was unlikely the golem took those. Rather, their removal confirmed her theory that someone had packed an overnight bag for Holmes's stay in a secret location.

Irene picked up a framed photo on Sherlock's bedside table, frowning. "He keeps a photo of his violin beside his bed?"

"He's a music lover," I said.

She scoffed. "He's a strange one, our Sherlock."

A final search of the sitting room unearthed one more possible clue—a small advertisement clipped from the newspaper, for the Oriental Emporium in Limehouse. She found it beneath a protective leather mat on Sherlock's lab desk.

"This clipping seems recent," I observed as she passed it to me. "I wonder why Holmes kept it."

"It might be worth a visit to this emporium, in case his business took him there in recent days," Irene suggested.

I nodded, glad to have a concrete lead to divert mind and body from fretting.

"Did our red-haired friend miss this?" I asked, waving the advert.

"We have to assume he's seen it," she said. "And that he will have it on his list of places to investigate, too."

I farewelled my guests on the street outside our residence, where we agreed to keep each other informed of any new information on Sherlock's whereabouts. While we talked, I glanced about furtively, searching for the German. However, he appeared to have vanished for the time being, which was a great relief.

I watched Irene Adler move along the busy road, so dainty and yet so intellectually formidable, and marvelled at all she'd managed to uncover while still ministering to Lestrade's bruised ego. Was it possible she had all of Holmes's deductive abilities, coupled with a superior insight into human emotion and motivations? If so, she was a truly fearsome ally. Or adversary.

"Doctor!" came a cry. Along the road, I spotted Dante dodging wheels and insults as he hurried towards me on his spindly legs. "I been lookin' for Mr Holmes in his usual haunts, but he ain't there. You want me to keep lookin'?"

I was reluctant to set the child on a course where he might encounter the golem, especially given the possibility Holmes might be safely under the protection of Her Majesty's agents. Instead, I invented a new assignment for him.

"Why don't you follow that lady there—" I pointed to Irene Adler "—and tell me where she goes." I handed him a few more coins. That gave him a task, and, if Irene were to encounter any danger, the boy could raise the alarm.

Dante tipped his imaginary hat to me and vanished into the teeming traffic.

Back inside 221B, I went straight to Mrs Hudson's door to warn her about the red-haired man. But if I'd expected her to wither in fear, I couldn't have been more mistaken.

"Let him come, the ruby-headed kraut," she said, "and I'll give him a welcome he won't expect." She wielded a heavy-based cooking pan in one hand and an umbrella in the other. "He'll find we English women are not the wilting flowers he imagines."

As she set to practising her "saucepan swing" and "umbrella poke", I couldn't help but admire her spirit. Of all the landladies in London, she was the right one for the city's famous consulting detective.

CHAPTER THREE

I had a few patients to see at my general practice, but after attending them, I set out across town and cultures to the Oriental Emporium in Limehouse in the city's east. By a stroke of luck, I managed to pick up a hansom cab right outside my door, though the driver was a voluble chap and particularly rude, making sport of insulting all those we passed. His exclamations constantly interrupted my train of thought as the cab's wheels churned through London's streets, where beggars overtaken by grime shared pavements with the primped, poised and prissy and the well-heeled rubbed shoulders with those down-at-heel.

"Move your arse or Mr Whip here will move it for you!" the cabbie called to some pedestrians.

Charming.

I wasn't sure what to expect at the Oriental Emporium. Perhaps nothing at all. It might have been no more than a fancy for a trinket that had caught Holmes's eye with that advertisement. I peered through the window of the carriage for signs of a red-headed monster in pursuit but saw none.

And if the golem did lay hands upon me? Well, I couldn't tell him anything, not for all his efforts to throttle it out of me. I knew nothing of my friend's whereabouts. In this, my ignorance was my greatest strength.

In the meantime, I regarded it as my job to lead the fellow a merry dance, so Holmes would be free to transact his business with the Crown jewels—if that was where he was— and for the plain thrill of it all. There was nothing like a mystery to quicken the pulse and get the blood pumping.

"Are you crossing the road, or takin' up residence! Out of the way!" cried the driver.

What was Sherlock up to, I wondered? Irene thought he might be involved in the refurbishment of the Crown Jewels, no less. That would be a boon for his reputation and career. A diamond, said to be the most valuable in the world, would be a financial and political triumph for England, too, adding significantly to its coffers, while boosting its stature upon the world stage. There had been whispers of war brewing abroad lately. Would a clear show of wealth and superiority by Britain quiet the dissenting voices?

"I've seen tortoises that would call you 'slow coach'! Get a move on!"

Damned if the fellow wasn't the most obnoxious cab driver I'd ever had the misfortune to engage. And there was some stiff competition for that title in this town. I was relieved when the vehicle finally came to a halt at my destination.

The Oriental Emporium was in a poor part of London where many Chinese businesses operated. A bell on the shop's door announced my arrival; several heads turned my way as if connected by string.

Barely a few steps inside, I saw this was no modest establishment. It was a converted warehouse, high-ceilinged and deep, stretching this way and that.

"Welcome, sir!" A man of Oriental persuasion bowed behind the counter. He had a long, thin beard and dark hair tied in a single plait that extended halfway down his back. He wore a high-collared silk shirt and matching cap.

"We have ornaments for your home and jewels for the ladies."

The man waved his arm across bowls containing colourful stones: all glass, I was sure.

My eye caught movement in the back of the shop. Young children practised acrobatic manoeuvres on mats—cartwheels, juggling, balancing on beams: circus arts from the look of it. A few were of Oriental ancestry but not all. And there were girls among those performing, which was highly modern.

"Can I help you with anything?" the man asked.

"If it's acceptable, I'd just like to browse your merchandise."

"Of course! We have clothes, too, for all seasons." He pointed to a rack at the side, with shiny Oriental-style dresses and shirts and bathrobes with dragon designs. There were winter coats with especially dense wadding, just right for London's relentless chill. I was tempted to purchase one for the cold nights in Baker Street. Except now was not a shopping expedition.

I perused a shelf of colourful bottles with Oriental remedies and a collection of painted statues—most of rural Oriental scenes. There was one, however, of a woman who seemed more western in her features. And oddly familiar.

"Excuse me." I held up the statue. "Is this a statue of Irene Adler?" The face shape, the hair, the lips bore an uncanny resemblance to the actress's.

The man frowned and shrugged, as if he didn't understand my question.

"I'm wondering if Mr Sherlock Holmes has been in here recently?" I tried to observe, as Holmes would, the man's first reaction as I said my friend's name.

"I'm sorry?" He remained blank, no trace of recognition.

"He's taller than me and thin with dark hair. Does that sound like any of your customers recently?"

The man smiled wryly. "Sometimes what you are looking for is right in front of you."

I wasn't sure whether he was merely spouting some Confucius-like wisdom or if his words held a coded meaning as he slid a large wooden bowl in front of me, containing crudely made paper boats.

"For a single coin, you can read what the boat of the future predicts for you," he said.

I reached in, drew out a paper boat and opened it. Inside, written in a fancy hand, was: "Meet me in Hyde Park at 4pm."

I knew it! A message from Holmes. My face flushed with pride that I had managed to pick up on a clue he'd left me.

"I hope your fortune pleases you?" the man intoned.

"Very much so."

The bell announced another customer entering. My view of the newcomer was partly obscured by shelving but I glimpsed the top of his head—and his bright red hair.

"Perhaps you would like to try the maze of mirrors," the serving man suggested. "It is not to be missed."

He pointed to the side of the room and I hastened that way, hunching low to remain concealed.

"Is there anything I can help you with today?" I heard the shopkeeper ask. I didn't wait for a reply; I slipped through the doorway to the maze.

A narrow corridor with mirrors on either side stretched ahead of me. Walking its length, I had the strongest feeling I was being followed. By myself! Looking left and right, my own image was reflected over and over. An army of Dr Watsons on one side seemed to face off against the same on the other. The effect was dazzling.

Heading deeper into the maze, I passed mirrors that rendered me as wide as a clown or as tall and thin as Holmes.

As if I'd summoned him with that thought, around the corner came my friend in the familiar deerstalker hat and cape.

"Sherlock!" I cried. With his back to me, Holmes held a hand up in greeting and continued on, taking a turn and vanishing from my sight once more.

"Sherlock!" I called again. He'd looked different somehow.

I stood astonished that I'd met my friend here in this strange world of mirrors. Rows of Watsons, gaping like guppy fish, appeared equally baffled.

There was no time to think further upon it as the whole maze rocked and rattled. Someone large had entered and begun thumping along the corridors.

I ran, taking this turn and that, banging head-first into a trick mirror. Cursing myself, I backtracked and found a new way through. The game had lost its appeal by now. I was heartily sick of my own image and desperate to escape.

Turning a corner, I got my first close-up look at the red-haired German I had seen from the window at Baker Street. His head was as square, as was his jaw, with deep eye sockets. The effect was simian and beastly, especially as, in that moment, he walked beneath a mosaic mirror ball dangling from the ceiling. It threw light and distorted images of him this way and that as it revolved.

My breathing was loud in my ears. I heard the man grunting nearby. And then he launched himself at me. I covered my head, anticipating a blow. Instead, a loud bang and a volley of swear words in German revealed he'd made the same mistake as I, crashing into a dead end.

And then I was out. I ran through the shop. The bell chimed as I left.

A cab was sitting outside—the same driver I'd had before, who'd taken a break while I was in the store.

"We have to wait!" I said. "For a friend of mine." I hoped to see Sherlock appearing at every second.

"Tall chap with a funny hat and cape? He shot out before you and ran off along the road."

"Really?" *Holmes left without me?* That seemed strange. I wasn't sure what to make of it. Without awaiting my commands, the cabbie started up. I felt fortunate he'd been there, even though he swore at the first person we encountered on the road.

Sighing, I leaned back in my seat and thought over all that had taken place. How the clipped advertisement had led me there. How Sherlock had appeared like a spectre in the maze and disappeared as suddenly. I pulled out his note and smiled at the fortune-telling ruse he'd used to deliver a message to meet him that afternoon.

I closed my eyes, slightly dizzy as I recalled the lights, the heady incense, the bouncing acrobats. In that moment, I felt like a circus performer myself, balanced on a high wire, with Sherlock holding one end and the red-haired agent the other.

Back at 221B Baker Street, Mrs Hudson brought in some much-needed refreshment and the paper.

"I've had a frustrating afternoon," she said, sitting down to pour.

She explained that she'd received an invitation to a teahouse in Bloomsbury, from a woman claiming to be a friend of her sister's. She attended the establishment at the appointed time but had waited almost an hour without the woman appearing.

"It's not the first time that's happened either," said Mrs Hudson. "A few days ago, an invitation arrived out of the blue from an old school friend—and I do mean old—inviting me to take tea at her home. I set forth to meet her, all the way to south London, only to find she'd never lived at that address."

"What do you make of it, Doctor?"

I scratched my chin and examined the facts. "Was there anything missing from your belongings upon your return?"

"Not that I could tell."

"Then perhaps she noted the address incorrectly on the invitation?"

Mrs Hudson pressed her lips together as she handed me a cup. "I'll ask Mr Holmes when he returns."

Deflated that despite training under the great detective, I couldn't fathom even the simplest mystery when called upon, I turned to a perusal of the paper. On the front page was a story about Sherlock Holmes and the Crown Jewels—Ms Adler was right!—with a sketch of the spectacular diamond from the Cape Colony in Southern Africa, to be set into the royal sceptre at a secret location the following day. Sherlock was to witness its authentication and placement in the royal sceptre, on behalf of Her Majesty and all her subjects.

"Sherlock Holmes is a consulting detective of formidable reputation," I read the piece aloud, "with no known political allegiances. Renowned for intellectual rigour and moral irreproachability, he is the ideal subject to act as the public guardian for this historic addition to the Royal collection."

"Not so sure about the 'moral irreproachability'," said Mrs Hudson, slurping her drink. "Whoever wrote that, clearly, has not met the man."

I laughed heartily in agreement.

"Well, Holmes would have no interest in stealing the diamond, so he is the safest person to handle it," I concluded. "Wealth, power, and prestige hold no allure for him. Of course, he might want the diamond to evaluate its geological properties."

Mrs Hudson cackled. "We'd find it broken into bits in the bottom of a test tube?" She slurped her drink. "Just be thankful, Doctor, that Sherlock chose to catch criminals rather than become one."

It was a couple of hours until our 4pm meeting. To occupy myself, I examined the living room to see if I could find any clues Irene had missed. There were none, of course. Not much escaped her eagle eye.

I moved on to an examination of Sherlock's bedroom to detail more closely which items were missing from his wardrobe. Among the things I could not locate were his smoking jacket, slippers and his violin.

I tried to picture the Queen's secret agents packing my friend's bag for a sojourn in a safe house. I had encountered such men during Holmes's investigations before. Most were ex-army, stiff-backed and unsentimental. I couldn't see them slipping the silk jacket and fur-lined slippers into his pack. Nor his violin.

Perhaps Sherlock packed his own bag? But that wasn't right either. Holmes was as disdainful of comfort as any army officer. And, besides, if he had gone to the trouble of including those items, he would have included his pipe, which had been so carelessly left in the sitting room, and the framed picture of his violin by his bedside. It meant a great deal to him.

How to explain this? I couldn't just now.

The answer continued to elude me as I arrived at Hyde Park ten minutes before four. Although Holmes hadn't specified where he would be, I knew he liked to attend concerts in a rotunda near the Serpentine River. I began there.

Within minutes of arriving, my spirits lifted as I saw a figure bobbing along in familiar deerstalker and cape. I marvelled that Holmes would attire himself in his most visible outfit for a secret meeting. But he knew best what he was doing.

As he drew closer, I detected a discrepancy in his height and weight, which confused me. This Holmes seemed heavier than I recalled. And the strong, determined strides were absent; he had more of a purposeless stroll. And then, Holmes walked right by me without any acknowledgement, and I saw this was not Sherlock, but an older man in his garb.

I was still marvelling at that—the coincidence of it, and the fact someone should so boldly have copied my friend's unique style—when I saw another be-caped individual. I was not in a moment's doubt about this person not being Holmes. He was young and short, with a beard and wisps of blond hair protruding from the deerstalker.

Over the next quarter hour, no fewer than twenty-five individuals dressed as Holmes appeared, laughing and posing, and puffing on their pipes in a very un-Sherlock way. I asked one what was going on and he informed me this was the appointed hour and location for a meeting of the Sherlock Holmes Appreciation Society.

"But aren't you Dr Watson, Sherlock's companion?" said one elderly pretender.

"No, I'm not," I responded rapidly. "But I think I saw him over there." I pointed to the other side of the river.

The Sherlocks stared across the water and I slunk away, concealing myself behind a flowering bush. All the while, I kept a lookout in case the true Sherlock had devised this scenario to provide cover for our meeting.

"There you are, Watson!" I turned to find a familiar face, though it took a few seconds to process who it was.

"Lestrade!" I exclaimed. For the officer was also dressed in a cape and deerstalker. "What on earth?"

"Does it suit me?" he said. "I almost fancy I think like the great man in this coat and hat."

Clothes maketh not the man. I resisted uttering the obvious. "It looks well on you, Lestrade. But what's going on?"

"I pulled another body out of the Thames today. Could have been Sherlock's twin," he said. "Through enquiries, I've established the corpse was last seen in the vicinity of the Diogenes Club."

Upon hearing the club's name, every organ shifted within me. I knew Sherlock frequented the Diogenes Club whenever he wanted to see his brother, Mycroft, about a case. I say "see" rather than "talk to", because club rules forbade any conversation within its walls.

"A red-headed man of large stature was seen near that location too. It seems our German golem is stalking all the known haunts of the great detective and anyone who looks like him is in peril." Lestrade hitched up his trousers.

"So why are you dressed like him, then?"

"I laugh in the face of danger," the officer boasted. "It's my job. Several of us at the Yard have kitted ourselves out this way and set ourselves up in spots Sherlock is well-known to inhabit. We are laying a trap for the killer."

I wasn't sure how to answer that, except to say my admiration for Lestrade increased at that moment. I knew Sherlock didn't think much of his deductive powers, but when it came to bravery, Lestrade was not lacking. His ferret eyes darted about, combing the shrubberies and walkways for the German golem.

For a short time, I eavesdropped on the assemblage of Sherlock impersonators as they discussed their hero and the various mysteries he'd solved.

"Of course, Dr Watson does much to help Sherlock," one impostor concluded.

"And what's that?" enquired another would-be detective.

"His dullness makes Sherlock seem to shine all the brighter."

They laughed like drains at that. But I didn't find it amusing, I couldn't be too angry though; at least they appreciated Holmes's remarkable abilities. Though I liked to think they might be underestimating my own small contributions to the detective's success.

When forty minutes had elapsed and my friend had not appeared, it seemed to me this was not a ploy to create cover. But something else altogether.

"Who called this meeting today?" I asked one Sherlock with a florid complexion and jowly aspect.

"I imagine it was a Holmes Appreciation Society member, but I couldn't tell you who."

I sniffed. *So much for detection.* Even I—blockhead though they thought me—knew good detective work involved asking the right questions. None of these pretenders had thought to ask that one.

As I was leaving, I spotted a redhead among the caped crowd. The German agent eyeballed each Sherlock as a potential candidate for his foul deeds. I watched from the side as he decided that the man with the jowls was the real Sherlock and made a grab for him.

"No!" I cried, lurching forward.

The golem hustled the man towards the carriageway. The fact his victim did not cry out convinced me his attacker held a weapon on him and had made threats if he did not remain quiet. The colour had drained from the man's cheeks as he stumbled along with his captor and his eyes bulged like peeled grapes.

"Lestrade!" I called—to no avail, the officer was some distance away—before launching into action. Fear vied with anger inside me as I charged after the abductor, hurling myself at the man's back and directing my blows to his kidney region.

"Leave him alone," I demanded.

"You don't want your friend hurt, Doctor." The man had a heavy German accent.

"I've never seen this man before!" I shouted. "LESTRADE!"

I felt all eyes upon me, as the officer's name was well-known among this crowd, with both the police and Sherlock devotees. I sensed rather than saw the detective speeding towards us, heedless of his own safety. Several others began to converge upon the redhead. The golem, realising the jig was up, let go of the Sherlock impersonator and attempted to flee. He moved surprisingly swiftly for a mountain of a man, I noted.

However, as two officers closed in—Lestrade in the lead—some mothers with prams chanced across the path, blocking access to the man. The police lost precious seconds veering around the group. And then—more ill luck—a bicycle rider barrelled right into the officers. They went down in a tangle of limbs and deerstalkers. By the time they had regained their footing, their quarry was lost.

I couldn't help feeling there was something familiar about one of the fresh-faced mothers with prams. Though, for the life of me, I couldn't think what.

Sleep was fitful at best that night, questions swirling in my head without answers. At some point, I became aware I was awake. And I was not alone. A creak in the floorboards and the faintest of nasal whistles confirmed it. An intruder was in the bedroom with me.

Casting off the cobwebs of slumber, I stared wide-eyed around the room, hoping to pick out details in the darkness. I vaguely made out a hulking form over my bed as a meaty hand grasped my throat and squeezed. I swung my arms wildly. My attacker repelled my blows as easily as if swatting away a mosquito on a summer's evening. I tried to cry out but barely a croak emerged. To silence me, he pressed down harder upon my larynx until I could no longer breathe.

"Quiet, Doctor," he whispered, "and I won't have to kill you. We're just going to take a little trip together, to bring the detective out of his rabbit hole."

He was planning to kidnap me to lure Holmes out of hiding. Not if I could help it! I redoubled my efforts to break free, thrashing about with arms and legs, though I felt my force ebbing and my consciousness fading.

"Unhand the Doctor, you devil!" a female voice demanded, followed by the *clang* of a saucepan hitting bone or skull. Through the veil of darkness, I thought I made out Mrs Hudson's shape and my landlady gripping an iron skillet as if it were a tennis racket.

"Now that's not very nice," she said, and—*thwap! thwap!*— delivered two more blows to the man's head.

I must have passed out then for I didn't recall anything more until I awoke hours later as feeble fingers of morning light reached into my bedroom.

I lay there for a moment, wondering whether I'd dreamt it all. Then I spotted on the floor a tooth, yellow and fang-like, with dried blood on one end, as if it had been knocked out of a head.

When I sought out Mrs Hudson to discuss the attack, however, she shook her head.

"Don't be daft, Doctor," she said. "If I had battled an assailant in your room, he wouldn't have got away. I'd have grated his tender parts and served them over fried bread for breakfast."

Mrs Hudson retrieved her pan for inspection. It was as clean and intact as on the previous day. I would have taken that as proof I'd imagined the whole incident but for a sore throat and red finger marks turning to bruising around my throat. And the tooth, left behind.

Was Mrs Hudson prevaricating? Could she be more formidable than she let on, perhaps secretly in the service of the Queen? Or had she sleep-walked her way through the entire incident?

More questions with no answers. If Sherlock were here, he would guffaw and tell me that though I looked, I did not see. That the answer was obvious.

Oh well, I'd just have to keep looking.

CHAPTER FOUR

I spent longer than usual in my bed and read the newspapers top to bottom, seeking anything I could find pertaining to the refurbishment of the Crown Jewels. After the secret ceremony to replace the diamond in the sceptre, it seemed the entire Crown Jewel collection would be displayed at Customs House for a select European audience—meaning the Royal Family would show off their shiny new jewels and watch their continental cousins turn green with envy.

As I threw down the paper, a note slipped out of its rear pages, in a familiar spidery scrawl.

"Meet me in the London sewers at 11am!" it read. "Where London's theatres meet its most skilled performers and audience of desperates."

The words propelled me to my feet. Holmes had called for help and I would answer. But first, I had to solve his riddle.

I paced, cursing Sherlock for playing games at such a critical time. It was probably a precaution, I reasoned, in case the note wound up in the wrong hands. Although, knowing Holmes, it could just be an exercise in showing off his superior intellect. Well, I'd be damned if I'd let it get the better of me!

London's theatres were in Drury Lane, of course. Its *most skilled performers*? They were there too. But the *audience of desperates*? Even for Holmes, it was a misanthropic label for theatregoers. Actors, though, were not the only performers. There were street shows, circuses, musicians? Still, I wouldn't call those who viewed them *desperates*.

And then, I remembered…Lincoln's Inn, where barristers—well-known for their showmanship—performed to an audience of the accused awaiting judgement. They were as desperate as one could be.

It seemed Holmes wanted us to meet in the underground tunnels somewhere around Lincoln's Inn. Why there, I wondered?

I changed into my worst shoes and oldest trousers, fit for the task, and galloped downstairs.

"Where are you going like the devil himself is after you?" Mrs Hudson asked.

"Nowhere in particular."

My landlady cocked her head. "Dr Watson, don't ever become a con artist, will you? I'd hate to see you starve."

As soon I hit Baker Street, Dante was upon me. "Doctor, I've been following that lady, Miss Adler. I know where she's been and where she is now."

"Thank you, Dante," I said. "I am very interested in your report, but later." I handed him a coin for his trouble. "Now, if you had any idea where the street entry point for the sewer system in a particular part of London was, that would be useful right now. Our other business will have to wait."

"You want to go into the sewers?" A grin broke out over Dante's face. "Well, them's like home for me. I can show you."

"I have a particular spot in mind."

"Try me, Doctor. I've escaped the rozzers more often in those tunnels than you've had hot tea."

Twenty minutes later, Dante had experienced his first hansom cab ride and I was about to enter "Stink River", as he called it. I'd checked and re-checked that the red-haired agent was not following but I glanced about one last time before lifting a grate upon the street which was the doorway to my meeting with Holmes.

The boy directed me accordingly—third tunnel on the left, second on the right, etc.—and promised to meet me back here afterwards. "Watch out for the rats, Doc. Nasty blighters."

As I descended below street level, the stench from the emissions of a city of a million souls grew so strong my eyes began to mist.

Dante pressed his face to the grate. "Jes' hold your breath, Doc! You'll be right!"

Plop. Slop. Slap. Squelch. The sound effects would have turned my stomach if it wasn't already twisting like a wet towel in the hands of a laundry mistress at the smell. There was no lighting in the tunnels, except that streaming in stripes from street grates above. I had to traverse long stretches of near darkness, touching the slimy walls to keep from banging my head. In all of my missions with the great detective, this was the most malodorous.

The *drip drip drip* of condensation on the walls into the ankle-deep murk was unnerving. As my eyes adjusted to the dark, I made out more detail—the brick work on the tubes, shiny in the reflected light; the bumpy surface of the water I wish I'd never seen. And rats moving with ease along the slippery sides.

"Oh, Lord," I muttered.

On the bright side, the stench was less noticeable the longer I lingered here. I imagined it seeping into my clothes, my hair, the pores of my skin.

I heard footsteps and stood still, trying to determine from whence they came. The tunnels were an echo chamber, the sound bouncing around in an unpredictable fashion. I decided the footsteps were ahead and pushed on. I was not one to fright easily, I reminded myself. And Holmes was waiting.

My resolve weakened as the *plop plop splash* grew louder. Whoever—or whatever—it was, they were almost upon me.

"Who goes there?" I called, fearing what might loom out of the blackness.

"Who goes *there*?" came the echoing call.

The voice seemed familiar. Limned by light from behind, I recognised the deerstalker hat.

"Holmes!" I exclaimed.

"Watson!"

Light glancing off the walls revealed it wasn't Sherlock, but

Inspector Lestrade, still in costume.

"Lestrade," I exclaimed. "What brings you here, to the very depths of our city?"

"I had a tip-off the golem was somewhere in this vicinity."

"Have you seen him at all?" I enquired.

"No, only rats and rubbish," he said. "Why are you wading about in the stink soup, Doctor?"

"I had an invitation from Sherlock to meet him."

"Really?" Lestrade seemed surprised. "But isn't this the appointed time for him to authenticate the diamond?"

"Yes," I replied. "I thought perhaps there'd been some delay."

"I guess you'll miss the meeting now," said Lestrade. "Not that you were invited to it, were you?"

"No, I wasn't."

"Although I bet this is one day Sherlock would want you there taking notes. For posterity and all."

In the distance, we heard the rhythmic slap of feet through the water. We tensed, scanning left and right as the sound ricocheted maddeningly about us.

Lestrade gripped his police truncheon in readiness; my fingers balled into fists.

Around the corner came a scrawny man, his clothes in rags, glowering at us with his one good eye. Just another one of the city's lost and rootless souls.

As he passed by, Lestrade and I exhaled in unison. I caught a gleam of teeth as the officer began to grin. "Here we are together," he said, "in mud and waste and who-knows-what up to our knees."

"Like a couple of clowns in a watery circus," I added.

I realised that, since the beginning, this case had been exactly that. A spectacle, a circus. The bedazzling mirror maze, the convention of Sherlocks, the drama of the sewers. Lestrade had even donned a costume for the show.

"Strange we're both here," I reasoned aloud, "at the exact hour Sherlock is to attend one of the most important meetings of his career."

"Yes, an odd coincidence that."

Coincidence. Holmes did not believe in them. The universe is rarely so lazy, he always said. When two unlikely strands of a story come together, it may be a random event. But more often it is through the careful work of a seamstress's hand.

Could it be that someone wanted us, Sherlock's two closest allies, underground and far away while the jewel authentication took place? And they had gone to a deal of trouble to get us here.

I could almost hear Sherlock's voice in my head. Keep the right hand busy and you're less likely to notice what the left hand is doing. The art of misdirection.

Neither Lestrade nor I had powers of reason anywhere near as sharp as Sherlock's. So, what were they afraid of? We knew nothing about diamonds and precious stones. Nor affairs of state, nor the twists and turns of international intrigue. We could not soundly apply Holmes's methods of detection to complex clues or Machiavellian mysteries. But we did know the detective...what he looked like.

"We have to get out of here, Lestrade," I said.

As we emerged from the tunnel, even young Dante, as inured to poor hygiene as he was, reared back. "Everyone knows that part of the tunnels is the smelliest," he said. "Them poor blighters in the court-house can't hold back. Want to hear my report on Irene Adler now?"

"Yes, indeed!" I said.

We followed the boy down alleyways, across busy roads, ignoring the disdainful looks of those we passed, to Bedford Square and an ordinary terrace house with no visible security around it.

"She's in there," he said.

I asked Dante to wait in the green across the road as Lestrade and I entered the house unchallenged. We made it through the doorway and down a stately hall without encountering a soul.

"Dr Watson!" effused a guard rounding the corridor. "Glad to see you, old chap. We were disappointed when you sent your apologies for today."

Apologies? What?

"But here you are anyway." The man slapped me on the back with undue familiarity. "Holmes will be happy to have his chronicler beside him on this historic day."

I felt Lestrade start at the mention of our friend's name. "Holmes? Is this...where the diamond is being verified? But weren't we in pursuit of Miss Adler just now? Is she with him?"

Yes...and no... was the answer, I suspected.

The man led us into a sitting room, well-furnished and elegant, though not as opulent as one might have expected for such an occasion. Locating the event in an ordinary house, with no visible security, was all part of the secrecy. For few would suspect what was taking place behind the ordinary oak door of a suburban home.

The guard ushered us to a sofa to witness the ceremony. Two statesmen in top hats and coats and a couple representing the Royal household stood either side of Sherlock as he conversed with a short man holding an enormous diamond. Sherlock placed a loupe to his eye and squinted through it to examine the jewel. Straightening, he nodded and smiled his assent. All the men visibly relaxed.

It was only then Sherlock saw Lestrade and I. And we saw him.

High forehead, aquiline nose, thin lips. All as they should be. But there was something...an eyebrow not quite right. A little too much style in the outfit he'd chosen. And a smile, with a hint of amusement in the corners. This was Irene Adler, if I wasn't mistaken, disguised—and very well—as Sherlock Holmes.

"Mr Holmes," said the Queen's representative. "You agree that this diamond is as it was represented?"

"I do," said Holmes/Adler. "The finest I've ever seen. My congratulations to Her Majesty."

The voice was almost flawless. But not quite. It wasn't just the way she spoke but the grace in the tone. Sherlock would have been more grudging. None of those assembled could tell, though. They didn't know the detective as I did.

I looked over at Lestrade, whose brow was creased. Something troubled him. But as the room broke into applause, he did too, taken in by Irene Adler's performance. A royal command performance. However, she knew that I knew and gave me a twinkly smile with just a smidgeon of concern.

"Who's for a drink?" said one official.

Formalities over, the Queen's jeweller laid out his tools to begin the job of replacing the old diamond with the new in the royal sceptre. He would complete the task before witnesses so there could be no question of deception.

But first, a bottle of champagne on ice was opened and glasses were charged for the official toast—to Queen, country and the Crown Jewels.

Two more glasses were found for Lestrade and I. The assembled guests said not a word about our wet feet and general reek. They were much too well bred to disparage us to our faces.

The policeman took great swigs of the golden liquid and became quite sparkling himself. Holmes/Adler, meanwhile, was all charm, impressing all who encountered her. Her eyes frequently sought me out, a tautness about the jaw betraying a fear that I might expose her.

I considered it. But I was trying to fathom what it all meant, where Sherlock was, whether he was in collusion with this? Or in some kind of danger? That was my prime concern.

I was baffled by what she hoped to achieve. The jeweller was present and had authenticated the diamond, which would shortly be secured in the sceptre. Unless she could effect an almost magical switch—the real gem with a fake—there was nothing to be gained.

"Dr Watson, my oldest friend," Sherlock/Adler stood before me. "You found me."

Sherlock would never have been so sentimental.

"Yes, although as you can see—" I gestured to my wet trousers and shoes "—I took a wrong turn along the way."

She could hardly hold back her laughter at this. If anyone present had known Sherlock at all intimately, this moment would have been her undoing. Her eyes were not the dull, focused beans of deduction, but full of light and laughter.

"And although it seems I sent my apologies to Her Majesty for today," I said, eyebrows raised meaningfully at her, "here I am. Though, I confess, I must be getting forgetful in my old age, as I have no memory of receiving the invitation." *For the simple reason it had never reached me. By design, I suspected. Irene's design.*

"You're a busy man, Watson, with many claims upon your time," Holmes/Adler said. "Perhaps Mrs Hudson received them on your behalf but forgot to pass them on. Landladies can be forgetful."

Of course! "Mrs Hudson"—or Ms Adler in her guise—must have taken possession of the Queen's invites while the real Mrs Hudson bestrode London on a goose chase for tea.

"Anyway," Sherlock/Adler said, "we're overjoyed to see you now."

Our smiles were painted on—part irritation, part amusement, and just a hint of a thrill that we shared a secret in this room of Her Majesty's officials and spies.

When I was sure we would not be overheard, I whispered, "Where's Sherlock?"

"Safe," she said. "This is for his own protection. We both want that, don't we?"

As she drifted off to charm the royal representatives in Sherlock's name, I sipped my champagne and wondered whether she'd just reassured me or threatened me. I was still trying to decide when a commotion broke out as the red-haired man stormed into the room, gun brandished.

"Give me the jewel," he demanded. He held his hand out and the jeweller, wide-eyed with terror, looked to us, unsure what to do. "Unless you wish to die in this room," the golem added.

That made up the man's mind. He offered the stone to the intruder, but as the German went to grab it, Sherlock/Adler lunged forward and snatched it. "No-one's taking that. Off with you now, you—"

We never got to hear what she/he was about to call him for the man drew a gun and fired. Sherlock/Adler staggered back with a look of profound shock. The golem snatched the diamond and ran. Sherlock/Adler slid to the floor, unconscious.

Bedlam ensued with guards pursuing the golem and officials hurrying out to watch. I rushed forward to attend Irene, sprawled upon the ground.

"Breathe!" I pushed down on her chest.

"Is he done for?" Lestrade had stayed with us rather than join the pursuit. "I can't believe it. Sherlock Holmes, dead?"

Neither could I. There was no blood at all. Which seemed strange. I undid Sherlock's coat and shirt to find a thickly padded vest beneath made of a tough fibre I'd never seen before. I felt something small and hard wedged within. The bullet.

And then Sherlock/Adler gasped and sat up.

"Sherlock," Lestrade sounded spooked. "I know you're clever and all, but to outsmart death...?"

Irene was too occupied with breathing to answer, so I explained. "Our friend was prepared for such a possibility, with a special vest, padded and of a durable material to stop the bullet reaching the body."

"I've heard of those," said Lestrade. "Might I inspect it, Doctor?"

"Perhaps later. Holmes needs a moment to recover."

By then, the others had returned, cursing themselves for the golem's escape. And Sherlock/Adler was back on her feet, if shakily, to the astonishment of the company. A rumour began after that night that Holmes had supernatural powers and bullets could not kill him.

"I could use that drink now," Sherlock/Adler whispered.

Lestrade almost tripped over his sodden feet to oblige, trickling the last drops of champagne into a glass.

In the silver bucket, the ice had almost melted, but for a lone cube refusing to succumb.

CHAPTER FIVE

Irene Adler did not appear on the stage that night. Her stand-in performed the role of London's most notorious female adventurer.

However, audiences were thrilled to see her back again the next night, more dazzling than before. When the final curtain fell, I went backstage, past the familiar props that from a distance had been so effective, but here seemed like cheap copies of life. Past the row of heads sporting facial hair and enhancements for a fuller cheek, a longer chin, a more forbidding eyebrow.

I knocked on Irene's door.

"Enter!"

She smiled, but I saw she was tired. The recent show—and not just the one where she played Moll—had taken a toll. Even drained as she was, though, Ms Adler was a striking woman—the cascades of amber hair (had she ever had the same hair colour twice?), the shapely lips that seemed ever-ready to laugh.

Looking into her eyes now, as brown as dark toffee, a question popped into my mind: "How do you change eye colour?"

"There are potions that can darken or lighten the eyes."

"With no damage to the eye?"

"None."

We regarded each other warily.

"I trust Sherlock will be home soon?" I heard the steel in my own voice.

"Perhaps even upon your return tonight, you may find him sitting in his usual chair, contemplating his next case."

"Or his last," I said. "He might be surprised to learn that he put himself in harm's way in the service of his Queen. I do hope he wasn't too badly hurt?" My concern for her was genuine, as a medical man and friend.

"He'll live." Irene threw off the wig, her dark hair tumbling free. "I daresay he's suffered worse at the hands of those thought to be respectable members of society."

I was disturbed to hear this. I'd imagined her life full of admiration and applause. But, evidently, it wasn't all opening nights and rose garlands for an unmarried actress in London.

"You've had a busy time, Doctor?" she observed. She leaned close to the mirror and, with a surgeon's steady hands, removed first one false eyelash, then the other.

"I've been running hither and thither, hastening after a phantom, searching, but not seeing what was right in front of me," I said.

"And what was that?"

"That I was a puppet in a comedy show."

Irene could compose herself no longer. She threw her head back and her unguarded laughter filled the room.

"It was educational," I conceded. "Especially the tunnels. I didn't like those trousers much anyway."

"You're a good sport. Not all men would take it so well." Now she dipped a cloth in a pot of cream and applied it to her face, washing off the paint on her cheeks and lips. "At what point did you realise your friend in Bedford Square was not as you'd expected him to be?"

"I had my suspicions before I entered the room," I replied truthfully.

"Really? How?"

I explained that, while enveloped in unpleasant fumes, up to my knees in muck in the sewers, where I could hardly see my (filthy) hand in front of my face, it had all become clear. That I was a player in a show—one intended to keep the eye fixed *here*, away from the action taking place *there*.

"Very good, Doctor. I see Sherlock is not the only resident of 221B with deductive powers."

"I daresay he would have arrived at that conclusion much sooner and without ruining his shoes."

"I'm not so sure." She slipped behind a screen to change out of her stage clothes.

"You didn't find the newspaper advertisement for the Oriental Emporium during your search of our apartment, did you?" I said. "You planted it there. I know because Sherlock doesn't snip things neatly out of the paper. He rips them out and half the page along with it."

"That must be very annoying," Irene called from behind the screen.

"You sent me to the Emporium to draw out Sherlock's pursuer?" It emerged as a question.

"I suspected someone would be after him," she explained. "And that they might follow you, hoping you'd lead the way. Lee, at the Emporium, is a friend of mine. I knew he'd play along. We could get a look at the agent in pursuit and keep him occupied long enough for you to escape safely."

"That Sherlock I encountered in the mirror maze? Was it you?"

"Yes, but a poor copy that day. I had to dress quickly. There was somewhere else I needed to be." She broke into a Cockney accent. "Oi. Move your arse! Or Harry the horse here will move it for you!"

I gasped. "You were that coachman?" I had been totally taken in by her as an odious hansom driver. "You truly are a master of costume arts, Ms Adler."

Indeed, as she stepped out from behind the screen, elegant in a lady's ensemble in brown tones, I doubted even those in the theatre's front row would recognise her. A chameleon, that's what Irene Adler was.

"And that circus of Sherlocks? Was that your doing?"

Leaning towards the mirror, she set about securing her hair with pins and attaching a hat to the crown. "Seemed like a good distraction. And with Lestrade there, you were safe. Although you didn't need protection." She turned to me with an admiring smile. "You were impressively fierce with that German."

Warmth flared in my cheeks at the compliment. "I don't know about that. And anyway, he got away."

"Shame." As I watched her attend to some rogue strands of hair resisting confinement, in my mind I heard the unmistakable tinkle of pennies dropping into place.

"That night I was attacked in my room—it was you, not Mrs Hudson, who came to my aid, wasn't it?" I recalled Mrs Hudson's voice—almost, but not quite, her own. "Your follow-through with that saucepan was most effective. Thank you."

She dipped her head and smiled, mischief in her looks.

"The golem escaped then, too," I said.

"At least I kept you safe, Doctor. If anything had happened to Sherlock's closest friend, he would be inconsolable."

She moved across the room to retrieve a bottle of champagne from a silver ice bucket.

"And the tunnels of waste?" I enquired.

"On the morning of the ceremony, it seemed wise to have you as far away as possible, to avoid complications," she said, easing the cork from the bottle, and pouring the contents into two glasses, one of which she passed to me. "Underground seemed the safest option. For while the officials at the ceremony didn't know Sherlock well enough to spot an impersonator, you and Lestrade did."

"Well, apparently not Lestrade," I said. We both laughed. Though in fairness to our flat-footed friend, I think he heard a false note and suspected something was amiss. But after a glass of champagne, he stopped listening.

"And speaking of Her Majesty's agents, I assume you were at the ceremony as one yourself?" I enquired.

Her quiet attendance to her glass was as close to an admission as I would get.

"Later on, I imagine, Sherlock will tell the press he attended and vouch for the diamond's authenticity?" I said.

"That's the idea."

I asked more about the vest. It was a Chinese invention. Lined with thick, light wadding, covered in a hardy fabric, it was a most ingenious thing and would have wider application in future, I was certain.

"And was it your idea to take Sherlock's place?" I enquired.

"Sherlock is a civilian," she said. "With the German on the loose, it seemed prudent. Though perhaps Holmes could have done better if he had been there." Her lips pursed with annoyance directed at herself.

"You stopped a bullet for him," I said, and knew it to be true. "As far as I'm concerned, you saved Sherlock's life that day. For you and I, Ms Adler, know Sherlock would never have worn a protective vest. His professional pride would not permit it."

"Call me Irene. Please?"

She put down her glass and began pulling on her gloves. "Now, may I ask you a question, Doctor?" said she. "How did you find the house at Bedford Square? Only a handful of people knew the location."

"When it comes to spies, Her Majesty is not the only one with agents in the shadows," I said. "One who answers to Sherlock, a resourceful and enthusiastic young agent, ghosted you over the past twenty-four hours and saw you entering this house."

"He must be resourceful indeed," Irene remarked, "as I have watched keenly for anyone on my tail."

No doubt she was looking for full-size pursuers, not a half-size street urchin like Dante.

"The same agent," I added, sipping my drink, "made enquiries at the Cafe Royale on my behalf. You said you were engaged to meet Sherlock the night he left our residence smelling like a spring garden. And that he'd stood you up. But according to the cafe manager, Sherlock was with you that night.

"So, tell me, was that when you and Her Majesty's agents 'took' Sherlock into custody? I know you could not have managed it on your own. For all that he admires and respects you, Irene, he does not trust you. He would have been on his guard, expecting skulduggery."

Far from being insulted, Ms Adler seemed delighted. "Oh, well. What's an assignation without some risk?"

Her similarities with Sherlock astonished me. I had no doubt my friend enjoyed Ms Adler's company because he was never sure whether she would flatter him or drug him and sell him to his enemies.

"But that red-haired golem was slippery, wasn't he?" I mused. "More slippery than one of Lestrade's eel dinners."

She drew the corners of her mouth up into a smile, like the curtains raised upon a stage.

"To think there were so many opportunities to capture the man. All missed." I listed them. "In the emporium, the park, in my bedroom that night, and in the final meeting, where he got away with the diamond.

"The police almost caught him that day in the park," I went on. "They would have, but for a group of mothers pushing prams, and a bicycle rider."

Irene listened but did not reply.

"And now that I'm back here, in the theatre," I said, "I realise where I'd seen one of the mothers before. It was your assistant, Rachel."

Irene fixed me with a hard gaze. "Are you saying I was in league with the German to steal the Queen's diamond? That I'm a traitor to my country?"

I considered that for a moment, then shook my head. "No. I felt the man's hands on my neck that night. There was nothing feigned about that. And I saw him fire that bullet into you. I examined you afterwards. There was no trickery I could detect."

"Do you imagine I wanted England humiliated?" Irene demanded. "Her enemies to have the means to finance a war on our shores?"

"No."

"Then what do you think?"

I paced, attempting to order my observations. "There was a statue in the emporium that looked just like you, you know?"

"An amusement. I did Lee a favour once."

"And the children learning circus arts? Where were their parents?"

Irene did not reply.

"Her Majesty has her agents," I elaborated, "of which you are one. And a very good one. But you have your own people, too. Lee and the children at the emporium, they're your agents," I stated. "And Rachel at the theatre. You take care of them. Her Majesty knows nothing of their existence."

Irene scoffed. "I can see the rational scientist in you has been over-taken by the writer tonight. One day, perhaps you'll turn your hand to drafting plays for the theatre, to thrill audiences with your florid imag-inings."

It was a poor attempt to discredit my logic; we both knew it. "You asked me why you would help the German escape?" said I. "For the same reason you had me running all over London. Because he pro-vided the spectacle, the show. He could step into the spotlight and take the blame for the theft. When really that had occurred before he arrived. You pulled off the robbery of the century, Irene. You stole the real diamond—the most valuable jewel in existence. And you did it right under the noses of Her Majesty's best agents."

"I...? What?" Irene's eyes grew big, her jaw tight.

"When the German came after me," I continued, "you saw an oppor-tunity. While you pretended to go after the man, you actually used your own collection of street agents to ensure he escaped. You wanted him at large and at that final meeting at Bedford Square.

"You kept him in play until the end. Somehow he found his way to the top secret location."

"You must have led him there, Doctor. He was following you," she asserted.

I shook my head. "If he had followed me that day, he'd have had sod-den trousers and shoes, like mine. His were dry.

"You suspected he might attack you at that final meeting," I con-tinued, "so you prepared yourself as best you could with Lee's vest. Meanwhile, you stationed your own agents to run interference across the street if the authorities got too close to him afterwards. According to reports, attempts to apprehend the thief in Bedford Square were impeded by a group of mothers wheeling prams on the green, an Oriental man on a bicycle and some children practising acrobatics—a girl among them.

"Lee had made a copy of the stone. After the diamond was authenti-cated, as we drank a toast to Her Majesty, you exchanged it for the real jewel. It was the imitation the German made off with. That's why you had your people there: to make sure he wasn't caught and the fraud exposed. Your people will presume the real jewel was lost. The enemy government won't discover the truth until later. And they can hardly complain then."

Irene smiled with her mouth, but not her eyes. "That's quite a story, Doctor. But if that were true, where did the diamond go? I was shot, unconscious. You examined me, unfettered, and presumably did not find a rock of unusual size upon my person?"

"No, I did not," I conceded.

"Well, then…?" She raised eyebrows, awaiting my answer.

As I chewed upon my bottom lip, uncertain, Irene began to relax. She was a cool customer that one.

Ice cool.

"I recall you were very keen to have a drink after that near-death incident," I said. "And who could blame you? I remember at the time looking into the bucket and seeing the ice had almost melted, but for a solitary cube."

"You made the switch and dropped the real diamond into the ice bucket to reclaim later. When you regained consciousness, that was the first thing you checked on."

I thought she might deny it. Instead, she was quiet for a time, then flashed me a dazzling smile, nothing held back. "You know, Sherlock underestimates you."

"In summary," I continued, trying not to succumb to flattery, "you were one of the Queen's agents charged with securing the jewel. But, secretly, you had your own people, your own agents, working to your agenda. As a result, a fake diamond has been set into the royal sceptre, in the Crown jewel collection. Sherlock will go on record as vouching for it. The Queen's agents will ask no further questions about it; they believe the German stole the jewel and will endeavour to keep the theft a secret so as not to discredit the government. But in reality, the real diamond was under their noses the whole time."

Irene chuckled. "Well, all the other jewels in the Crown collection have been replaced with copies to pay gambling debts for this royal cousin or that duke. At least the proceeds for this one will go to a good cause."

"Your people?" I asked.

"London's an expensive city to live in, as I'm sure you know. But a cheap place to die."

Without funds to pay their way, many paid with their lives, I knew. We drank a toast, sizing each other up, as allies. And enemies.

"If you repeat that wild theory to anyone, Doctor," Irene said, "they'll never believe you. And if Sherlock were to investigate further, well, it might end badly for him."

Was she was making threats? Against Sherlock? It was my turn to smile now. Irene Adler was formidable and as ruthless as any male, I had no doubt of that. However, I did not believe Holmes was in any present danger.

He always said when you eliminated the impossible, whatever remained, however improbable, must be the truth. I knew a bag had been packed with some of Sherlock's belongings for his stay in protective custody. Included in that was his smoking jacket, slippers and violin. Neither the seasoned secret agents, nor Sherlock himself, would have bothered with such fripperies. So, who did? It had to be a particular agent, concerned not just with his survival, but his comfort and contentment. Irene Adler had packed his case.

And someone who had demonstrated that much care would not harm him without a most pressing reason. For now, at least, I reasoned, he was safe.

I laid out my argument for Irene, who made no attempt to deny it.

"Well, next time I want to blackmail Sherlock," she said, "I know what to do. I have but to steal his violin and threaten to harm it, and all my demands will be met. That framed photo by his bedside reveals where his heart truly lies."

Indeed.

But for all her cleverness, she'd missed the most important clue. If she'd used her Sherlock logic, she would have noted fingerprints on the glass in the frame revealing the picture was handled frequently. The photo on display was fractionally askew, as if placed there quickly and carelessly. Which should have given her a hint. Beneath the picture of the violin was a second photo of something Sherlock valued even more than his instrument. It was a portrait of Irene herself.

The two of them liked to think they were adventurous and brave, disdaining "love" as a commonplace illusion, somehow beneath them. But in this area, I was the master and they the students.

For I knew love was the ultimate risk. It demanded you lower your guard and reveal your vulnerabilities, effectively placing the secret of your destruction in the hands of another. Neither of them had the courage to take that risk. To trust anyone to that extent. Not yet, anyway.

I did not divulge Sherlock's secret to her. It was not mine to reveal.

At this point, Rachel, the rose-cheeked beauty I'd met during my last visit backstage, rushed in. "Irene, a gentleman begs your attendance," she said. "He says he is tired of lingering by the stage door and his generosity tonight will be seriously curtailed if he has to wait much longer."

"Offer him my apologies," said Irene, "and tell him I will not be attending him tonight. Or any night. Until he learns some manners with me and my people."

The girl smiled. "I would love to tell him that, but I fear his reaction."

"Very well, I'll tell him myself." Irene turned to me. "Excuse me, Doctor?"

She got up to leave, turning back briefly to give me a wink and a playful smile—a gift from one of the strongest and smartest woman I've ever encountered—before heading along the corridor.

Rachel and I waited together awkwardly.

"Are you studying to be an actress?" I asked.

"Yes, sir."

"You have a good teacher in Irene."

"Yes, sir."

"And what do your parents think about that?"

"I have no parents. Irene takes care of me."

I wondered how many more there were like Rachel, under Irene's protective wing, who would otherwise perish in the city.

"Well, good night to you, Rachel. And say good night to Ms Adler for me." I put my hat on and prepared to leave.

"Ms Adler?" The girl seemed confused.

"Irene Adler."

"Oh yes, Adler's her stage name. We know her by her real name."

"And what's that?"

"Irene Moriarty."

It's My Funeral!

GENRE: GHOST

PROMPTS: BUYING A PLOT OF LAND, A GLUTTON

♡

Griffin has heard the expression before, but after a killer day at Bondi Beach, the words take on a whole new meaning for him.

Oh man! That was the mother of all nights out. What a headache! I can't remember much about it. Must have been a great night!

But where am I? In a place with dark carpets, velvety wallpaper, fussy gold mirrors. Some woman's house, I suppose. A sexy babe who whisked me back to her place for a nightcap and a game of *hide the sausage*. Was it the surfer chick from Bondi in the barely-there bikini? Talk about hot. And the way she rode those waves.

I'd better find a mirror to see how bad I look and whether I need a shower. Don't you hate it when the girl gets her first peek at you in day-light and throws up?

That's weird—a trick mirror which shows everything in the room, but not your reflection. *Cool.* Girl has a sense of humour.

I'm wearing blue board shorts but can't see my shirt anywhere. We must have gone partying straight from the beach. Or cracked open the

113

icebox on the sand and got stuck in early. *Sweet.* And it would explain why I don't remember much. I can't wait for Tom to tell me what happened.

I'm scratching my head, trying to guess which of the three closed doors might be the bathroom when an older woman in a black suit barrels past followed by, of all people, Mum and Dad. To say I'm shocked doesn't come close. Who wants to be caught by their parents *in situ, in flagrante*, as Tom would say. He's a wanker with words but not a bad bloke for a lawyer.

"Mum, Dad!" I call. They ignore me and follow the woman through the left door. Must be bad when your parents won't speak to you. I can't help grinning. At twenty-nine, I thought I was slowing down, getting old and boring. Good to know I'm still the party animal who can gross his parents out.

I wonder who the lucky lady was. Not that old girl, was it? Is that why my parents look grim? She'd be fifty if she's a day. Still, I wouldn't say no to all that experience.

Another woman walks by—mid-twenties, pale blonde hair and wispy white dress, carrying a clipboard. And when she smiles, she has a real twinkle going on. That must be my girl. I grin and wink. Though I have absolutely no memory of her. But how on earth could anyone forget a smokin' babe like that?

Blondie heads into the room with the others and signals me to join them. Bit weird, but where she goes I can't help but follow. *Woof.* We're in an office with serious furniture and a framed embroidery reading: *Love Never Dies.* The older women—Vera, according to her name tag—talks in low tones. My parents nod and listen. Mum sniffles. She seems upset about something.

"Mum, what's wrong?"

Hot Stuff touches a finger to her lips. "Shhh."

"How can I make a decision like this?" Mum says. "It's…too much."

"There are three plots available," says Vera, passing some papers to Dad. "One has an ocean view. That's the premium option."

"We want that one," says Mum. "Griffin loved the beach."

Is she buying me some land with a view of Bondi? What a generous mum! The woman in white scribbles something on her clipboard and smiles at me. She's impressed, I can tell. All that love and generosity, who wouldn't be?

"Why does he need a view?" says Dad. "What's the budget option?"

"It's a very nice plot," says Vera, squinting through pince-nez, "under an oak tree, next to a gentleman who was a father of three, divorced and—" she clears her throat "—a serial killer."

"What? My boy can't rest next to a serial killer," says Mum.

"He was a crime reporter," says Dad. "He'd probably find it exciting. We'll take it."

"We've got an opening for a funeral tomorrow at 4pm," says Vera. "Does that suit?"

"Funeral? Mum? Dad? Who died?"

They don't look at me. But the blonde does and shakes her head in that *Get with the program* way so many girls have done during my lifetime. A lifetime which, it seems, is now at an end.

After breathing into a paper bag for five full minutes, I gasp: "So I'm dead? A ghost? But, how? Last time I looked I was in great shape. Well, not bad. I wasn't at death's door anyway."

Blondie refers to her notes. "It seems you drowned on Bondi Beach."

What the—?

"It was unusually big surf," she says. "A girl with a very small bikini expressed fear about entering the water. You said you loved danger and this was nothing compared to the waves you'd bodysurfed in Hawaii." She flicks through the pages. "Which is strange, as there's no record of you ever having been to Hawaii."

Uh-oh.

"Careless with the truth are we, Griffin?" she asks, pen poised.

"Well, I'm a journalist. But I don't let the truth get in the way of a good story."

"I see."

She makes more notes. I'm starting to hate the sound of her pen scraping against the board.

"Can I ask, who are you?"

"You can call me Angel," she says.

"Short for Angelique?"

"Just Angel. I'm an assessment officer for *In-betweeners*. Like you."

"A *'tweener*? What's that?"

"Most people clearly belong upstairs, or down. But a small group hover somewhere around the middle. We have to decide where to put you."

"Oh, My Fucking God! Sorry, I mean...Gracious, what a conundrum!" She makes more notes.

At 4pm the next day, a group of about thirty people I know gather round a grave—mine, I suppose. Everyone looks sad. Mum sobs into Dad's chest. Tom is glassy-eyed and quiet, which is weird as I've never seen him not joking around. Ruby, my best friend since school, has a new black dress on which looks great with her golden hair, though her face is a mess, black eye makeup streaking down her cheeks like a horror film extra. I'm touched by their emotion. Angel takes more notes.

A casket sits in the grave. It's made of cardboard with a beach scene printed on it. It's actually pretty cool but I know, because I wrote a story about it once, that it's a cheaper option than a wooden casket. Three guesses who chose that.

"Does the amount spent on the funeral have any bearing on my final destination?" I ask Angel.

"*Some.*" *Thanks again, Dad!*

A few family friends are here and a girl I was dating casually, Cherie. Plus, a group from the office. There's my boss, Julianne, who's like a second mother to me and keeps deodorant, razors and a new shirt in her bottom drawer in case of "emergencies". There are a couple of women I dated who gave me the "Let's be friends" treatment. My arch rival is here too—Lucien, the city reporter. The guy's a total sleaze who lies and cheats to get what he wants. Well, I do that too, I suppose. But he's worse. Once, he was interviewing a grieving mother and when she went off to make him coffee, he nicked a photo of her dead daughter. It was a low act.

"Quite a good turnout," says Angel. "I'll add fifteen per cent because it's a weekday."

"So, when it comes to funerals, *size* is important?"

"Well, of course," she says. "Though we all pretend it's not."

"And how close am I to going...upstairs?"

"Let's see how it goes here and at the wake, shall we?"

Tom makes a good speech about me, mentioning the bingo calling I do at my Nan's nursing home and my "literacy work with underprivileged kids" (really just hanging with some cool kids and correcting their spelling occasionally). Angel twinkles at that. Thankfully, he doesn't do his usual top ten vomit stories or mention our naked swim at *Sea World* at the end of high school.

As the first handful of dirt is sprinkled onto the casket, Ruby steps forward and throws a red rose into the grave. She looks more broken up than I've ever seen her. I really wish I could console her.

Angel has something like a lipstick tube which she points at people.

"What's that?"

"An emotion gauge. It measures units of genuine sadness."

Everyone is still and serious but most are dry-eyed.

"Cry, you buggers!" I want to yell.

The wake is held in my local pub, *The Stoned Crow*. Mum booked the entire back section, which is like a French garden. Many of my favourite snacks are laid out—mushroom arancini, calamari, pizza, zucchini fries. And there's an open bar.

"Can you limit people to three drinks?" Dad whispers to the barman. "They can pay for their own after that."

Angel overhears and makes notes.

"What you have to understand," I say, "is that Dad can't help being frugal. It's no indication of the degree of his love or anything. It's just he comes from a poor family. They were so poor all his school shoes had holes in them."

"Interesting," says Angel. "Though I'm not seeing any holey shoes in my records."

So, Dad made up that story to justify being cheap for his whole life? *Seriously!*

The family friends have a drink or two, a few nibbles and go on their way, but my office and school buddies settle in for the night.

Tom sits at the bar with a large vodka. "Cheers, mate," he says, raising his glass. "I'll miss your ugly mug. You made me look good."

"You too, mate," I say.

Tom chokes on his sip and looks around, freaked.

"Can he hear me?" I ask Angel.

"When people have a special bond, some low-level intra-zone transmission is possible. A bit like an echo or a breeze."

Lucien hits the food table, pops two arancini in his mouth and, after a sneaky look around with his lizard eyes, slips a few more in his pocket. Bloody thief. Not that I blame him. The arancini here are to die for.

I cruise around, shamelessly eavesdropping on conversations.

"Griff. He was the best," says one of the women I dated.

"And the worst," says another.

"Like a puppy who wees on your carpet, he's annoying, but you can't help liking him."

"If only he could be neutered too."

O-kay. Heard enough there.

Cherie revels in her role as the grieving girlfriend. "Griffin could have been the love of my life," she tells a group with a dramatic sigh. "Now I'll never know."

Not a word of it's true. The pair of us didn't really gel; we both knew it. Then again, though I love women—and not just like *that*; I have more female "friends" than males—I've never really gelled with anyone romantically. Not quite sure why that is. Or *was*.

While Angel's attention is elsewhere, I do what any red-blooded male ghost would do—check out cleavage. There's Olivia, the office secretary and her heavenly mangoes. She's talking to Ginette. Hers are more like beach balls, perfectly spherical. They can't be real?

When they head into the ladies' loos, I follow. I've always wondered what goes on in there. Olivia gets out a makeup purse the size of a brick and sets to work with brushes, pencils and tweezers. If this is a reincarnation deal, *please Angel, don't send me back as a woman.*

The cubicle door is a tad open so I peek at Ginette sitting on the toilet.

"I bet Lucien makes a move on Ruby tonight," says Olivia.

"Really?" Ginette says, pulling off a long piece of toilet paper and leaning forward. I step back. Some things even I don't want to see.

"Lucien has always had the hots for Ruby," she continues. "But he knew he didn't have a chance before."

"Because she was in love with Griffin, I suppose?" says Olivia.

What the—? Ruby, my best friend since Year 5, was in love with *me*?

"She should have said something to him," says Olivia. "Just goes to show. Life's too short to hang about."

Back in the bar, I watch in horror as Lucien sits down next to Ruby. Angel hovers at my shoulder.

"So now you know," she says. "How does it feel?"

Like I died again.

"Here's to Griff," says Lucien, raising his glass. "Departed this world too soon."

Ruby has managed to stay staunch all day but now she breaks down completely. Lucien wraps his arms round her, a python embracing a deer.

"Can't we stop him?" I say.

"She has to make her own decisions," says Angel.

"GET AWAY FROM HER!" I shout in Lucien's ear. He doesn't react, but Ruby's brow creases. She definitely heard something.

I go over to Tom, slumped on the bar. "RUBY NEEDS YOUR HELP! GET UP!" He looks around, rubs his ear then flops back.

"Okay, I've seen enough. Time to take this to the committee," says Angel.

"We can't go yet. Ruby's about to be devoured."

"We have a deadline here. A dead line."

"A bit longer."

"You know, not following protocol will go against you. And with the lying, laziness, lack of responsibility—"

"I'll take my chances."

After a tussle over the credit card with Dad, Mum orders cappuccino for everyone. My favourite drink.

"Is there cappuccino upstairs?" I ask Angel.

She snorts. "Would it be Heaven without?"

By now Lucien has his hand on Ruby's arm.

"GET OFF HER!" I shout.

He doesn't blink.

"What can I do?"

"Accept it. It's no longer your worry."

"Apart from that."

"Well, with training, you could make a small breeze."

It's not much but... "Okay, show me how."

She tells me I have to picture a golden tunnel between myself and the person I want to contact and fill it full of love. Sounds a bit like bovine excrement to me, but *what the hell*? I try transmitting to Tom—the love thing's a tad embarrassing. He feels something, waves his hands around as if shooing a fly, but doesn't budge.

"You know, Griffin is probably interviewing the serial killer in the plot next to him right now for the *Heavenly Times,*" Lucien says, edging closer to Ruby. "That guy had great journalistic instincts."

"He had no respect for my writing," I say. "He'll say anything to get what he wants."

"And you wouldn't?" says Angel.

"Not like this, no. Not taking advantage while they were down."

Angel raises an eyebrow, unconvinced.

"How are you getting home?" Lucien asks Ruby. "We could share a cab. I'll stay with you tonight, if it will help."

"NOOO!"

The whole room rumbles. Everyone looks around.

"O-kay," says Angel. "Time's up."

"Just a bit longer."

"None of this is your concern any more, Griffin. Let it go."

"I can't."

She throws her hands up. "It's your funeral!"

If she thinks I can walk away, turn my back on a friend in trouble, she doesn't know me that well. I may be a bit mucky—more than a bit. And take things too far sometimes—most of the time. But I'm not like Lucien. Some things I would never do. I really hope Ruby and Tom know that about me. As I know the best and worst about them.

And then I have it. Of course! I know Ruby. Her strengths *and* weaknesses. One of which is that she's ticklish. Especially on the back of the neck.

I stand behind her, picture a tunnel and fill it with love. It's easy because I have so much for her. She's the first person I call when things go well or spectacularly badly in my life. She's a worse cook than me—and that's saying something. And the bravest person I know, though she hates the sight of blood and once fainted when I showed her some crime scene photos. She beats me in every category of Trivial Pursuit—except *Game of Thrones*. No-one I dated has ever come close. Why didn't I see it before?

I have so much breeze to give, but I hold it until just the right moment—as she picks up her coffee—then release it in a slow, steady stream. The golden hair on the back of her neck wavers, then ripples. She giggles wildly and jerks and spills her hot coffee in Lucien's lap.

"Fuuuck!" he says, jumping up.

"Sorry." Ruby flaps a serviette at his groin.

"Leave it! Fuck!"

"Keep the language down, mate," says Tom, coming over. "This is not the time or place."

As Lucien heads to the bathroom to blow-dry his scorched crotch, Tom takes his seat. "Hey, Ruby."

They smile at each other. They've known one another a long time, but this is a new look. A spark, perhaps?

"Farewell, Griffin," says Tom. "We'll miss you, mate." He and Ruby clink mugs.

"And I'll miss you. All of you," I say. "But especially you, Ruby."

Ruby puts her mug down and looks right at me. "Griffin, is that you?"

She can see me. I reach out for her, but Angel slaps my arms back and shakes her head.

"Let me say one thing," I ask.

"No."

"Please." Just, *I love you.*

"No!"

Ruby stares at the spot where I was, blinks and rubs her eyes. "I could have sworn he was standing right there. In his blue board shorts."

Tom looks around. "He probably is here," he says. "I've never known him to miss a drinking session. Griff, if you're listening, mate, you still owe me fifty bucks. I'll ask your Dad for it, shall I?"

As Angel and I exit the bar, we're no longer in my local suburb, but on a road so white it's dazzling.

"Whoa, give a bloke some warning!" I say, holding my hand up against the glare. "Do they have sunglasses in Heaven? And cleavage?"

"I'll pretend I didn't hear that."

Angel leads me uphill towards a mass of fluffy, white clouds.

"Where are we going then?" I ask her.

She turns to me with a smile that is anything but angelic.

"Wouldn't you like to know?"

Electric Love

GENRE: SCI-FI

PROMPTS: A DEALERSHIP, AN EXTENSION CORD

♡

Tired of flawless beauty and absolute obedience?
Then, have I got a deal for you!

The EC shopping precinct was heaving today—despite reports of an unexpected turndown in demand for Electronic Companions. Lindsay weaved around potential buyers inspecting—or flirting with—companions displayed in store windows.

Glancing at the crumpled street map she held, she turned it upside down and frowned, unsure which way to go. *Is this really how people moved around before computers?* She'd only tried this dinosaur navigation because she needed to stay offline in case fellow student Christiana or one of her lackies tracked her to the EC area and saw what she was up to.

Tonight was the Retro Ball at Glenhill High. Students would dance to old songs, eat retro food, revel in the "cool" past. And they'd been asked to bring real human dates instead of ECs.

"Have you ever even had a real date?" Christiana asked Lindsay the previous day in front of her mini-brained friends. "Or are real humans too messy for a precious thing like you?"

Lindsay had lined up Benne, a neighbourhood friend, to accompany her to the ball, but he pulled out last minute. Now, she was desperate to find an EC that could pass as human so she could flip the bird at *pissy Chrissy et al*.

"Ah." Lindsay spotted her destination across the road—*Connections*. The biggest EC dealership in town.

From beneath a sign *Where Dreams Come True*, an E-sales agent, a robot himself, emerged to greet her. "Each showroom features a half-decade of design, going right back to the earliest companion models."

The first room showcased new releases. EC males/females/hybrids, all preternaturally beautiful, chatting or flirting with potential clients.

"Do you like pink champagne?" a middle-aged woman asked a young EC male.

"That depends," replied the model suggestively. "Do you?"

ECs were displayed in ascending decades from twenties up to elderly. The busiest section was the twenties/thirties/forties models. There was little appetite for over-seventies designs, even among older clients.

As Lindsay headed towards the doorway to the next room, a twentysomething EC female with a perfect face called: "Woo-hoo! Miss Right!"

"Don't go! Stay!" A stunning thirtysomething male waved coyly to her. The robot attention made her feel grubby, as ever.

Moving swiftly through the showrooms, she stopped to inspect the older, cheaper ECs in the penultimate display.

A human salesman—quite a novelty—greeted her. "Welcome! Vance Grantham, at your service. Are you looking for male/female/mix?"

What would impress Chrissy more?

"Male," said Lindsay. She perused a dozen ECs with hairy arms, greasy hair, crooked teeth and surly looks. "They're…" *imperfect.*

"The word you're looking for is 'unique'."

They were indeed a contrast to the perfection of the previous rooms. *Predictable perfection.* "Is it due to decay of materials?"

"Oh, no! These models are in pristine condition," Vance replied. "It was a design decision. To look more human."

Lindsay inspected the male models along the line. They were kind of "hot" in a human, imperfect way. *A bit of rough.* That ancient expression came to mind. The flaws seemed oddly appealing.

The cost, too, was a pleasant surprise. "They come with wardrobe to suit your purposes. And electronic safety log," said Vance. "But there's one thing I should tell you..."

A loud *zizzing* filled the room, followed by a *thwap*. And everything went dark. It was electronic overload, Lindsay knew. The new EC models used more power, especially during the sex act. When enough engaged in it at the same time, the overload shorted circuits across the city.

Lindsay huffed. *I don't have time for this!* She needed to go home, get dressed and prep the EC with a rock-solid legend to convince Chrissy he was human.

Barely a minute later, lights and all ECs sprang back to life.

Except the models in the line before them. Their heads lolled, eyes glazed.

"What happened?"

"Because they're an older model, they need physical rebooting."

Oh no. If this happened during the ball and her "human" partner slumped in the middle of the dance floor, outing himself as an EC, it would mark her as a Loser forever.

"But there's a solution!" Vance held up an electric extension chord. "If you keep the EC plugged in during the mostly likely surge times— around noon or 9pm most nights—that will negate the need for rebooting."

He showed her the EC's power plug just beneath the left sleeve, around wrist level. "The shortness of the plug was the reason this model was phased out. But if you plug the extension in here and connect it to the power, your EC will sail through the night without interruption."

Lindsay huffed. *No, it's too risky!* If Chrissy spotted the cord...?

But then, at the end of the line, an EC model she hadn't noticed before caught her eye. He had light brown hair, tanned skin and a wry expression, as if he was struggling not to laugh at some joke only he understood.

"You," Lindsay addressed him. "What's your name?"

"Levi. But you can call me Honey."

Arrogant. He even had bitten-down nails...*like her.* Perhaps it was that detail?

"Can he dance?" she asked Vance.

He looked over at the EC. "Can you?"

"I can definitely shake my booty. No worries there."

"Will he pass as human, do you think?" she asked.

Vance scratched his chin. "Well, he's full of himself, prone to laziness. Cheeky. Amusing at times; he thinks so anyway. Not overly bright. Yeah, he'll pass."

Full of himself? Cheeky? Somehow that sounded like a challenge. After decades of EC perfection and obedience, she wasn't the only one craving something different. But were human foibles really the answer?

Only one way to find out.

"I'll take him."

"Him?" Vance seemed surprised.

Lindsay transmitted payment via secure brain wave and, watching her EC's smug smile, wondered whether she might regret this.

As she collected four suits of clothes for him from the wardrobe assistant, she saw Vance and Levi chuckling and wondered what they were talking about.

"See, Dad," said Levi. "You thought I was too human to ever get a date with a real woman."

And Levi looked over at Lindsay and winked.

All That Glitters

GENRE: DRAMA

PROMPTS: A COIN COLLECTOR, A SWING

Dealers at the Sydney Coin Expo offer gold and silver treasures to satisfy the pirate lust in any buyer, and no-one asks how they came by the booty. But this year, Isaac will be making enquiries.

"Isaac, when will I see you? It's been so long!"

Only six months! And it would be six months more if I could stretch it that far. "Can't do it today. There's this thing I have to go to."

"Okay." Mum sighed. "I bought a leg of lamb, in case."

And I'm vegetarian.

"Gotta go. Call you later, Mum."

The "thing" I had on was the *All that Glitters* festival, Australia's second largest coin expo, held in Sydney's Darling Harbour Convention Centre.

Thousands of coin collectors—or numismatists—came to trawl the tables of gold, silver and bronze coins and listen to lectures on the secrets of our pocket change. They're treasure hunters all, myself included. Though I was looking for just one particular coin, from a not-so-particular dealer.

A quick glance around confirmed the usual suspects in attendance. The older die-hard collectors, quirkily dressed, greeting each other like old friends and rivals. The get-rich-quick hopefuls in well-made suits, Google running hot in their hands, seeking the deal of a lifetime. And the "tourists" gawping at the booty, with no clue about its history, mythology or value. They drifted from table to table, eyes round as 20c pieces, gold and silver flickering in dark pupils.

How the dealers came by the glittering merchandise, no one knew. Or cared to ask. Just so long as some of it ended up in our pockets.

Roasted coffee and fried onions scented the air. With a bitter tang beneath. Metallic, like blood.

"Isaac!" Evie's sand-blonde head bobbed through the crowd. "Good to see you here. Looking for anything in particular today?"

"Might be." I grinned. "But if I told you what, I'd have to kill you."

She chuckled politely, which was more than the joke deserved. Evie, thirties, the festival PR manager and a collector herself. Sparky, eager to please, with a teasing smile, she was a treasure herself.

"Is that for me?" She reached playfully for the takeaway coffee I held.

"Sorry." I pulled back. "It's a bribe."

She nodded, intrigued. "Well, if you need anything at all...?"

Does she mean more than just coins? "I'll come to you," I said.

"Promises, promises." She grinned and headed back into the fray.

Ooh, very nice. Remember the mission!

I squeezed past a crowd at Newlands' stall admiring the Spanish gold—pieces of eight and doubloons—the show's superstars. A couple had dressed up as Jack Sparrow. Pirate loot never lost its shine.

And then I saw her—Maisie, sixties, joking with a customer. When she spotted me, her smile faded like the last firework on New Year's Eve.

"Maisie!" I shouted. "Cappuccino with five sugars, for you." I plonked it down in front of her.

"Thanks." The Coin Queen snatched the coffee. "But, I only take four and a half now. I'm sweet enough."

Debatable.

"And to save your breath," she said, "I'm not selling it."

The "it" she referred to was right there under glass. A gold coin, part of a commemorative set for the Sydney Olympic Games in 2000, of a swimmer. But on this coin, the water lines didn't end at the neck, they covered the athlete's face. It was a flaw, a minting error. In coins, though, unlike in life, blemishes increased desirability.

"I think we got off on the wrong foot," I said. *On the previous three occasions.*

"You mean you had your *foot* in your mouth and I had mine on your butt when you accused me of stealing?" The woman's stare was as cold and hard as metal.

"Could we start over?" I asked. "I'd like to buy the coin. I'm happy to pay whatever you think's fair."

Maisie raised her eyebrows. "Appreciate the offer, but I'm keepin' it. For sentimental reasons. My dead husband gave it to me. It ain't perfect, but neither was he."

Maisie slurped the drink loudly, then turned to another customer, dismissing me.

Walk away! Don't say anything you'll regret!

My legs carried me to a stall a few rows along. I scanned the merchandise without seeing it. Maisie was keeping the coin *for sentimental reasons?* The woman was about as sentimental as Ma Baker. And as honest.

By rights, that coin was mine. And one way or another, I'd have it before the day was done.

"How'd it go?" Evie was back, with her own cappuccino. "Not giving Maisie grief, I hope?"

"I was a complete gentleman." *Just.*

"Everyone loves Maisie. What is it between you two?"

"Can I have a sip of that?" I reached for her cup.

She pulled it away. "Get your own."

This was a tough side of Evie I'd never seen. *I like it.*

In the cafe at the side of the hall, I slugged down a double espresso and tried to explain.

"I might have called her a thief, once or twice," I said.

Evie grimaced. "You used the 'T' word?"

We didn't say that around here.

My phone buzzed in my pocket. I whipped it out. *Don't forget, you said you'd call later.*

"From my mum," I explained. "We don't get along."

Evie sipped her drink, assessing me over the rim of the cup. "If Maisie won't sell the coin, I know two other dealers with Olympic coins." Evie scrolled through a list of exhibitors on her phone.

"You don't understand," I said. "I don't want any Olympic coin. I want *that* one. It has…sentimental value." To borrow Maisie's phrase.

"Well, if Maisie won't deal with you, maybe she will with me? As your agent?"

"Great idea."

When Evie put her cup down, she had a little froth moustache.

"Better make you presentable." I wiped her top lip with my napkin and watched her cheeks turn deep pink.

She had a lovely smile. And a missing tooth I'd never noticed before. Which was cute.

"Give her whatever she wants," I said.

But minutes later, Evie was back. "She saw me talking to you. So, no dice."

I spent the day buying some coins for my modest collection. I wouldn't become a coin freak like some around here—just like King Midas, thinking of nothing but gold.

At 5pm, the dealers packed up and headed home.

I watched Maisie wheel her trolley away, the coins secured in locked cases.

Time to take things to the next level.

"Isaac, you're still here?" Evie seemed pleased. "Any luck with Maisie?"

I shook my head and showed her some coins I'd bought, which included another Olympics swimmer—standard mint variety—and some gold 1988 two-dollar coins engraved with the artist's initials.

She whistled. "Must have set you back a bit?"

"Do you think Maisie would accept them as a trade?"

"She'd be up on the deal," Evie said. "But will she go for it?"

Should I tell her? Bring her in?

"She won't have a choice," I said. "I have her address and I'm going to slip in quietly and swap my coin with these."

"What?" Evie was horrified. "You're going to break into her house?"

"I can only do it if you keep her busy at the front door."

"I don't know, Isaac."

"No-one will get hurt. Maisie will make a tidy profit on the deal. And I'll take you out for dinner to thank you."

She licked her lips, somewhat tempted by the last.

"I need a reason," she said.

I leaned closer. "I'll just be stealing back what's mine."

And so I told her. My mum left us when I was nine. Dad raised me. Though we didn't have greens with every meal, he always had my back.

The two of us struggled to connect. Coins gave us something to do together, a common interest. On my 10th birthday, he gave me a set of six Sydney Olympic gold coins and said they'd be worth something one day. They were my "inheritance".

"Were they really so valuable?" Evie asked

"No. But the flaw on the swimming coin was worth something."

During my teen years, I was a typical teen; I didn't want to be around Dad. When I started a career in finance, I didn't have much time to see him.

She listened hard, a line of concentration appearing between her brows.

He was drinking a lot. I didn't have much patience with that. Just before he died, he rang me to say someone had broken into the house and stolen my coin set. He was very upset. It was all he had to give.

"I didn't care about the value," I explained. "That set was special to us. He died not long after that. That was five years ago. This year, I decided to buy the coins back if I could. As a way of remembering the best parts of Dad."

Evie stroked my shoulder. I put my hand over hers.

"I located five of the six coins. When I asked the dealers how they'd come by them, they mentioned the same source: Maisie."

Evie pulled her hand away. "Maisie's no thief."

"Maybe not. But it seems like she bought stolen goods from the thief. And asked no questions. I can fix this," I said. "But I need your help?"

At around 7pm, we pulled up outside Maisie's house—a two-storey place that had seen better days. She'd lived there alone since her husband died the year before, Evie said.

I stayed in the car while Evie knocked on the dealer's front door. Maisie answered in her dressing gown and the two chatted on the front step. I heard Evie declining an offer of tea or whisky as I slipped into the shadows and around the back of the house.

Moonlight glanced off an old swing set in the yard. A protest of rust as it shifted in the breeze made me shudder. Or was it because the scene seemed eerily familiar?

Like any old playset.

The back door was unlocked; thankfully, I didn't have to smash anything. I turned the handle slowly and went inside.

On the wall ahead was a framed embroidery of a koala. Which seemed familiar also. I shook my head. *Like many old folk have on their walls.*

Creeping along a corridor, I turned, almost by instinct, into the second room on the right. And gasped. The old sofa. The battered wardrobes. A painting of African elephants on the wall. I'd seen them before. *But how?*

Maisie's coin cases were neatly stacked by the sofa. Ignoring the spooky *déjà vu*, I burrowed into them and found the flawed gold swimmer, replacing it with the regular minted version and the two-dollar coins. I snapped the locks shut. *The old girl might suspect me, but she'll never prove anything.*

As I turned to leave, I spotted some drawers with fussy gold handles.

What the—? I know them. I couldn't help myself. I opened the first one. And there, on top, lay the wallet folder for my Olympic coin collection. And, no, it wasn't any coin folder: it was mine. My name and address on the back written in my ten-year-old hand proved that.

"What the hell?" Stark light flooded the room as Maisie appeared in the doorway, Evie at her shoulder. "I'm calling the police." She tapped on her phone. "To report both of you." She glared back at Evie.

I thrust the wallet folder in Maisie's face. "*This* is me! This set was stolen from my father's house. Let's get the cops here and you can explain to them how it ended up in your drawer."

"Oh. My. Lord!" Maisie clapped her hands to her cheeks. "You're little Isaac Montague. Davey's boy."

"That's right," I said. "And these coins are mine."

"Emergency services!" a tinny voice answered. Locking eyes with mine, Maisie disconnected. "I'll get the whisky."

Evie and I sank to the sofa. "What's going on?" she whispered.

"I have no idea."

But a vague memory stirred.

Maisie splashed golden liquid into three glasses. "Bottoms up!"

I've heard her say that before.

We took a hefty slug.

"Someone broke into my father's house and stole this set," I began. "Are you going to tell me it wasn't you?"

"It wasn't me."

"Bullshit," I said. As if saying it strongly enough would make it true.

I didn't know what was coming, but I sensed I wouldn't like it. Especially not when Maisie's expression had changed from anger to… pity.

"I'm sorry to tell you this, Isaac, but no-one stole those coins. My husband, Dennis, won them off your father in a game of poker."

A gut punch.

"No way. You're lying."

"Your dad suffered like my Dennis. They had the gambling bug. It's a disease."

What the—? Dad gambled away my inheritance?

One look at Evie, hand over her mouth in horror, and I knew it was true.

"We're both victims here, Isaac," Maisie said. "My husband won the coins off your father. But if Davey'd had more time, I'm sure he'd have tried to win them back."

As if that's any consolation. I gulped my drink. It burned my throat on the way down, which felt good. And I realised I had been in this room before. Dad used to leave me here while he transacted "business" in a separate room.

"How's your mum?" Maisie asked. "You know, it was her who bought that coin set for you. Sourced it through me. Cara couldn't cope with your dad's gambling. She hated leaving you, though. She tried to take the coin set before she left. But thought she'd lost it. I guess your dad had it somewhere."

So. Mum bought the set and Dad took credit? He was a gambler and a thief?

Evie reached over and touched my arm, but I shook it off and stood up, draining my glass.

"The coin's yours, Isaac," Maisie said. "Keep it."

"I don't want it anymore." I tossed it onto the seat next to her.

Maisie picked it up. "I see this is a shock to you. To find out your dad wasn't perfect. That your mum might have had good reason to leave. But we need to face the truth about people we love. And love them, despite that, if we can. That's why I liked that flawed coin. It reminded me of Dennis. As quickly as I brought money in, he'd gamble it away. He wasn't perfect, but there was a lot of good in him."

But all that time, I've been angry with Mum. Like a spoilt child. All that time…wasted.

Evie's eyes had a misty sheen. Or was it seeing them through my eyes?

"It's not too late to fix this," she said, as if reading my mind.

"Would you mind if we had dinner another time?" I said. "There's someone I need to see tonight."

Sweet and Sour

GENRE: ROM-COM

PROMPTS: GENTRIFICATION, A FORTUNE TELLER

♡

There are two sides to every love story.

EXT. SUBURBAN STREET – DAY

A street with a mix of old houses, new mansions and trendy townhouses.

A rundown single-storey brick house, with paint peeling on the window frames and an old car on the lawn, sits beside a funky double-storey townhouse with a metallic pink car on its cobbled drive.

The clang of a cheap screen door banging shut as HUNTER, early 40s, ruggedly handsome, emerges from the brick house. He wears a paint-spattered shirt as he kneels to work on a garden bed at the side between the houses. His side is full of weeds and neglect, while his neighbour's is well-mulched, well-tended with pink flowers blooming.

A second clang as his son, LOGAN, long hair, grungy, 10, emerges to shoot baskets in an old hoop in the yard.

From Hunter's POV, the sound of a more solid screen door opening and closing and high heels clacking on cobblestones towards him. Pretty feet with painted toenails in immaculate shoes appear at ground level. He admires the curve of an ankle and the flow upwards of a shapely female leg.

SARA (O/S)

Good morning, Hunter.

SARA, late 30s, is attractive in a sunshiny, just-scrubbed way.

SARA

In the garden early this morning?

HUNTER

Well, it was kind of overdue.

SARA

I'm hopeless, me. Wouldn't know one end of a plant from the other. Luckily, I have a gardener to help with that.

Hunter gives her a tight smile and continues weeding. The *bang, bang* of the basketball hoop continues behind him.

SARA

It's another lovely day. Makes you glad to be alive, doesn't it? What are you and Logan planning to do today?

HUNTER

I don't know. Car's broken down. I have to fix that.

SARA

You fix cars too? You're useful to have around. Whenever Pixie—that's what I call my car—breaks down, I call Walt, the mechanic. He comes to my rescue and lends me...

                    SARA (cont)
… a car to run around in while he does the repair. I
couldn't go a day without my wheels. If you need a lift
anywhere, I'd be happy to oblige.

                    HUNTER
Thanks. I'm okay. And if Logan needs to go anywhere,
he's got two legs to take him.

                    SARA
You are so right, Hunter. Our kids don't do nearly
enough exercise, what with all the screen time they have.

Logan blows a gum bubble. It bursts audibly.

Sara's daughter, VIOLET, 10, neat and girlish, emerges. She and Logan
stare openly at each other like creatures from alien worlds.

Logan thumps the ball into the hoop. She watches intently but does not
react.

                    SARA
Violet, sweetie. Do you want to pick some flowers for the
hall vase?
(to Hunter)
We like fresh flowers. It brightens up the house.

                    HUNTER
Until they start to wilt and die.

                    SARA
Don't worry. As soon as they start looking sad, out they
go. That dead-flower vibe? No-one needs that.

Violet picks flowers. Logan watches her, expressionless.

> SARA

I'm loving this neighbourhood. Have you been here long?

> HUNTER

This was my parents' place. I've been round the area for most of my life.

> SARA

Really? I move every five years or so. I get bored in one place. But that's just me—short attention span. You're a more steady guy. Which is admirable.

INT. HUNTER'S HOUSE – DAY

Hunter's place is full of old furniture, inherited from elderly parents. It's messy and the walls need painting. There's some quirky art on the wall. Logan slumps on the sofa, playing with the ball as his dad paces angrily.

> HUNTER

Did you hear that?
(Imitating her)
I get bored in one place. But you're a more steady guy.
(shakes head)
Bloody cheek.

INT. SARA'S KITCHEN – DAY

In a neat open-plan room, with pinks and pastel shades, Violet arranges flowers in the vase. Sara paces, tense.

> SARA

I sounded like such an airhead out there. I'm a psychologist. I speak to doctors at conferences and I do business seminars. But that man turns me into a babbling idiot. It's just, I find him so…attractive, in this animal kind of way.

Violet squirts the flowers with a water spray, eyes wide.

INT. HUNTER'S HOUSE – EARLY EVENING
Hunter puts chunky sausages on his son's plate and they sit down to eat. Scattered on the table are lots of papers, including a letter which Hunter picks up and reads.

> HUNTER
>
> I get two or three of these letters a month – from real estate agents wanting properties in this "sought-after" area. Maybe I should sell, take the cash, move out west where people don't have gardeners to help them because they "don't know which end of the plant is which". And there are no Walts to fix their pretty pink cars. Do I sound bitter?

Logan has a big mouthful of sausage and can't answer, but he frowns deeply.

> HUNTER
>
> Yeah, I'm bitter.

INT. SARA'S KITCHEN – EARLY EVENING
Sara opens the fridge to reveal a super-neat arrangement of food. There are stacks of plastic containers. She takes out two, as Violet gets plates, cutlery and napkins.

> SARA
>
> I'd really like to ask him out. For dinner, or a drink? But what if he says no? That would be awkward.

EXT. SARA'S FRENCH HERB GARDEN – EARLY EVENING
Sara and Violet eat salad and cupcakes at a tiled French table amidst gravel and herbs.

> SARA
>
> I hope he doesn't see all the salad containers in my garbage. He'll think I'm totally hopeless, that I can't do a…

> SARA (cont)
> ...thing for myself. Well, he'd be right. I'm not very
> domestic. And he's so self-reliant. And speaking of
> garbage, I have to put the bins out later. Better make
> sure I wear something nice in case I run into him.

Violet has a mouthful of cake and can't answer.

INT. HUNTER'S HOUSE – NIGHT
Hunter works at a canvas on an easel, throwing paint at it like he's trying
to hurt it.

> HUNTER
> Every time we have a conversation, she's so condescending.
> Like I'm an idiot, a simpleton. It makes my blood boil.

Logan appears, sucking on a lollipop, his frown deepening.

> HUNTER
> I should go round there and tell her what I think of her
> and her domestic staff. Tell her where to stick her
> gardeners and flowers which brighten up her day. I was
> here first. I'm as good as her, or anyone on the street. No
> matter how many convertibles they have in the driveway.
> I don't have to take that crap.

Logan crunches his lollipop, brow trenched in anger.

INT. SARA'S LOUNGE – DAY
Violet is focused on an iPad as Sara enters, dressed up.

> SARA
> Do I look okay? I'm going to put the bins out now. I prob-
> ably won't even see him. But if I do...? Should I ask him
> over for dinner? Only I can't cook. And dinner sounds a
> bit intense. Maybe it should just be tea? Mum didn't . . .

SARA (cont)
...teach me much in the kitchen, but I do make a good cuppa. That's if I even have the nerve to ask.

She stops, distracted by a painting on her wall of a sunken New York City with weird human fish around it. Signed F.T.

SARA
I have one of his paintings on the wall. Is that a bit stalker-ish?

Violet shrugs and keeps staring at the screen.

SARA
I'll have to tell him about it before he comes over. If he comes over. He's just so talented. He really deserves more commercial success.
(breathes deep)
Anyway, wish me luck.

As she leaves, Violet puts the iPad down and follows.

EXT. HUNTER'S HOUSE – NIGHT
The door bangs shut as Hunter storms out of his dark yard into hers, triggering a blaze of security lights.

EXT. SARA'S HOUSE – NIGHT
Sara emerges with a garbage bin and a few plastic containers to find Hunter on the front stairs.

SARA
Oh, I was just going to put the rubbish out. Is it containers night tonight?
HUNTER
I think so but, err...

He's distracted by how good she looks.

> HUNTER

Are you going out somewhere?

> SARA

No, err... The truth is I was going to ask you over for dinner one night. Or afternoon tea, if you'd prefer. There, I've said it.

> HUNTER

You want me to come for dinner at your house. Why?

> SARA

You're a smart guy. You'll figure it out.

As Hunter twigs what's going on, the frosty demeanour changes to flirtatious.

> HUNTER

Well, it wouldn't be to help with the gardening—you have a gardener. Or to fix your car. Walt does that.

> SARA

You remember his name?

There's another bang of the screen door. Violet peers around her mother and sees Logan slip out and disappear into the dark. Violet goes out to see where he is.

> SARA

Before you come over, though, I have a confession to make. I have a painting of yours on my wall.

> HUNTER

Really? Which one?

                    SARA

New York, New York. With the city underwater. Let me just
say, I admire what you do so much. A lot of people have
tried to get the message out about global warming. But
your paintings do it so well. I can see why they call you the
Fortune Teller.

                    HUNTER

Well, thank you. I wish more of the art-buying public
thought so. But hearing an intelligent, and beautiful,
woman like yourself say that— sorry, may I say that
about you?

                    SARA

You may.

                    HUNTER

It makes it all worthwhile.

As Violet moves towards the pink car, she hears a hissing sound. She
goes round to the other side. The rear tyre is totally flat. And Logan is
working on letting the air out of the front tyre with a screwdriver.

Violet glares at him. Logan glares back. Their parents' voices are a
background hum of flirtation.

Hunter is smiling broadly at Sara now. Sara smiles coyly back.

                    HUNTER

Well, I think…dinner would be lovely.

                    SARA

Yes, it would be.

                  VIOLET (O/S)

Mu-um!

I, Spy

GENRE: SPY

PROMPTS: A PICKLE, AN OIL TANKER

♡

Brigit Hastings knows risk and danger are part of a spy's job. But what happens when the jeopardy flows onto those you love?

On a dark suburban street washed silver by moonlight, I await my signal.

The mission will be dangerous, I know. Possibly lethal. I should be focusing on that. But I'm not.

I'm thinking about Luke.

Not for the first time, or even the second, I check my phone. Still nothing.

It's been nine days since our date. Just recalling that night makes my face burn, like the sunrise we watched together. He went straight to the airport for an overseas business trip afterwards. But I know—in ways I really shouldn't—that he's been back for forty-eight hours. Without contacting me.

"Standby, Hastie," a voice crackles in my earpiece.

"Copy that, Jez."

I force my mind back to tonight's mission. A mysterious truck delivering an unknown liquid to an oil tanker nearby. Intelligence suspects the load is nasty—so nasty, it could hasten global warming by a decade or so. Why anyone would want to do that, with millions of lives lost, I can't imagine. But my job is not to reason why. It's to find out what's going on and stop them. Permanently, if necessary.

A possum scurries along a wire across the street. Will it get down safely? Or be up there as a power surge hits, melting its innards like candle wax?

"Hurry up, little fellow," I whisper.

"Hastie? Did you say something?"

"No."

"Well, anyway, it's time. You're up."

I feel my phone, warm, against my left leg, and my gun, cool, against my right, as I plunge into the night.

With a can of aerosol acid, I cut a hole through the metal security fence around the merchant port and climb through. I know that down on the water my colleagues are creating a diversion to distract the guards so I can do my job.

"How long have I got?" I ask.

"Five minutes. Maybe less."

I creep along the path towards the guard's box-like office, my dark clothes blending with the shadows. The huge red and blue tanker sits on water as black and shiny as the oil it carries, in a sleepy cove surrounded by bushland. This place would be a hiker's paradise if not for the blinding day-to-night lighting and ugly lift-and-pump mechanisms of the port. Voices echo around the bay. Further out to sea, a distant bell clangs.

I dart across the path to the guard's office.

"I'm in."

"Copy that," says Jez. "Now, you're looking for a ship's manifest or anything that will give us a clue about the mystery cargo."

The office is sparse—a battered desk, computer, messy paper pile, metal cabinet in the corner.

"Don't bother with the computer," says Jez, "our hackers would have found something if there was anything to find. You're looking for a paper copy."

I flick through some logbooks then spot a chart Blu Tacked to the wall.

"This could be something. Contents: tank one, oil; tank two, oil. Wait, tanks seven and eight are blank."

"They're our babies. I'd bet my life on it," says Jez. "But we'll need more to get the go-ahead for a tap and wrap."

"Tap" their brains with bullets—"wrap" their bodies in a body bag.

"Look for anything that can tell us who's behind it and exactly what the load is," says Jez. "But do it quickly and get out of there, Hastie."

"Copy that."

A flicker on the right catches my eye—a security camera in the corner.

How did I miss that?

I climb onto the desk and spray black paint onto the lens.

"Watch out! Someone's coming!"

As I start to get down, I'm aware of footsteps behind me. And...

When I wake up, I'm tied to a chair. A man paces in front of me. I recognise him from pictures on the news—James Bartram, of Clean Green Industrial waste. In his forties with a square jaw and eyes as blue as the Barrier Reef, he's the pinup boy of the environmental movement.

"Who are you and what are you doing here?" he says.

"I was walking my dog. He got off the lead, a block back. And I—"

Bam, he hits me in the face. I wince and turn back, chin high.

"No tears?" he says. "What are you? Government agent?"

I scoff. "You've seen too many Bond films, mate."

Anger scuds across his face before the fake charm returns.

"You'll tell us who you are before we finish here," he says. "Oh, and if you thought someone might be coming to rescue you—" he waves my earpiece in my face, then drops it, and stomps on it "—think again. Because no-one's listening anymore."

If I don't make it out of here, I'll never know if Luke would have called me.

Whether he was The One.

"Since I'm no longer a threat," I say, "is there anything you want to get off your chest?"

There is, of course. Megalomaniacs love bragging.

He tells me the liquid in the tanks is industrial waste "concentrated like a good stock". The world thinks he disposed of it but, really, he stockpiled it. When released, in a particular spot on Earth, at a certain temperature, it will massively expand a hole in the ozone layer, making global warming a reality twice as fast.

"If you succeed and bring on the destruction of the planet, won't you be destroyed along with it?" I ask.

"Not everyone will die in the cataclysm," he says. "A few will live on. They'll get the chance to create a better world."

"I see…" I say, nodding, "…that you're insane."

Bartram snorts. "All great thinkers have been called that at some point."

"As have all residents of the locked ward."

I ask him what chemicals are in his end-of-the-world cocktail and encourage him to go into detail. It means nothing to me—I'm not a chemist. But it will to someone listening. The top button of my shirt is a radio receiver. Everything he says is being monitored by my colleagues at HQ.

This was plan B all along. Get myself captured, let the target find and destroy the obvious listening device, then, as they divulge their criminal plans in the time-honoured narcissistic way, we get the justification we need for a full takedown. Bartram doesn't know it yet but he and his nasty load are now dead in the water.

"You don't feel guilty about the millions of people who'll die because of your actions?"

"Because of the world's inaction, you mean. That is. . .unfortunate. But those who remain will have a chance to build a better place, with proper planning and the right leadership to steer our course."

"The right leadership? That would be you, I suppose? Kill me now."

"What's your hurry, Ms…?" he says. "What did you say your name was? Oh that's right, you didn't."

Now his blue eyes shine with real enjoyment. I have a sick sense something bad is coming.

"But I know it starts with a 'B'."

Uh oh!

With a flourish, he pulls out my phone. "You sign off all your texts: *Cheers B.* So, what is your name? Brogan? Bailey? Bella? Maybe I should contact—" he looks down at the screen "—Luke Edgerton at 17 Vista Street and ask him what to call you?"

I try to keep my expression blank. But my skin is clammy and I can feel I'm not blinking enough. Bartram licks his lips, tasting victory.

"Interesting that you have a phone dedicated to a single caller," he says. "That means one of two things—either you're married and having an affair. Or you're *very* keen to keep business and pleasure separate. In which case, you're a hooker. Or a spy."

His eyes are all over me, taking in the black leggings and long-sleeved black T-shirt. "Personally, I'd pay top dollar for you if it was the former. But I'm going with option B: spy. So, who do you work for?"

I give a big, growly open-mouthed yawn as if I'm bored breathless. He sniggers, not buying it. As he scrolls through the texts, his eyes soak up all my carefully composed, casual messages to Luke. I want to lunge at him and snatch the phone back so badly. But I try to appear cool.

"Forgive me for saying this," he says, "but you seem to send him more texts than he sends you. *How was the trip? All going well? Have a safe flight?* I can't see answers to any of those. Could it be you're keener on him than he is on you?"

The bloody cheek.

It's one thing to kick me, or kill me in the line of business, but this…is out of order.

"Tell me, what are your hopes for this man?" he says. "A few wild weekends?" His gaze travels up and down my body. "I bet you can be wild when you want to be."

Let me out of these ropes and I'll show you how wild.

"Or are you looking for something more?" he says. "A commit-ment—mortgage, couple of kids, Sunday barbecues in the park? I've got bad news for you, B. People like us don't get to have that.

"Your average idiot walks around with a blindfold on," he continues. "He doesn't see— or even want to see—what's really going on, how far people like you and I have to go and the things—the terrible things—

we do to keep them safe as we take part in the war between good and evil raging on in the wings.

"I suppose you think I'm evil. I believe I'm on the side of the angels. But that's beside the point."

"Can we get to the point?" I say. "Unless you're planning to bore me to death."

He smiles but a muscle on his jaw clenches. I've hurt his feelings which is something, at least.

"My point is," he says, "once the blindfold's off, you can never put it back on again."

He shuts up to let me chew on that for a moment. I try not to.

What's keeping you, Jez?

"Who do you work for?" he says, moving closer. "If you won't tell me, maybe Luke will. My boys are on their way to his place now for a chat."

No, no, no! Never acknowledge anything, no matter what! Spycraft 101.

"He knows nothing about my work," I blurt out. *Fuck protocol!* "And anyway, he's probably still overseas."

Bartram grins, a big *guess-who's-in-control-now* kind of grin.

"Are you sure about that?" he says. His face drifts closer still, his lips grazing my ear as he whispers: "Could it be that he is back home, that he has been for quite some time, but is just not interested in contacting you?"

Bam! I head-butt him. He staggers back. I jump up, knock him down and out, still wearing the chair.

"Jez! Send people to Vista Street now!" I shout to my top button. "Luke Edgerton must not be harmed. Repeat. Save him. Or you'll have me to answer to!"

Agents swarm the docks. The tanker is going nowhere fast.

Fifteen minutes later, I receive confirmation that Luke's visitors were "intercepted" in the car park of his apartment block. He's safe.

Leaving the mayhem behind, I head back to my car.

The buzz of an incoming text shatters the silence on the street.

"What are you up to? Can I see you?" From Luke.

Yes, yes, yes.

He wants to see me. Bartram was wrong. *Hah!*

I call up the keypad, pausing to reflect on what a close call we had tonight. If those guys had got to Luke first...

Bartram's words swirl round my head like alphabet soup. I don't want to believe a thing that psycho says, but there's an idea there somewhere—like a bullet stuck in a bent barrel which won't go down fully, but you can't get out again either. He said people like us could never have a normal life. That once you've seen the dark side, you could never unsee it.

Rubbish.

It's just a job. I can leave any time. I'll quit. Put it behind me. Start afresh. With Luke.

"How about tonight?" I type.

My finger hovers over the *Send* button as, like an evil jack-in-the-box, Bartram pops up again in my mind, strutting about, vomiting out his vile vision for the future. He came close to realising that sick, twisted vision tonight. His charming demeanour hid a heart so dark, it was like a black hole: one the entire world could have been sucked into. If we hadn't stopped him.

If I hadn't stopped him.

And now I know why James Bond is always alone.

I delete the words on the screen and retype: "It's not going to work. Please don't contact me again."

Luke and everyone I care for will be safer with me out here, fighting in the shadows.

I am Brigit Hastings, Spy.

As the phone clatters to the road, the possum on the wire, outlined by the moon's silvery hand, looks up and freezes.

The Bodyguard

GENRE: DRAMA

PROMPTS: A HOBBY, A SECURITY GUARD

♡

As a former cop, Jackson expects his job as security guard to a science researcher will be an easy gig. Until he finds out what she's researching.

My brief was clear. Keep myself and the woman I was guarding under the radar. Off the grid. In the dark spaces between the bright city lights.

Am I doing that now, I wonder, as I lift her up and carry her like a baby in my arms through a gym studio full of women clapping the "hero" who saved their Zumba classmate?

Did any of them know, I wonder, it was that same hero who'd felled her in the first place during a misplaced merengue manoeuvre? Or in plain terms...Sarah and the Zumba class went one way, I went the other. Hard. Onto her foot.

I was meant to be protecting her. Instead, here I am carrying her away from carnage I created.

"Sorry," I tell her.

151

She glares and shakes her head. "Why the hell wouldn't you let me show you some of the steps before we came, like I wanted to?"

I'd arrived at her place—a one-bedroom apartment in a small art deco block in Kirribilli, overlooking Sydney Harbour—at 7.30 this morning, slipped inside as someone left the building and found myself outside her door (noting the security was slack).

"Hi, there," I beamed when she opened up. "I'm Jackson, from Up Close and Personal Security Service. Are you Sarah Lockhart?"

She scowled as she looked me up and down. Perhaps she didn't warm to my casual vibe—black jeans and T-shirt, with denim jacket, longish brown hair flecked with grey. Or she'd detected on my breath the splash (or two) of bourbon I liked in my morning coffee. But that wasn't it. Not entirely.

"I don't need a bodyguard," she said. "This is ridiculous."

Slight, sandy-haired and unremarkable in that I-could-be-gorgeous-if-I-tried kind of way, she wore black leggings and a loose grey tank top with *Rock My World* in rainbow shades.

"May I come in?" I asked.

For several long seconds she stood firm, then stepped back with an audible sigh, slamming the door in protest. In my line of work, I was used to this. No-one likes a stranger hanging about peering over their shoulder, judging their activities (and we do judge).

The flat was liveable, but not loveable. IKEA furniture, nothing on the walls. Lots of books, though.

"You've been getting death threats," I said, leading with my ace. "Is that usual for—" what was she meant to be, again? "—a scientist?"

She tipped her head, like a bird. A pretty, pissed-off bird. "No. It's probably just someone's idea of a joke." She squatted down to tie her trainers.

"So," I said, "where are we off to?"

She was going to a Zumba class at the gym, she told me—whether I liked it or not. Outside of science, this high-energy dance class was her one passion. Going was non-negotiable.

I shrugged. "Well, I'm coming with you."

"And what are you going to do," she asked, "stand at the back of the room like a bar-room bouncer?"

"Well, not exactly like that. I...err..."

"No. You'll put the others off and only draw attention to me." Her brow puckered. "I suppose you could stand outside and watch through the glass walls."

Gracious of her. *Not.* But that wasn't how I worked.

I stretched my cheeks in imitation of a smile. "It's okay. I keep some workout gear in the boot for emergencies. I'll do the class with you."

Now she inspected me a tad more seriously.

"Do you do Zumba?"

"No."

"Then can I at least show you a few basic moves before we go so you don't stand out like a cockroach in a bowl of sugar?"

Whoa! *I've been called a lot of things in my time, but cockroach?!* On the plus side, she was smiling now.

"I'll figure it out as I go," I said.

She's quiet on the drive back from class. As we climb the stairs to the first floor, I offer her my arm but she chooses to lean on the stair rail instead. Inside the flat, she hobbles across the room and flops onto the sofa.

I get us both a coffee—it's the least I can do—admiring the view of Sydney Harbour through the kitchen window as the kettle boils. It's dazzling blue today, sunlight flaring like diamonds on its surface as ferries and yachts cut through the water, past the Sydney Opera House, which looks like a stack of rowboats awaiting a renter.

I hand her the coffee. "We need to elevate your leg." She watches warily as I place her foot onto a cushion, then clamp a bag of frozen peas wrapped in a tea towel over the ankle.

"It's not that bad." She goes to stand up. "I need to get on with my work."

"Relax at least while you have your coffee?" I say.

For a moment, she seems about to argue, then she sinks back into the sofa cushions, huffing in irritation. As she blows delicately on her drink, her phone tings. She snaps it up to read a text, her lips twitching into an impish smile. A lover's message, perhaps? I pretend not to notice.

"So...a scientist?" I say. "What kind of science?"

"A chemist."

"Chemistry?" I grimace. "My least favourite subject at school. Mr Bertrand, my teacher, did NOT like me. And the feeling was mutual."

"I suppose because of all the clever tricks you did with the Bunsen burner." She rolls her eyes, unimpressed. Smart-arsery doesn't amuse her, then? I wonder what does.

"So, are you researching the cure to some terrible disease?" I ask. "Cancer? Greed?"

"No, medicine's not my field," she says. "I study fuel sources."

She's had a breakthrough, she tells me. Early testing is encouraging...results will go to a government committee...for presentation at the *Future of the Planet* conference in Toronto. As I listen, it's like the molecules freeze in the air around me.

By the time she's done, my lips are as dry as the Aussie outback. "You've come up with an alternative to petrol? Is that what you're saying?"

"That's the hope. One that's more planet-sustaining."

I put my cup down carefully and walk to the window overlooking the street, standing well back so as not to be seen. Pulling out some pocket binoculars, I focus on a van parked across the road. It has *Stern's Electrical* on the side, but if I've ever seen anyone who looked less like an electrician, it's the hulk of a guy with the broken nose in the driver's seat. His gaze boomerangs to Sarah's window, hand touching his ear as he mutters to himself—or to some kind of partner on a communications device.

"Can you walk?" I ask Sarah.

"Yes, I think so. But—"

"Get your things! Your laptop, phone. Anything to do with the research. We need to go. Now."

"What? Why?"

I help her track down what she needs. She's moving pretty well, if a little slowly.

"Is there a back way out?" I ask.

"No."

I send her to the bedroom to hide.

"What's going on, why do I have to—"

"Just do it. I'll explain later."

She watches me prime my gun, her eyes morphing from irritation to dread as she slips under the bed.

I head out the front door and march purposefully across the street to the guy in the van, thrusting an old police ID through the window. "Officer Caraway of Armed Response Unit," I say. "I'm afraid I'll have to ask you to move on. We've had a report of a crime underway in the area and we'll need this space for police cars, which will be arriving shortly."

"What?"

"Mate, why don't you go to your next job and come back later, after my colleagues and I—" I raise my arm and wave along the road behind him, as if I see someone approaching "—have dealt with the criminals."

"Fuck!" the guy mumbles and starts his car.

I see his hand touch his ear and lips move. Not long after, a skinny guy hurtles out of the building, jumping into the car's passenger seat before it drives off. *Speaking of cockroaches…*

I've bought us time. But not much.

I take the stairs two at a time to Sarah's apartment.

"Quick, come now!" I say, peering under the bed. We sneak out of the flat into my car. I put a cap on, as a disguise.

"Better stay down," I hiss.

"What's going on?" She's hunches below the dash.

"So, well, errr, it looks like the threat made against you wasn't just a random thing." I keep my voice measured. "That was a professional crew going after you."

"After me?" she asks, pink-faced. "Why? Who'd want to hurt me?"

"In my opinion?" *It could be anyone. From a wide range of countries.* "What you're doing will change things. A lot of people don't like change. Especially not to the megabucks they get for oil."

She sits up, her creased brow gradually smoothing as she considers my words. "But I'm just a researcher. It makes no sense."

We drive to my apartment in Glebe. I figure no-one will look for her there. It's not much to see but at least it's well-stocked with wine and beer.

I pour Sarah a glass of sauvignon blanc from New Zealand—I developed a taste during a trip to the Marlborough vineyards a few years back. As much as I'd like to join her in a glass, I refrain. I need to stay sharp just now.

"I can't believe this!" She shakes her head and gulps down half her wine. "Have you done many of these jobs? Protecting clients from people wanting to…hurt them?"

The question throws me for a moment. I haven't done this kind of serious protection since the force. *And how did that work out for you?*

"Errr, not recently. I usually do low-key stuff." *The lowest.* "Mostly TV people and low-ranking celebrities. I stop the paparazzi bothering them. Or corporate types who think they're important enough to need a bit of muscle. Though, usually, there's no real danger."

But for Sarah, the threat is real. She smiles and asks questions about which celebrities I've protected. I give her a few names—some are quite well-known—but she looks blankly at all of them. Seems she's been staring down a microscope way too long.

She picks up her phone and starts texting. Quite soon, a shade of flamingo pink washes through her cheeks. She's speaking to "him". Or "her". *The One.* I place my hand over her screen and lock eyeballs with her. "You can't tell anyone where you are."

"We can trust Alain, my boss." She pulls the phone away, glowering. There's something about the way she says "boss" that suggests he's more. "I'll just let him know I'm safe."

When she's done, I take the phone and switch it off. "People can track your signal."

She glances around my apartment. There's not much to see. Cheap furniture. Nothing on the walls. Some film mags and books. A bunch of junk mail I haven't thrown away. She and I have the same decorator—disinterest.

"Is this guy, Alain, also your boyfriend?" I ask.

Given my job here, I figure I have some right to know who the main players are.

She swigs her wine. "None of your business. And it's complicated."

Complicated?

"He's married then?"

She doesn't reply, just sucks on the wine and keeps her eyes fixed on the blank walls.

"Oh, come on!" I say. "You deserve better than that."

"You don't understand."

"I understand lying very well."

"Well, that's not something to be proud of."

Maybe not. But at least I didn't lie about lying.

I persuade her to have a quick shower (despite the lack of a lock on the bathroom door). "Not too much hot water on the ankle, or it will swell!" I call.

While she's in the bathroom, I retrieve her phone, punch in the password (I'm good at reading people's keystrokes upside-down) and scroll through her messages from Alain.

"Miss you, muffin." "My universe is dim without its brightest star?" "Take a photo where you are, so I can picture you."

I check first to make sure she hasn't sent him anything, then type: "Fuck off back to your wife and don't call me again!"

And switch the phone off.

Sarah comes back in, looking refreshed and cool, sits down and rubs her ankle.

"Still a bit tender?" I ask. "Shall I get some more ice?" I always have plenty of that.

"No, it's okay," she says.

"So how did you come to make this scientific discovery?"

As she talks science, her eyes fill with light and a dimple in her cheek appears, hinting at a playful side. I wonder how I didn't see it right off the bat—she is beautiful. And completely unaware of it.

The mood sours when I pop out to refill her glass and she sneaks a peek at her phone, discovering a dozen wounded responses from her boss to my message.

"Did you write this to Alain?" she asks. "How dare you? You're supposed to be protecting me, not ruining my personal life!"

"Trust me, this won't stop him." *Lowlifes like him get keener with a few obstacles thrown in their path.*

"Well, genius," she says, "in one of those messages, Alain says he saw a picture of me on Facebook being carried by some guy through a gym.

Some Bigfoot with a big mouth."

Uh-oh. She shows me a post from one of the Zumba women. "Hero saves fallen classmate." With a clear picture of our faces. *Not good.* Whoever is after her will know we're together and may be able to track us here.

"We have to move," I say.

We sneak out through the laundry on the ground floor, then cross the garden bed. I can't spot anyone on the street as we slip into my car. Though, as I change lanes on the main road, I see another vehicle leap-frogging a few cars back.

My phone rings. A picture of Mark, my boss, flashes onto the screen. I answer, driving one handed through the traffic, one eye on the rear-view.

"Hey Jackson, you on the job?" he asks. "Wanna make a little extra? A few people are interested in the location of your client." I look over at Sarah, staring through the window, oblivious. "There's a grand in it for you," he adds.

A grand? Double what I usually get for tipping off the paparazzi about my clients' movements. Then again, the result here won't be just an embarrassing photo on social media.

"Sorry, no can do."

As I go to click off, I hear. "Jack!" I bring the phone up again. "These people are seriously keen to hear from you." Some heavy breathing. "Ten grand."

Ten grand! I know Mark takes a cut. I wonder how much he'll personally make for throwing Sarah to the wolves.

I watch my client. The light from the traffic dances across her face, illuminating tiny lines of worry around her eyes. No doubt she got them from hours hunched over test tubes, fathoming out complex problems to help the planet. All of which will be for nothing if I allow her to be found.

"Can't help you, mate."

"What the fuck!" he says. "Since when are you a hero? Why do you think you were hired for this job? To save the damsel in distress? No, it was so you could give her up, like you usually do. Like you've always done. So why don't you be a good, bad bodyguard and—"

I hang up and switch off.

It's an effort to keep my expression blank, my breathing even. That was tough to hear—that it was my reputation for betraying the people I was meant to protect that had won me this job. Had I really moved so far over to the debit side of the balance sheet?

I grip the wheel and press my foot down more firmly on the accelerator. Sarah senses it.

"Jackson? Is everything okay?" Sarah asks.

Is it?

"Never better."

I know now what I have to do.

Spotting a small street on the right, I glance in the rear-view mirror, then cut across the traffic and swing down it. Then turn right again, into an underground car park. I squeal down several floors, then pull up in a shadowy spot. I bundle Sarah out and get out a lockpick to break into the car next to us—a blue Mazda. In a few minutes, I get the engine purring and we head back out into the traffic again.

"Where are we going?" she asks.

"To the city." *We need to lose ourselves in a crowd. To buy us some thinking time.*

"I noticed you have a police ID in your wallet," she says. "Is it fake?"

I shake my head.

"Then you were a police officer? What made you switch to security guard?"

There's disappointment in her voice, or maybe it's in the filter through which I hear the question.

My eyes range around the traffic, searching for any vehicle in pursuit. We're okay for now. "I did something I shouldn't have."

She's silent as I explain that I used to work in witness protection. "I was protecting a guy who'd seen a well-known figure commit a crime. When I finished my shift, I had a drink with a police mate of mine. He asked me where the safe house was, where the guy was being kept."

"And you told him?"

I nodded. "I'd known the cop for years." *I thought he was a good friend.* "During the night, the safe house was raided and the witness was killed. The charges against the public figure had to be dropped due to lack of evidence. And I was discharged from the force."

"Your cop friend was corrupt, and you got the blame?" Sarah sum-marised it coolly. I lost my job, which was bad enough. But the guy I was protecting lost so much more. "It wasn't your fault," she says. "Your only mistake was trusting the wrong person."

In my business, knowing who to trust is everything. I'd let the witness down.

Since then, in my role as security guard, I'd let quite a few others down, too. For a price.

I change lanes frequently yet smoothly, so as not to draw unneces-sary attention to us. On the edge of the city, we abandon the car—the cops might be looking for it—and catch the tram into town. It crawls along the main street, slow as regret.

"What I don't understand is why they'd want to hurt me," Sarah says, a crease forming between her brows. "I'm just a researcher. If I die, someone else will just carry on with my work."

"Someone like the married guy you've been texting? Alain?"

She nods, a muscle on her jaw taut as she clenches her jaw. "He's in charge of the project."

The city shops glide by, the Cinema Multiplex, the Queen Victoria Building with its stained-glass windows, ever busy with shoppers, as I think this through. With a scientist's logic, Sarah has homed in on an important truth. There's no point coming after her unless it means the project will end when she does. Someone would have to lose the research, discredit her work and get the whole project shelved perma-nently. Someone senior to her, who knew all about what she was doing. Okay, so I had a suspect.

"I know you trust Alain," I say. "But will you let me do a little test to put my mind at ease that he's worthy of that trust?"

"Are all security guards as interfering as you?" she asks.

"Just the good ones."

She folds her arms, lips pert. *Is that how she looks when a science experi-ment doesn't go the way she thought it would?*

"We'll give him some false information and if he does nothing with it and nothing bad happens," I say, "I'll be confident he's okay. And you'll have gloating rights."

She presses her lips together so tightly they turn white. She doesn't like it. But as a scientist, she can't deny the logic.

"All right, I'll do it. To prove you wrong."

Over cappuccinos at a grungy midtown cafe, we watch video surveillance of my flat on my phone screen. I use Sarah's phone to text Alain: "Here's the address, I'm not supposed to tell you. Kiss." And switch off.

"I never say kiss at the end like that."

"You think he'll suspect something?"

She doesn't reply, just remains sullen as we drink coffee and watch the screen.

Before the froth has settled on our drinks, two men with necks like bridge supports break in through my front door, guns brandished. They move from room to room, looking for someone.

One man speaks on a phone. "No-one's here. Yes, I'm sure. We'll wait here for a while in case they come back."

"That doesn't prove anything," Sarah says. "Whoever made the threat against me might have seen the Zumba post online and figured out where you live. You don't know Alain told them anything."

I nod, and don't disagree. She put a lot of effort into coming up with that explanation. A good scientist should explore all possibilities, I know. But they also have to acknowledge the truth, no matter how unpalatable it is. Something about the way she's twisting her lips and gnawing on the inside of her cheek tells me she's doing that privately, even if she won't admit it.

But if Alain is the bad apple in the barrel, Sarah's in deep trouble. Who can she turn to, who can she trust? And—more to the point— what's the best way to keep her safe?

"When do you need to deliver the results to this government committee?" I ask.

"In three days' time," she says. "There's a meeting scheduled at the Ministry for Climate Change."

Three days. *She'll never make it.*

"You know what?" I say. "There's no time like the present. Let's deliver the results early, shall we? But we'll do it my way."

Sarah frowns as she considers this, then nods. "Okay," she says. "What's the plan?"

Her sea blue eyes are alert; she's ready to listen to me and face whatever we have to face, together. I feel a twinge of pride at her confidence in me and something else—the strongest desire to be worthy of that trust.

I ask Sarah for the name of her contact at the Ministry of Climate Change. It's the Minister's political advisor, Colson Janus. I don't like the sound of him. Not just because it's a hokey name, but because in my experience political advisors often have their own agenda, serving their own interests before anyone else's. I make a note of Colson's name. A bit more googling, and I learn that there's an event at the Opera House tonight. A concert for climate change. The Minister is bound to be there, with Colson by his side, glad-handing the donors and celebrities. And posing for a few media pics. A call to the Minister's personal assistant, an efficient-sounding woman of middle years, confirms it.

"We're going for drinks at the Opera House," I say.

"We are?"

"But we'll need to dress for the occasion. What's your go-to store in the city for clothes for fancy affairs?"

"My what?"

I look at Sarah, still in her gym gear, worn at the knees from overuse, and make a wild guess that she doesn't have a go-to upscale boutique.

"We'll just have to explore." I grin.

Drinks are to be served at sunset, overlooking Sydney Harbour, so we have a couple of hours to prepare. As a security guard, I go to a lot of swanky functions, so I know the kind of gear we're looking for. When Sarah emerges from the change room in the first shop, in a green cotton dress my grandmother would not even wear to do gardening in, I frown and shake my head. "We can do better."

She might be a genius at science, but when it comes to glamour, she needs help.

I lead her back onto the street and take her to *Roxanne's*, a designer shop on the first floor of the Strand Arcade with a lot of sequins in the window. My own outfit is easy—black trousers, white dress shirt, bow tie and jacket. But the eponymous Roxanne takes charge of Sarah to find her something appropriate for cocktails with Sydney's glitterati. I sit back on a leather sofa, sipping tea, while she tries on dresses in one of three luxurious change rooms.

Emerging in the first dress, her eyes dart about as if terrified someone might see her. *Which is the general idea.* She's a vision in a strapless, silver-sequined dress, shaped at the bottom like a mermaid's tail. I can barely tear my eyes away.

"Is this really necessary?" she says, frowning in the mirror.

Not totally. "Oh, yes, absolutely," I say.

"Have you seen how much it is?"

"Just part of the cost of keeping you safe." *I've made more—from selling clients out.*

"Cherie," says Roxanne with a broad Aussie accent, "gorgeous! But don't make a decision till you've tried the red."

"The red" is scarlet and dramatic, with feathers among the sequins and a split up the side almost to the waist.

"Spectacular!" says Roxanne, clapping her hands together.

"No way in the world!" says Sarah, eyebrows tight.

Sigh. "What else you got?" I ask Roxanne.

The next dress is not as showy. It's a rich blue, to her knee, in a sparkly figure-hugging material that somehow accentuates the colour of her eyes. *Perfect.*

"Not bad," I say.

I'd like to say more—a lot more—but I sense compliments will only send her back to the change room again.

Roxanne locates shoes and a bag to match for Sarah. I look through the jewellery on display and pick up a chunky necklace with a sun and moon in it.

"Appropriate for a climate change concert, don't you think?" I say, clipping it at the back for her.

"It's pretty," Sarah concedes.

No, you're pretty, I want to say. But I don't.

I hand over my credit card—aware this might alert anyone tracking us that we're in the city.

We won't have much head start.

As twilight descends, we approach the Sydney Opera House, its sails like eggshells catching the sun's last rays. The Minister's cocktail party is on at the rear, with the full glorious sweep of Sydney Harbour on show.

We follow a stream of well-dressed people approaching a security checkpoint. Ahead, someone flashes an embossed invitation at the guard on duty. Just as I thought— drinks, *by invitation only*.

I take Sarah's hand and lead her to the railing by the harbour. We look out at the water turning golden as the sun slips towards the horizon. The Harbour Bridge stands sentry before us, lights winking as cars whizz back and forth. To anyone observing, we look like any couple having a romantic moment at sunset. I'm slow to release Sarah's hand and tell myself it's to keep up the illusion.

"What now?" Sarah asks. "Do we create a diversion, or pickpocket the invitation from someone going in?"

I cough out a laugh in surprise. "Well, look at you, Ms *Ocean's Eleven*."

"Ocean's what?" She's genuinely confused.

"Oh, girl. You have spent way too much time in the lab," I say. "One day, someone will have to fill you in on all you missed while you were burning those Bunsens." *Please let it be me.*

A wry smile breaks out on her face, the dimple making a brief appearance, like a glimpse of pirate treasure before the casket lid bangs shut. But when her watery gaze fixes on mine, all playfulness ebbs. "Before I get to things I missed, we have to get through today. So, tell me, Mr Bond, how do you propose we gatecrash this soiree of the great and not-so-good?"

I ask her to wait by the entry. Then head into the Opera House building. I've body-guarded a few celebs at events here and I know where the catering staff work. Putting on my best "here-to-serve" face, I stride into the kitchen and snatch up a tray of hors d'oeuvres. No-one gives me a second look as I emerge in the middle of the party, offering spring rolls and arancini to the sparkling guests.

When my tray is empty, I scan the long drinks table for what I need. A half dozen women's handbags sit on the table unguarded—their owners immersed in conversations nearby. I see one sparkly red bag with The Event invitation spilling out. I grab it, ditch the tray and head for the security entrance.

But Sarah's not where I left her. Panic sluices through me as I consider she might have been taken already. My eyes scan the line of people waiting to enter. She's not there. I look further along at the people strolling on the Opera House walk—she's not there either. I narrow my eyes to scan the cars cruising along the road nearby, checking she's not in one of them.

"Hello." Sarah's in front of me, unharmed and grinning.

"But how did you get in?"

"I told the man on the door I'd left my invite at the office," she says. "He let me in. I'm not totally helpless, you know."

I chuckle. This is a woman who's competent at anything she turns her mind to, I suspect. Except perhaps interior design. And making the most of her appearance.

I place her arm through mine—we have to continue the charade, after all—and we stride through the crowd, mixing with the glitterati.

For a moment, I imagine how nice it would be if the fantasy were real, if we were simple partygoers attending a concert on climate change. Clinging to each other like a life raft in turbulent social seas.

But she's the one here for climate change. Not me. What she's doing could help repair the world. As long as no-one stops her in the next few minutes. And that's where I come in. My job is to mess with anyone who tries to mess with her.

We swipe some champagne and nibbles and look around for our target. It's not hard to spot the Minister for Climate Change—he's surrounded by lobbyists and sycophants. His personal assistant, Ruth—a well-dressed, middle-aged woman I recognise from Google images—lurks nearby, keeping watch in case he needs rescuing. To the right, I see Colson Janus, the political advisor. Porkier than in his last photo, he quaffs finger food and slugs down free booze as if it's his birthright.

Everyone is in place.

And then I spot...bridge bollards one and two—the thick-necked heavies who were at my house earlier—in the queue to get into the party. Their suits are a size too small, and they look like rent-a-thugs as they scan the crowd with predators' eyes.

"Keep your head down, and go see the Minister's assistant now," I instruct Sarah.

From my experience, personal assistants are fiercely loyal with integrity to spare and a finely tuned bullshit meter. There's usually no love lost between them and political advisors like Colson, whose breathtaking pragmatism they recognise for what it is. Sarah needs to trust someone here; I'm hoping Ruth is the one.

I watch Sarah introduce herself. The assistant listens and frowns, not sure at first what to make of the stunning woman before her with the Ziploc file. But after a few minutes, Ruth's face relaxes into a smile. She's drawn to Sarah's intelligence and passion for her subject.

Meanwhile, I loiter around Colson, who's scrolling through his phone messages and doesn't notice me over his shoulder. I need to keep him well away from Sarah until her research is safely in the Minister's hands.

The big boofheads are through security now, head-bobbing, trying to spot Colson in the crowd would be my guess. I stand between him and them, blocking their view, to buy more time.

I'm keen to know whether Col really is working with Alain. So I switch Sarah's mobile back on. Half a dozen messages from the guy are waiting, expressing concern that, even from this distance, has a whiff of fakeness to it. "I'm so worried about you." "Tell me where you are, sweetness." "I'll come get you and keep you safe."

I message a reply: "Hi Alain, I'm going home now. But my body-guard Jackson is delivering our research tonight to the Minister, at a drinks function at the Opera House. Isn't he brave?" *Couldn't resist that last part.* I send a photo of me, smiling with the Opera House behind me. Then switch off. And wait.

I start counting to ten but only make it to seven before Colson's phone rings.

"He's here? Now?" I hear him say. His snake's eyes slither over the crowd. "Haven't got a photo of him, have you?"

A few seconds later, my mug fills his screen—proof my suspicions were correct and Alain is selling Sarah out. "I'll take care of him," says Colson.

He holds the phone up, comparing the photo with the faces of the men in the crowd. I'm directly behind him and move around as he does, so he doesn't see me right away. I stop when he's almost done a 360-degree turn. He's taken aback to find me right there in front of him. Smiling.

"Colson Janus, I presume?" I offer my right hand to shake, and as he takes it, I jab him hard in the solar plexus with my left.

"Oof." He doubles over and I hold him down and jostle him away from the crowd. "A few too many hors d'oeuvres was it, mate!" I say loudly for anyone watching nearby.

We move to the railing overlooking the harbour, where I deliver a blow to his lower back for good measure.

"That's for trying to hurt Sarah."

"Who the fuck are you?" he says.

"I think you know." For a second, his face is a picture. It could be a Google image of Guilt.

"I'll call security," he says.

"Good idea," I say. "And we can explain to them why you have a picture of me on your phone." I snatch his phone while I'm at it. "And how you promised to 'take care of' me. And how your friend Alain got some of his friends to go round to my apartment earlier to 'take care of' both Sarah and I."

"I don't know what you're talking about."

"This phone might say differently."

"Give me that!" He leaps for it like a child jumping for a confiscated toy. I pull it away with a parent's relish and, as he lands, I stamp on his foot—hard—in a move I perfected in Zumba class earlier.

"Fuuuck!" While he limps around, moaning in pain, I look back at the crowd and spot Ruth and Sarah hovering near the Minister, waiting for a chance to interrupt his conversation with some people.

Almost there. I just have to keep Col busy a bit longer…

Unfortunately, the two thugs have spotted us and cross the Opera House concourse with a Terminator eye lock on me. Their thighs are so large, they walk with their feet wide apart, I note.

"Smile!" I snap a picture of them and quickly send it off to a journo I know. One of them rushes forward, grabs my phone, and flings it out into the harbour.

"That's littering," I say.

He swings a punch at me. I duck and kick him in the shins.

His friend, the other bulldog bookend, grabs me from behind, gives me a couple of good poundings on the cheek that make my world spin and a couple of teeth rattle in their sockets. Before I have my bearings again, he lifts me off the ground and starts moving towards the harbour, with his brother bollard blocking any view of us. I brace my legs on the metal railing and try to push back as I stare down at the dark waters of Sydney Harbour, wondering what lies beneath. Fish? Sharks? Discarded rubbish? I really don't want to know.

"I'll be over with the Minister when you're done," Colson mutters.

He might still get there in time to ruin Sarah's introduction. I need to delay him a bit longer.

"There's something you should know," I shout.

Col crosses his arms and tips his head, dubious. "What." Spitty on the "t".

"Just a warning," I say. "If you have any more ideas of harming Sarah, I'd think again. Half a dozen lawyers and journos around the city have copies of her research—and instructions to release it with a big song and dance if anything happens to her."

It's true. I sent a copy of her research summary to everyone I could think of before we came out tonight, figuring the more who knew about it, the safer she'd be.

"Fuck!" says Col, pacing and raking his fingers through his hair.

"Time for a dip!" says Apeman number two, lifting me higher and plonking my butt down on the railing, with my feet dangling like a kid on a tall chair. I grip the rail with my hands and fingernails as he exerts pressure. I resist with all I've got, but I won't be able to hold on much longer.

"The journos have your picture too, guys," I say. "As do the people just over there." I incline my head backwards

The meatheads and Col can't help but turn around. No-one's there, but in that split second, the guy's grip on me eases a smidge. I lean back, grab Col's shirt and launch us both forward.

Over the rail, into the harbour.

I hit the water hard, a full body slap. The shock of the cold makes me gasp. Even six feet under, I'm none the wiser about what's lurking here. It's too dark and murky to see much—and for that I'm truly grateful. Looking up through the water, I see the Opera House, wobbly and ghostly white against the liquorice sky. As I rise to the top, I grab Col's arm and pull him up with me.

We break the surface together, gasping for breath.

"You fucking psycho!" he says.

Half a dozen people have rushed to the edge and peer down at us with O-shaped mouths. Col sinks under again and I drag him back up, putting him in a lifesaver headlock as I tread water, to claps and cheers from the crowd.

"Fuckwit!" Col hisses.

"Smile for the cameras."

A few people take pics—of me grinning and Col coughing up muck—and post them on social media #OperaHouseHero.

"Are you all right?" someone shouts down.

Sarah's face appears over the railing, full of concern and surprise and then something else—amusement.

"Never better."

A small boat delivers Col and I safely back to Circular Quay where Sarah is waiting.

"You made quite a splash there," she says. She tries to smooth my tangled hair. "You really don't know how to dress for a swanky event, do you?"

There's the dimple again, not going away this time. I feel heat rising from my neck to my hairline. And I didn't think I could still blush.

"So, tell me," she asks, "what did I miss?"

The Woman Who Fell to Earth

TIME TRAVEL NOVELLA

♡

On her 25th wedding anniversary, Cassidy wonders whether she would do it all over again. But some questions should never be asked.

"If you could go back twenty years, what would you change? Or would you do everything again, exactly the same?"

Someone posed this question at our Friday work drinks. I forget who. Jasmina, maybe? It was not particularly original and completely pointless. I mean, why worry about things you can't change, right? But the question stayed with me. Like a fly trapped between the glass and screen doors, it buzzed round my head. I couldn't get it out.

If I had my time over, would I change anything? Had I made the best decisions in my life? Did I have any regrets?

It was on my mind as I stood at the back door of our Roseville home, looking out at our elegant backyard. With its well-trimmed hedges and French-style plantings in pinks and purples, it was a Sydney home buyer's dream. Just before sunset, the scent of rosemary was sweet and the paved area seemed incandescent, almost otherworldly, as the travertine surface soaked up the last rays of daylight.

Two nights from now, this space would be filled with tables, set with white tablecloths, seating thirty close friends and family. We would share a catered meal to celebrate my twenty-five years of marriage to Vaughan, the world's best husband and my best friend. He and I had met at a party at Sydney University. From that first moment, we were in love. He was my first, my only, lover.

"Reckon all the tables will fit?" My eldest, Matilda, twenty-two, was not usually an organiser. She kept her head down while the work was done and popped up again with the first champagne cork. However, she had stepped up to shoulder some of the "load" for this event so I could enjoy the evening more. I wasn't sure whether to be happy she was growing into a more considerate person, or sad, as it meant I was that much closer to being completely redundant.

"If the tables don't fit, we can plonk a few in the flower beds," I said. "Close friends go near the gardenias. You can put Jasmina in the middle of the rose bush, on the thorns."

Matilda chuckled. "Why do you invite her if you feel like that?"

"Because she's my friend. Most of the time."

"And what if it rains?" Matilda asked.

"We'll all have to squeeze onto the deck and into the living room as best we can. Don't worry, honey, it will work out."

Matilda tilted her head, a deep crease between her brows. "Who are you and what have you done with Mum?"

Okay, so I wasn't usually laid-back about things like this. I was a planner. I fussed and worried and worked hard to make sure everything in our lives, every detail, was just right. From the family dinners and holidays to Christmas celebrations, kids' parties and big life decisions, I liked things to be perfect, or as near as I could get to it. It was a crazy and ultimately doomed ambition. I could no more shield my kids from the cruelty of high school than I could save Dad from the Parkinson's disease that eroded his quality of life and took him in the end. But I kept trying.

Until recently, when my youngest, Ryan, eighteen, finished his exams. Just like that, the day after the test, getting everything 110 per cent right seemed unimportant. Was it my age? I was forty-seven. Was wisdom finally kicking in? Or was it something else? The sense, both satisfying and terrifying, that my job as a mother was done now.

So... what next?

"You and Dad have been married for twenty-five years!" Matilda shook her head in awe. "Not long enough though, hey?" It was something I usually said; she got in first.

"And I hear the second twenty-five years are the best." I completed our script.

"Yeah, well, let me get through the first twenty-five days with a guy, then I'll think about that."

"No rush."

Snap! Where did that come from? I was usually all about the rewards of love and commitment.

"You were married by my age," Matilda said.

"That was me. You don't have to do the same. Go out, party. Chase a few wild oats."

"Don't you mean 'sow' my wild oats?"

"Chasing... sounds more fun than sewing. Which is my point."

Ryan emerged, shirtless, eyes glued to his phone, a white chord dangling from his messy blond hair.

"Auntie Nicky called earlier," he said. "She won't be bringing a date to the dinner after all. But can you please not put her at the old farts' singles table?"

"Auntie" Nicky wasn't really my sister, but my best friend. She'd never married or had kids of her own but had been as good as an aunt to mine.

"You don't have to call her 'Auntie' anymore," Matilda said. "We're grown-ups now!"

As Ryan turned her way, half-listening to something on his headphones, she shook her head. "He probably thinks her first name is Auntie."

And then—*boof*—he walked into the glass door. We rushed over, checked he was not too dazed ("How would you tell the difference?" Matilda asked), before Band-Aiding a cut on his forehead.

"Tell me if you start to feel dizzy," I said.

"Oh, no!" Matilda pointed to a small hole in the glass with fine cracks emanating like spider webs. "We'd better call the emergency glass guys pronto."

"Don't worry. We'll tape it up and deal with it after the party," I said.

Two sets of eyes—hers blue, his hazel—went pug wide at me.

"Are you feeling okay?" Matilda said.

"Yes, of course."

But when I asked myself that question, later, I wasn't so sure. I hadn't sounded like my old self, then.

Maybe I wasn't okay at all.

After work the next day, Jasmina cracked open some champagne for the office to celebrate my anniversary.

"Twenty-five years together! Impressive," she said, though the droll twist of her lips hinted at amusement. "Perhaps you can give Brodie and I a few tips?"

"Me? Give *you* tips? You're much more experienced at marriage than I am. Anyway, isn't the third time meant to be a charm?"

"Husband number three is nothing if not charming," Jasmina said. "Let's hope he doesn't turn out to be nothing in the end."

Brodie, who she'd married six months before, got better looking with age. A sprinkle of salt and pepper in his dark brown hair, some fine lines on his tanned face, gave him a Bond suaveness. At uni, he'd been two years above us and the It guy (as opposed to the I.T. guy). Completely out of our league. Since then, he'd gone on to do some big finance deals and was now quite well-off, though a tad arrogant for my taste.

"To true love! Long may it last!" said Jasmina.

"True love." We raised glasses.

Through the glass walls, I watched Jasmina moving about the lab, checking results, instructing technicians. She was so self-assured I was in awe and a smidge jealous.

We'd graduated together from Sydney University and begun our careers, side by side in a private lab. That was before my children were born and I gave up work to be a full-time mum. "These kids are the most important science project I'll ever have," I'd said at the time.

I realised now how sanctimonious I must have sounded to Jasmina, who had children but didn't have the option of staying home even if she wanted to. She'd raised three kids, with two different husbands, and worked the whole time, much of it as a single mum.

Now, she was second-in-charge of a government research lab and head of its Future Technologies Division. While I—after almost two decades out of the field—couldn't get a research position and had to rely on her for something in public relations.

"I haven't thanked you properly for this job," I said.

She waved away my gratitude. And, as I reached for the champagne bottle once again, she pulled it out of reach. "Don't you think you've had enough?" she said.

It was eight o'clock. The only people still here were her and I and Marcus, a young researcher with a thick beard and thicker glasses that refused to stay on his nose whenever he looked down—which was most of the day.

"Let me enjoy the moment." I wrestled back the bottle. "I've spent a quarter of a century doing what everyone else wants. Isn't it time I do what I want?"

Jasmina tipped her head. "Wasn't that what you wanted? To be a wife and a mum? You had a choice."

"Yeah, I know."

I emptied the rest of the bottle into my glass, watching the bubbles rise to the surface and burst.

"Remember the conversation we had at drinks a couple of weeks ago," I said, "about what you might do differently if you had your time again?"

"Vaguely."

"I haven't been able to get that out of my head."

Jasmina picked the last broken pretzel out of the snack bowl and popped it into her mouth. "And would you change anything, if you could?"

"No, nothing really. I've been pretty lucky." I watched her load the empty glasses onto a silver tray. Once sparkling and new, now they were smudged with lipstick, greasy fingers and saliva. "Though maybe I should have worked more when the kids got older. So I still had some sort of research career at the end. When they no longer needed me."

"I've worked the whole time I've had kids," Jasmina said, "and, between us, I never felt like I did anything properly. Work, home. It all felt half-arsed. I was jealous of you. You and Vaughan and your perfect kids. Your perfect life."

"Really? I thought you were self-assured and sophisticated while I was Mrs Mop."

Jasmina smiled genuinely now. It was a rare moment we weren't niggling each other.

"But, thing is," I said, watching the golden liquid swirl in the glass, "in all my planning—holidays, running the kids to extra-curricular this or that, researching the perfect lunch box—I never imagined coming to the end of their childhood. Or what I'd do afterwards."

"You do whatever the hell you want. You and Vaughan are free agents now."

"I suppose. Though not so free that we could go to Paris for our anniversary. We had a trip booked, but he cancelled last minute because he has some important board meeting. "

"There'll be other trips."

Jasmina picked up the tray. The glasses rattled against each other.

"There is one thing I regret," I said. "If I had my time again, I'd like to have had a few boyfriends before Vaughan. I wouldn't be in such a hurry to close off all other options."

Jasmina leaned closer, checking that Marcus, at his microscope, couldn't hear. "Way I see it, it's like buying a dress for a special occasion. You go to the shops, see one, try it on. It looks good. But do you buy it there and then? Or do you keep looking in case there's something better elsewhere?"

"You'd have to try a few shops, at least."

"But how many do you try? What's the magic number to make you sure enough? And what if, after hours of searching and trying on dresses that are too tight, the wrong colour, or make your hips look like a hippo's, you realise the first one was the best all along?"

"You go back and get it."

Jasmina shook her head. "But you can't, because someone else bought it while you were away. You see, somewhere between grabbing the first dress you find and looking eternally for some elusive perfection…that's your problem."

Jasmina carried the tray to the lab door. I raced ahead and opened it for her.

"Anyway," she went on, "haven't you seen those memes saying you should be happy with what you've got?"

"This from the head of a division called Future Technologies," I replied. "Since when are any of us content with that?"

"Have one more drink with me?" I said.

Marcus looked up from his microscope, pushing his glasses back up to the bridge of his nose for the zillionth time.

"Just one?" I pleaded. "So I don't feel like a sad, lonely drunk?"

I didn't want to go home yet. The kids were out and Vaughan was on a business trip. I'd be alone, as I was more often lately. I gave Marcus a flirty smile, which made the cheeks above his Ned Kelly beard turn eczema pink. Tipsy as I was, I knew he was half my age and not my type anyway. I was courting him for reasons I couldn't articulate just then.

"Okay. But just a small one," he said.

I poured. We tinged glasses.

"What are you working on at the moment?"

"I'm not supposed to say."

"You can tell me. I'll have to promote whatever it is when the time comes."

He licked his lips and glanced at the door, checking Jasmina wasn't about. Then he showed me—the world's first time and space machine.

"A time machine?"

"And space."

"You're joking?"

Marcus shook his head. He didn't do humour.

It was similar to an iPhone only thinner, with lights on the screen exploding like fireworks. "How does it work?"

"You put the destination co-ordinates here." Marcus brought up the prompts. "The date you wish to travel to, here. And to blast off, press *enter.*"

"Has anyone tested it yet?"

He shook his head. "We've sent objects through time and back. And mice in cages. We're just waiting for a human trial."

"You must have some security in place to stop people stealing it?"

"You need to know the Continuum Interface Code. Only Jasmina and I and two other techs know it."

I felt my heart thudding a drumbeat of warning. "What is it?"

Just like that, I asked him. And he answered. (No, I can't tell you for your own sake!)

From a far room, Jasmina called him. With an uneasy glance back at me, he left the room to answer the call.

So, there I was. Bold with drink. Clutching the world's first time and space machine.

Where would I go for my first trip through time? Just for fun, I tapped in a destination— Sydney University—and a date in 1988, two days before I met Vaughan at that party. A prompt asked for the Continuum Interface Code.

I entered it.

Then hit *enter.*

CHAPTER TWO

I was inside a tube of light which seemed to stretch upwards to infinity. The air inside had the stale, metallic quality of plane travel. Outside was a swirling mist. I heard clattering and rumbling and a scream that left me shaking. Gingerly, I reached out and touched the walls, which were cool and throbbed like a heartbeat. In the mist beyond, faces from the past whipped by—my father in pain, my grandmother laughing, my best friend from primary school in an Easter bonnet.

About twenty terrifying minutes later, the world went quiet and still. As the fog cleared, I found myself on an expanse of well-tended lawn, surrounded on four sides by classical buildings. It was the quadrangle at Sydney University.

Sound filtered through: of talking, laughter. Young people with lots of hair—permed, crimped or gelled into strange shapes—clutched books as they passed. They wore shirts tucked into jeans, puckered at the waist, with thin, brightly coloured belts. One guy with black hair short on one side, long on the other, had a giant boom box on his shoulder pumping out a Robert Palmer song—*Simply Irresistible.*

"His poor ears!" I tutted, mother-like.

Beneath the flowering jacaranda tree, a girl stopped mid-chew to gawk at me. She looked as if she'd seen a ghost. Or an alien. Or someone who wasn't there one minute, then was. Time to get moving.

I walked along university roads lined with cars I'd last seen in a vintage display—Holden coupes in a rainbow of colours, Ford Fairlanes with chrome trim and furry dice dangling from the mirrors.

Is this real or some kind of delusion?

My head was buzzing. I took a breath, held it, then exhaled slowly, steeling myself for a closer look. Fact 1: No-one had mobile phones. Fact 2: All the students struggled with knapsacks filled to bursting with thick books (which would keep physiotherapists like Nicky busy in the next decade). Fact 3: So many people were smoking. Fact 4: A lot of people had shaggy perms of a type I hadn't seen for decades (and for which I was truly grateful).

Almost by muscle memory, I found myself at the university's main cafe—or cafeteria as we called it then. The room smelled of overcooked vegetables. Soggy peas and carrots stewed in silver trays next to fries shiny with grease and a tray of lasagne curled and hardened at the edges. Fact 5: No quinoa or kale in sight! (Not all bad then!)

I needed a coffee. But as I watched the cappuccino machine dispense amber liquid into a paper cup with a last-minute spurt of froth, like old dishwater, I decided to pass. Fact 6: No barista in my time would serve that. This, more than anything else, confirmed I had to be in the past.

Whoaa! A heart-stopper.

But when exactly was I?

Scanning the long, plastic tables strewn with dismembered newspapers, I picked up a page of the *Sydney Morning Herald*'s Books section (with a review of Isaac Asimov's *The Robots of Dawn*) and my gaze flew to the date at the top: *2 April 1988.*

What the—?

Barely an hour before, I'd been tipsy in 2018. Now, here I was thirty years in the past and as sober as I'd ever been!

What about my family? The anniversary dinner? Could Matilda handle things while I was gone? They'd be out of their minds with worry. Then again, Vaughan was away, and the kids were so focused on their own lives they might not notice for a while. Would I even make it back for the dinner? Would I ever see my husband and children again?

Dazed, I ordered a toasted sandwich and tried to pay with some two-dollar coins. "We don't take foreign currency," said the cashier. As I passed over a ten-dollar bill, she sucked in a breath. "I've only seen a couple of these new plastic notes. This one's different."

Lucky for me, she accepted it and gave me some old-style currency as change. What the Treasury would make of the future note when it filtered back to them, I couldn't imagine.

"Can I have a bottle of water?" I asked.

"We've got Coke in bottles."

I looked around. No-one had the familiar clear bottles. The whole plastics nightmare had not yet begun. Though at this point, I don't think anyone drank water. Period.

I stumbled through the afternoon in a haze of self-recrimination. I'd often wished I was more easy-going and impulsive. But why did my first spontaneous act in decades have to be while I was drunk in a Future Tech lab?

More than once, I headed into a toilet block, panting like I'd run a marathon, to reactivate the time machine and go home. Each time, I stopped before hitting *enter*. What sort of scientist would I be if I left the time period before I'd made any worthwhile observations? Perhaps if I learned something interesting while I was here, they'd give me a research job rather than firing me for misuse of government equipment!

In the afternoon, I drifted back to the science block, where I'd spent most of my time as a student, and wondered if I'd see anyone I knew. Like young Jasmina, or Nicky, my bestie, who I'd known for about a week by now.

Or Vaughan? Would I see my husband lurking around the corridors? At that thought, my stomach did some travelling of its own.

But was it even safe to meet someone from your past?

The old warnings from time travel stories surfaced in my brain: like how any changes made in the period, even small ones, might lead to still more changes, the effects rippling through the space-time continuum with devastating effect. I'd have to be very careful in all my interactions here.

Though, surely there was no harm in observing?

As I sat on a bench, waiting for students to file out after class, I pulled out my key ring with a framed picture of my family on it. The photo had been taken just before sunset, on a Hawaiian beach, where we'd gone to celebrate Matilda's high school graduation. Looking at it now, I could almost smell tuna on the barbecue, coconut oil smeared on caramel bodies. To the right of the picture, I knew, a giant turtle lay sleeping.

I sniffed away the beginnings of a tear. *Get a grip.* These days, I teared up so easily. When I was a student, I was much tougher; the maternal hormones hadn't kicked in yet.

And speaking of me here, I wondered whether I'd see myself around campus. That was a weird thought. Could something bad happen if you met yourself? Like, could one version of you wipe out the other? In full panic, I hurtled towards the ladies toilets, determined that this time I would power up the machine and start for home. It was just too risky.

However, as I lurched through the doorway, I came upon three young women giggling in front of the mirror. One of them was Me. I hung back in the entry to observe.

My permed and blonde-streaked hair reminded me of a cavoodle (which had not been invented yet). The cerulean blue trousers I so loved at the time with matching "kill me" heels were way too loud for my taste now. But check out my neck and skin! Not a sag in sight.

The two girls with me were Jasmina—her dark, wavy hair in a ponytail on the side— and Nicky—going for the Madonna look with a pink head band and shock of blonde fringe.

"Do you think we'll meet anyone at the party tomorrow night?"

That was me. My voice had a higher pitch.

"Try stopping me." Jasmina tucked a few loose strands into the ponytail. As bold and determined as ever.

"Who do you fancy?" Nicky asked.

"That's easy," Jasmina said. "Brodie Milton. And his leather jacket."

"But he's a third year, isn't he?" I said.

"All the better. He has...*experience*." Jasmina's husky drama brought on a fit of the giggles. I couldn't help smiling myself. Jasmina caught my eye then, so, head down, I made my way to an end cubicle, where I could watch the girls through a gap around the door hinge.

"You wouldn't know what to do with an experienced guy, Jasmina," Nicky hissed.

"True, but hopefully he would. Which is the point."

"What would your opening line be?" Young Me asked.

Jasmina bit her bottom lip. "I don't know. I could sit on his lap and we could talk about the first thing that popped up!"

Gales of laughter followed. I shook my head and tried to hold the laughter in. I'd forgotten all this bawdy fun we used to have. *Have I become such a prude in my mid years?*

"There's this guy—I think his name's Vaughan," said Nicky, blushing. "He's in my bio tutorial. And he's got this lovely smile." *What? Nicky fancied my husband? I didn't remember that.*

"And is he...*experienced*?" Jasmina asked.

"There's only one way to find out!" I said, the dare evident in my voice. Was I encouraging Nicky to go for Vaughan? I had no recollection of that at all. I wondered if older Nicky still did.

"What are you going to wear?" Jasmina asked.

I didn't catch their answers, as they moved away then. I hurried out to watch them cross the grass—three girls full of hopes and dreams, many of which would be lost in the mists of time. Several heads turned their way; they didn't seem to notice. And probably wouldn't for another twenty years, until the looks stopped.

When a couple of guys made lewd comments at them as they passed, the girls scoffed. Young Me walked away, arm raised, middle finger pointing skywards, to a "Whooo!" from the guys.

You go, girl!

I was so proud of myself. I had a lot more nerve back then. I wasn't always so keen to please everyone, to do the right thing and be the perfect mum, with the best healthy cakes at bake sales, kids who knew their Ps and Qs and looked scrubbed. I wasn't always the keeper of upstanding morals and ethics, all of which looked slightly tarnished now with the passage of years. Dull, lacklustre, rusting.

As the sun sank behind the university skyline, I knew I should head back to my own time. But I wanted to stay a little longer. See a bit more. I was dog tired by then, from the adrenalin coursing through me all day. Or was it from the temporal travel itself? Perhaps that was one scientific observation I could take back to my colleagues, so my unauthorised journey wouldn't be a complete waste.

I sat down on a bench near the library to figure out my next move and close my eyes...just for a moment.

An image of Vaughan came into my head. Smiling. So loyal. We'd been through a lot together in twenty-five years—babies, sickness, parental deaths, plodding on when at times it seemed all the juice had been squeezed out of life. We kept going. Ironically, now that it was our turn to grab some happiness together as payoff for all that hard work, it was like we'd run out of things to say. On Vaughan's last business trip, he didn't call once in four days. That hurt.

But if the romance between us was waning, it wasn't just my husband's fault, I knew. Over the years, there'd been times I was too much the Super Mum, not enough his partner, his lover. Like the weekend when he booked a romantic getaway for us at an exclusive coastal resort and even arranged for his mother to babysit. But it coincided with Matilda's Year 10 netball final.

"It's important we're there to share it with her," I said.

"And what about sharing with me? Isn't that important too?" he asked.

In retrospect, we could have gone. Matilda was in a grumpy phase and didn't want us around anyway.

We'd both made mistakes. But could we come back from them? That was the question.

"Excuse me." A man in his thirties, with dark, cropped hair, gently shook me awake. He had a scent of sterilising solution and burnt chemicals about him—a lab worker, perhaps? "Are you okay, ma'am? Can I call someone for you? Help you get home?"

Home? Now there was a thought! Perhaps I could phone my parents? How great would it be to see Dad again, and Mum with all her mental faculties. But it might unsettle them and, anyway, Mum could never keep that secret through time.

"No. I'm okay. I'll get going."

"Are you walking to the station?" he asked. "Because I'll go with you. The streets around here can be a bit dodgy after dark. I'm Baxter, by the way."

"I'm Cassidy."

As he went back into the library to get his bag, I rested my eyes a bit more and pondered his name—Baxter. It was unusual for this time, but within a decade, it would become quite fashionable. There'd be three Baxters in my son's preschool class alone.

CHAPTER THREE

That was the last I remembered until I felt warmth on my right cheek and forced my eyes open...and found I wasn't on the bench anymore. I was in a single bed in a small room. The hot spot came from the morning sun lasering in through a rip in the curtains.

What the—?

The room was simply furnished—a battered wardrobe, upturned plastic crate as a bedside table, a desk and chair in the corner. Most of the furniture was from IKEA, I knew, because I'd bought it myself—thirty years before. This was my old university room.

I jumped up and twirled around. Once, twice. Then flung open the wardrobe door to find the full-length mirror I knew would be inside. Staring back at me was...Me! *Younger Me!* I looked around for myself—Older Me. Under the bed. Behind the wardrobe. But I was nowhere. Young Me was the only Me here.

"Oh, my freaking God!" My younger self mouthed the words with me.

I was her—Young Cassidy. Inside this skin, I felt fantastic—no aches, no tightness in the hip or neck. I could see more clearly and read everything, even the small print on the books littering the floor. And I had so much energy. It sloshed about inside me, waiting to gush out.

Like a crazy person, I danced around the room, up on the bed, trampolining for a while. My reflexes were top notch, as were my joints.

Bang, bang. Someone from the room below thumped a protest through the floor.

"SO-RRY!" I called out. *Not sorry!*

This was weird. I had all my teen memories and my future ones— marriage, children, press officer job. I moved closer to the mirror and inspected my tight neck and jawline. *Wow!* That old expression—*If I knew then what I know now*—that was me! I had the maturity and experience of an older woman in the body of a young one.

"You're dangerous!" I said to my reflection and began whirling around the room again. The banging from below started immediately.

But how did I get here? I was in my favourite Mickey Mouse satin nightie. Older Me's clothes were scattered on the ground. And—epic relief—the time machine was there too. It wasn't that I'd traded places with Young Me. It was like we'd merged. Was that what the scientists expected? Well, I certainly had something to report back now.

The question was, though, would I be able to unmerge when I needed to.

Panic kicked in—a middle-aged woman's *what-ifs* vying with a teenager's *it'll be all right.* What else could I do but hope for the best and worry about it when the time came? My kids would be proud: I was going with the flow. I wasn't sure whether this was growth or regression. Both, I supposed.

A thump came from the door. I opened it gingerly, expecting my grumpy neighbour. Instead, Jasmina swept in, bringing a cloying floral scent I recognised—*Anais Anais,* the perfume of the day.

"Still not dressed, sleepyhead? We have a lecture in five. Wouldn't want to keep Moody waiting." She imitated our chemistry lecturer's deep drawl. "I had the courtesy to turn up punctually. I'd appreciate it if you would too!"

Laughing so hard my ribs felt sore—though Older Me knew it wasn't that funny—I threw on a pink shirt with a cat design and jeans with a thin, hot-pink belt.

"Eeoo!" I whipped out the belt and flung it away.

"You loved that belt yesterday!" she said.

"Well, I've changed my mind."

"You've had it—" she checked her watch "—seventeen hours. And people call teenagers flaky?" Always the snarky jibes, even from the start. Jasmina and I were born rivals.

We collected Nicky on the way to class and slid into our seats in the theatre as class began. The girls paid scant attention to the lecture. Jasmina doodled a caricature of the teacher's face and Nicky read a music magazine inside her notebook with INXS on the cover.

But I found the lesson riveting. All this knowledge! Ours for the taking! Looking around at the bored students in the room, I had to smile. *It's true what they say. All this is wasted on the young.* Give people a few decades of drudgery and domestic minutiae, then see how they respond to big ideas, the sweep of history, advancements and questions of science, a world of literature.

When Nicky leaned over and whispered something about what she was wearing to the party that night, I put a finger to my lips: "Shhh. The lecturer's talking." I felt my friends' disbelieving looks in response.

And all day, I revelled in it. My mind was ravenous for new information and I had the fresh brain cells to eat it up. The first time around, romance had seemed more important to me. The lectures were filler between nights at the bar, flirty glances across bookshelves. This time was different. I had a whole new set of priorities.

After a tutorial on Future Technologies, where the lecturer, Aaron Palmer, hinted that one day time travel would be possible, Jasmina yawned and whispered, "I thought it was supposed to be science, not science fiction."

"Come back to my room when this is done," Nicky urged. "We can get ready for the party together."

"I'll see you there," I said. "I need to talk to the lecturer."

I invited Aaron Palmer for a coffee at the cafeteria.

"I enjoyed your lecture," I said as we attempted to slurp down the execrable machine beverage.

"I'm glad somebody did. A lot of people think I'm crazy."

"All great scientific thinkers have to deal with sceptics," I said.

He spooned one…two…three teaspoons of sugar into his cup. "Not many students think like you. Nor, unfortunately, do many in the science faculty. My tenure's up for review and, well, anyway, I'm glad you enjoyed it. Makes it all worthwhile."

It would be decades before anyone took his ideas seriously. The disappointment and humiliation would lead him to commit suicide in the car park of the university one cold July night fifteen years from now. Leaving behind a wife and two sons—one of them named Marcus, who would work at the CSIRO on his father's discredited ideas.

What was I meant to do here? Leave things be? Allow a good man to die of a broken heart? Old and Young Me were in agreement—no.

"What I'm going to tell you now may sound strange…" I checked no-one was nearby to overhear "…but don't give up on your ideas. Because they will be reality one day."

"Thanks," he said, slurping down the last of his coffee with a grimace. "I'm glad someone has confidence in me."

He stood up.

"Wait," I said, picking up my bag and leaning in to whisper. "I know your ideas will become reality because…I'm from the future."

His right eyebrow pinged up and he nodded. "Well, I have to go." He headed for the exit. Fast.

I followed him onto the road and struggled to keep pace with him. "I'm not delusional. Or mentally unwell," I said.

"Glad to hear that."

"It's hard to believe, I know," I said. *What could I say to convince him?* "Look." I pulled out a two-dollar coin. "That's a coin from the future when we change over from two-dollar notes."

As he noticed the markings—an Aboriginal elder on one side, the Queen's head on the other—his frown deepened. "Is this a joke? Has someone come up with this to make me look a fool?" He looked around wildly, as if sniggering colleagues might be hiding in the bushes, slapped the coin back at me and strode off.

"I travelled here in a time machine," I said, jogging alongside him, "which was built using principles similar to what you described in your lecture. So, no matter how difficult things get in future, no matter what other scientists say, this coin proves you're right and they're wrong. Take it. Please. Even if you don't believe me now. You'll see. Eventually. Take it."

He glowered, then snatched the coin and continued along the road. I stopped. I'd done all I could. A little further along, he slowed and turned. "Can you tell me anything more about the future?"

I shook my head. "And you of all people should know why."

"I'm not eating anything but diet milkshakes for the next two weeks."

Nicky had seven pink and brown sachets lined up on her chest of drawers. As she snipped open a sachet, the too-sweet smell of sugared flavouring filled the room. "I bought a pair of size-eight jeans and I'm going to get into them."

"Got the coat hanger ready?" asked Jasmina.

Nicky held up a wire hanger in triumph.

I'd forgotten this one. *The old lie on the bed and use the coat hanger to do up the zip trick?* Quickie diets were all the rage now. I read the ingredients on the pack. It was high in sugar and suspicious colour additives.

"You're better off eating more fruit and vegetables, cutting down on treats and exercising more," I said.

"Well, thanks for your encouragement, *Mum*." Jasmina snatched the pack with a disapproving glare.

And then the conversation turned to—*what else*—guys.

"What do you want in a boyfriend?" Nicky asked Jasmina.

"He has to be tall," said Jasmina. "With brown eyes and a car—preferably a convertible. And a spunk, of course." Which was eighties-speak for "hot".

"Cassidy?" Nicky asked. "What's your dream guy?"

"Someone sexy and fun, who loves housework, especially cleaning bathrooms and vacuuming. And cooking. Oh, and who loves planning meals for the week ahead."

Both girls looked weirded out by that. "How is that sexy and fun?"

They didn't yet get that sharing the drudge work was the real sexy—but they would. In the meantime, though...

"Or someone who'd fly to Paris at a moment's notice," I said. "And call me every night if he was away on a business trip."

"What about you, Nicky?" Jasmina asked.

"Oh, you know, just someone nice. I'm not too fussy."

"You must have some preference? Or shall I set you up with Frankenstein's not-as-good-looking twin?"

"Okay, maybe no sewn-on dead body parts," Nicky said. "I just want someone I get along with who's kind and makes me laugh."

They moved on to marriage—both of them wanted to get hitched by their mid-twenties and have two kids. Nicky liked Bailey for a boy's name and Chantelle for a girl's. Which broke my heart as I knew she'd never have them. Somehow, though she was—hands down—the nicest of the three of us, she never found the right man.

When the subject changed to hairstyles and favourite band members, my attention wandered. "Don't you have any assignments to do?" I asked.

"Did you take too many boring pills this morning?" Jasmina said.

I told them I had some errands to do and headed off. And it was true: there were a few things that needed my attention.

First, I wrote a couple of notes to slip under students' doors. One was to Christian Parker, telling him not to go to Bali in 2002. And that if he did, he should stay well away from any clubs in Kuta Beach. He was one of hundreds killed in an explosion there.

The second note was to Gail Bryant, telling her that Martin Phelan had a contagious sexual disease. He didn't really have one, but I hoped it might make her stay clear of him. In the future, Martin would become a violent husband who got her hooked on drugs. She'd die in a junkhouse in Kings Cross aged thirty-one.

Should I be making changes like these to the timeline, the scientist in me wondered? I'd read stories on time travel with those dire warnings about not changing the past in case it changed the future in unexpected ways. But I reasoned that their premature deaths and misery had no broader significance and that altering their futures would have little, if any, lasting impact on the space-time continuum. Regardless, it would be an interesting scientific conundrum to discuss back at the lab— making my trip less of a breach, more of a field study.

Next, I headed into town to buy something to wear to the party. I could hardly turn up in a ghastly red or purple fashion faux-pas from my wardrobe with puffy sleeves and ludicrous belts. When I met my husband for the first time, I wanted to look hot.

Central Sydney 1988 was a hoot! The biggest difference was a lack of moving ad images around the malls. There were no phone or computer shops, but a lot more book and video stores. With quite a few camera shops offering "4-HR PHOTO" development. *Oh my!* And telephone booths on every corner—though most of them would be vandalised or out of service, if memory served.

The window displays of the dress shops on Pitt Street Mall made me chuckle behind my hands. Most of it was too colourful, too puffy. *Too much.*

I found just what I was looking for on a Sale table in a small arcade—a black T-shirt dress, size 6. Short and very tight.

"Are you going to a funeral?" Jasmina asked when she saw me in it, her lip curled as if she'd smelled something bad.

I managed to stop myself making a dig about her shiny, blue coat with square shoulder-pads ("Take me to your leader!"). Nicky wore a loose red blouse and tight black leather skirt—totally ghastly, but it was the times! And, anyway, she was gorgeous in anything.

"Let's party!" said Jasmina.

CHAPTER FOUR

I felt the bass throbbing through the ground before I heard the music spilling from the hall. *Of course!* The eighties was all about live bands and heavy rock music—the speakers pumping out music so loud your ears rang for days afterwards (and kept audiologists and ENT specialists in business for decades!).

"Have fun, sweetheart," said the doorman, slapping me on the bottom as I entered. *Eighties sexism!* I didn't miss that.

We were in a long, church-like room with vaulted ceilings and stained-glass windows. First-year students crowded around a trestle table which served as a bar. I had an impression of teeth, moon-white in the light of a revolving disco ball. A girl with a poodle perm and hot pink lipstick blew smoke in my face as I passed.

All around the room, specks of orange burnt through the blackness as people lit up cigarettes. I coughed madly, horrified that we ever put up with this passive smoking nightmare. In the smoky fug, I caught a whiff of something sweet and earthy—it wasn't just nicotine they were smoking.

For a moment, I thought I spotted Baxter, the guy who'd offered to take me to the station the night before. The whites of his eyes looked unnaturally large in this lighting, as if he'd seen something disturbing. It couldn't be me, could it? We'd only met briefly. There was no way he'd recognise me in this younger body. It got me wondering what the guy must have thought when he came out of the library with his bag and found me gone. Did he think I was rude? Or…had I vanished right before his eyes? That would freak anyone out. I looked for him after that, hoping to find out what had happened, but he seemed to have gone.

At the far end of the room, a rock band in horror film makeup cavorted about on a slightly raised stage, singing Foreigner's *Feels Like the First Time*. Seemed appropriate.

"Band's pretty good, hey?" A tall, skinny guy with blue hair looked me up and down.

"Not bad."

"Can I get you a drink? I'm Brad."

"No, thanks. I'm waiting for someone."

My first meet with Vaughan would be happening soon and I needed to be free. Besides, this guy looked familiar. And not in a good way.

Concealed by darkness, I studied the faces around me. There was Peter Telefares, with long dark rock star hair. He would be almost completely bald within five years, but one of the nicest guys you'd ever meet. And who was that pretty girl, smiling sweetly and drinking through a curly straw? *OMG*. Zelda Meekham? By her thirties, she'd only ever open her mouth to make cutting comments at others' expense.

David "Bucky" Reid made caveman noises at every girl who passed, preparing to become a *Give-Em-Nothing* divorce lawyer of the future. Rosalind Johnson was mousy and unexceptional now, but in fifteen years, she'd be a leading advocate for gay marriage.

It was so weird to see everyone and know what the future held for them. The drunk, the musician, the Lotto winner (perhaps I should ask about her favourite numbers while I had a chance).

I hadn't seen Vaughan yet. Any time now, he'd come through the door. We'd meet at the drinks table and have our first conversation, which everyone in our family knew word for word.

I drifted over to the two punch bowls. One was signed *Non-alcoholic*, the other *Alcoholic*. I filled a plastic cup with drink from the first bowl.

"Playing it safe, then?" Brodie—Jasmina's third husband—emerged from the shadows. He was a third-year and hadn't spoken to me first time round. If he had, I would have run away. Not this time though.

"Thought I'd take it slowly," I said. *Keep a clear head for Vaughan.*

"Slowly…sounds good to me," he said suggestively. Brodie grinned and sipped his drink. His lips were dark red like a vampire's. With his lopsided smile on a strong jaw and short, dark hair swept back, he was hot, no question. But I didn't need that sort of complication tonight.

I moved away.

"He's so gorgeous!" Jasmina shouldered people aside to get to me. "And you spoke to him! What did he say?"

"Nothing much."

"Have you seen Vaughan anywhere?" Nicky asked, looking around.

"Not yet."

I chugged the sweet drink, hoping it would still the bubbling in my tummy. Was I nervous about meeting a man I'd been married to for twenty-five years? Absolutely! And with good reason. I should have left last night, before the merge with my young self happened, and let things play out as they were meant to. It was too late now. All the balls were back in the air. It was up to me to catch them and make this right.

I returned to the punch bowls just as blue-haired Brad switched the labels around. Now I remembered him! He'd be locked up one day for crimes involving date rape drugs. *The lowlife.*

"Leave it alone or I'm calling a supervisor," I said, putting the labels right again.

"Just having a bit of fun. Uptight bitch!"

He gave me a death scowl. I gave him one right back. He looked away first.

"Ooh, you are a force to be reckoned with, aren't you?" Brodie appeared beside me, beaming. "You look as sweet as that drink there. But I bet you've got a stronger punch than it does."

"I don't see why he gets to choose whether people have alcohol or not." *Did I sound like a mum?* Probably. Because I was one. Even though I was young enough to be my own daughter.

"Will you have a drink with me? Alcoholic or non-alcoholic, it's up to you." Brodie asked. "No judgements."

"Maybe later."

I hurried away.

"Look at Mr Right," Jasmina said, frowning behind me. "He can't tear his eyes off you. Why? What's so special about you?"

"Nothing." Except I had a grown woman's confidence in a young person's skin.

And then Nicky went still, her gaze fixed on the entrance. And I turned just in time to see Vaughan entering.

As if in slow motion, I watched him. He nodded hello to people he passed and laughed with the guy beside him. Even at this age, he had all the mannerisms I knew so well. The way he slapped his friend's shoulder to get his attention. How he threw his head back as he laughed, like it was the best joke he'd ever heard. That quick scratch at the top of his left ear when he was nervous. With his messy, brown hair and slight build, he was not the best looking guy in the room, but he definitely had something. A calm confidence that stood out when most others ran on nervous energy. Several heads turned his way—Nicky's among them.

I thought she might move over to talk to him but at the last moment, another girl distracted her.

Leaving the field open for me.

I swigged my drink and wished I'd chosen the alcoholic punch. I wanted to savour the moment. Vaughan's green eyes were wild with reflected light. His smile was warm enough to melt all the ice in all the Eskies around the room. As he threaded his way through the crowd, I did the same. We both reached for the scoop on the alcoholic punch at the same time, hands touching. Warmth fizzed through me just as it had the first time. I fancied him all over again.

"After you," he said.

Under his intense gaze, I was nervous and spilt some.

"Let me help with that." He filled my cup and handed it to me, looking

into my eyes with complete focus, like I was the only one in the room—
in the universe—that mattered in that moment. Or ever would. This
was not the gaze of a man who would postpone a trip to Paris for a
company board meeting.

"What's a nice girl like you doing in a place like this?" he asked.

There it was—The Line. (I never said it was a great line!) Now, it was
my turn to respond: "Looking for a bad boy like you." And we would
laugh, because he was so obviously not a bad boy and this was such a
cheesy beginning.

Over his shoulder, I spied Brodie trying to catch my eye, bottom lip
curled in a playful pout that made me smile.

I looked back at Vaughan. I was sure—100 per cent—I would do it
all again with this man. Marriage, kids, a million loads of washing, a
trillion shopping lists. Lifts to school sport at ungodly hours without
caffeine, arguments about what subjects the kids should study, which
parents we should visit for Christmas, friends we should spend most
time with. The many thousands of negotiations—big and small—that
made up a shared life. All over again.

But does it have to start right this minute? Couldn't it wait a few weeks
or months, while we had some light-hearted fun?

If I felt that way, Vaughan probably did too. If he knew that this
would be It. The last time he ever got to deliver a cheesy pick-up line,
the last charming stranger he would meet at a party, or bar, or conference—he might want to squeeze in a few more clumsy or sweet or
memorable encounters. Wouldn't he? Something to warm his private
moments and bring a glow to his cheeks thirty years hence.

Here and now, I could give us both that chance to see how we fit
with others. For a little while. It would make us that much more confident later that we'd made the right choice.

And maybe it would give Vaughan something to reflect on in the
future, when he was too tired on his business trips to dial my number—
that he hadn't been my only option.

I smiled at my future husband. "Just getting a drink. Have a good
night." It took force of will to turn away from that gaze.

And then...the weirdest thing happened. The lights buzzed loudly, the
speakers boomed, the room plunged into darkness. Everyone screamed.

Thirty seconds later—*thwap*—the power came back on.

Standing beside me was Brodie. Very cute, very close.

"He didn't seem your type," he said. "Too nice."

"You wish," I said.

"I do actually."

We danced a bit, flirted a lot, and left the party together after eleven. He snuck me into his college room. His roommate was still out, so he pushed a set of drawers against the door to give us more privacy.

As he drew my face to his, I trembled with excitement and fear. For one part of me, this was only the second man I'd kissed in my life. For the other, it was the first. He kissed me shyly at first, but as he grew more confident, he became more passionate.

I switched off the bedside lamp. Brodie's room was on the fourth floor, overlooking a sweeping lawn. Moonlight streaming through the blinds painted silvery stripes on him, like an actor from a black and white film. His arms and body were well-toned and strong from youth and activity rather than gym workouts. As he coaxed me into his embrace, I found he wasn't as "experienced" as we'd imagined. Not as much as me, anyway. So, I took the lead.

Every cell in my young body urged him on. Older Me was happy to go with it, too, without the need for it to lead anywhere. I had a husband and kids, a life I was quite content with. This was no more or less than the passion of the moment.

Did it feel like I was cheating on Vaughan? Ever so slightly. Though I told myself we weren't married yet or even going out, so it couldn't be. And what about Jasmina? This was her future husband. Was I doing wrong by her? However, I reasoned that by the time the two of them married, she'd already have had two husbands and three children and he'd had too many lovers to count. One more would make little difference.

Sometime after midnight, his roommate thumped on the door.

"Open up, Brodie!"

"There's no-one here by that name," Brodie called out in a high pitch. We giggled like primary schoolers under the blankets. I don't know where the poor guy slept that night. Brodie and I had the room to ourselves and we made use of it.

Very little sleep, a whole lotta love.

CHAPTER FIVE

"Well, you are a dark horse, aren't you?" Brodie squinted as the sun came at him through the blinds. "Such a sweet innocent face. Not so innocent on closer inspection, though?"

"Does that bother you?" I quite enjoyed being painted as the scarlet woman for once.

"No," he said. "I like it. I loved it. Three times loved it. But how is it, you're so...err...?"

Right! Now I remembered. The eighties was a time when sexual "experience" diminished a woman but elevated a man. Double standards.

"Sometimes I feel like an old soul, you know," I said. "Like I've lived a whole other life before."

"A life where you were a stripper? Or a hooker?"

His hair was tousled, like a just-washed puppy. He smelled of alcoholic fruit and luscious late night. But as he moved towards me, on all fours, his tawny limbs rolling one way, then the other, he was pure predator. He kissed me lightly on each cheek before jumping onto the bed, gyrating and shimmying, humming *The Stripper* song.

We had a good time together.

But he wasn't Vaughan.

At lunch the next day, Nicky could hardly wait to tell me her news.

"Guess who I had the slow dances with last night? Vaughan. And then...he kissed me."

"How was it?" It was hard to get the words out as my breathing felt constricted.

"Mmmmm," she purred dreamily.

I forced myself to stay calm. The bond Vaughan and I shared could withstand a bit of fooling around with others. Besides, if I knew him, it would be relatively safe for a while. He wasn't a fast worker.

"And where did you get to last night?" Nicky asked.

"She went off with Brodie," Jasmina said, her eyes narrowing to slits of jealousy as she looked me up and down. "What have you got that I haven't?"

"Brodie for one." Nicky winked at me.

During the next week, I tried to block out my worries about Nicky and Vaughan and enjoy my time with Brodie. And it was fun. He might become arrogant and insufferable as he got older, but right now he was sexy and playful with enough self-confidence to take my teasing and still laugh at himself.

His father was a mechanic, and he knew a lot about engines, so he went about town on a shiny black motorbike he'd fixed up himself. With me clinging onto his back. Young Me loved the wind through my hair, the rush of the road, the way students' heads turned our way as if connected with string each time we pulled up. Older Me constantly reminded him to "Slow down!"

"You think you're really It, don't you?" I said one day as we dismounted on the quad. Dressed in his leather jacket, with his mirrored sunglasses and that confident smile, he looked great, and he knew it.

"Can't take my eyes off myself," he said. "Unless you're around, of course."

Part of me hoped Vaughan was nearby watching and experiencing, if not actual jealousy, then a twinge of cosmic yearning or something. I gazed around slowly but couldn't see him or Nicky anywhere.

As we crossed the quad, however, I felt mascara-ed eyes following our movements.

"I'm getting the evil eye from a few girls," I said. "I'm guessing you've had a few other female friends before me. And not all those encounters ended well?"

"With some people, you have a good time but once is enough." He flung his arm around my neck and tickled my ear as he whispered. "With others, you can never get enough."

Over his shoulder, I saw a girl with Cindy Lauper-style spiky red hair—having anything but fun—as she watched us together. "What happened with her?"

His eyes flicked back and he grimaced. "She said the 'L' word."

Love.

As we got to his building, we raced each other up the four flights. Brodie kept trying to pull me back to get ahead. The cheater. I did the same but was better at it than him.

I made it to the room first and flopped on the bed, panting. He lay down beside me, leaning up on his elbow. "I guess maybe it wasn't the 'L' word so much as the person saying it." He sighed and swept a rogue strand of hair behind my ear. "Who knows? If it came from the right person, I might feel differently."

The shrill squawk of a cockatoo made me start. I drew back as it flew by, shocking white against the blue sky.

"Do you think you'll ever say it?" Brodie whispered.

"Say what?"

"The 'L' word."

"Maybe one day." *Not today.*

Later that evening, painted in zebra stripes of moonlight, he whispered: "You're not like any woman I've ever met before."

As if that was a good thing.

Meanwhile, Nicky updated me daily on her progress with Vaughan.

"How are you two lovebirds going?" I'd ask.

"Good," she'd say, with a twinkly smile. She wasn't big on personal description. I tried not to worry. It would take more than "good" to derail our timeline. But when, later in the week, she up-scaled her answer to "Really good", my anxiety rose too.

No longer content with spending the bulk of daylight hours in Brodie's room, I found myself inventing excuses to range around the university grounds, hoping to glimpse Vaughan and Nicky and take action if necessary.

We were all invited to the science faculty's drinks under the jacaranda tree. Brodie and I, Nicky and Vaughan and Jasmina clustered together.

"Brodie, Cassidy, this is Vaughan," Nicky said. *So weird.*

"Pleased to meet you," I said.

Vaughan shook Brodie's hand. When he turned to me, his eyes grazed mine for the briefest moment, as if we were total strangers—no trace of recognition from our encounter at the punch bowls—before boomeranging back to Nicky. Where it stayed all night.

Jasmina wore her hair loose and looked gorgeous in an off-the-shoulder spotted green dress. I tried to steer Brodie away but she was as persistent as a puppy awaiting a treat. And so, I introduced them.

"Brodie, this is Jasmina."

"Hi, Brodie." Her eyes were like chocolate Rolos, lashes working overtime. "You're in third year, right?"

He nodded and smiled at her, but didn't look at her long enough to recognise her if he ever saw her again.

"What are you looking for out there?"

I was at Brodie's window again, scanning the crowd of students on the grass for Nicky and Vaughan.

"Nothing. I'm just looking," I said.

"Well, look this way." He patted the bed beside him, a wolfish grin on his handsome face. "I'm not finished with you, Missy."

I smiled weakly back, but I knew—I was done with him.

It had been eight days since I'd merged with my young self. Eight days in which all my carefree fun had morphed into fear that my best friend was stealing my husband.

Every day, every hour, the feeling grew that I needed to do something about it. Before a new timeline with them as a pair gained too much momentum.

As for Brodie, he was lovely, but he was only 20. I couldn't have the far-reaching conversations I did with Vaughan. Things that still awed him, like the first job on a career ladder, a serious relationship, held no more mystery for me. Being with him, I felt a little bored and a lot guilty. Like a cradle snatcher in a youth suit.

My gaze swept over the colourful specks on the grass below as I searched for the words to let him down gently. And then, a flash of bright light drew my focus to the right. I squinted towards the source. It seemed to be light flaring off glass or a mirror somewhere. I looked closer. Oh, yes. It was a pair of binoculars pointed straight up at us. Held by Baxter—the guy I'd met on my first day.

"Back in a minute," I said.

Taking the steps two at a time, I was downstairs within minutes, lurching through the stone archway where I came face to face with the guy. Baxter stopped dead, gawped, then turned and ran.

"Wait!" I shouted as I took off after him.

He was faster than me but I knew this university well—this was my fourth year here. So, I took a short cut, slipped behind the Humanities building and emerged on the road ahead of him.

"Please, can't we talk!" I said.

Doubled over to catch his breath, he eyed me with suspicion.

"Were you watching me just now?" I asked.

"No, I was looking at the detail on the building."

I noticed his trainers—vibrant blue and green with gel cushioning. *High tech.* Most other trainers around about this time were white with red or blue stripes?

"Do you recognise me?" I asked.

"No?" It was obviously a lie and he didn't have the face for it.

"Then why did you run?"

As he twisted his lips left and right, struggling to answer, my eye caught a flurry of movement on his watch face.

I grabbed his hand. "Is that...a heart-rate monitor?" He tried to pull away. I kept hold of him. "And number of steps taken? I'm pretty sure they didn't have those in the eighties."

"Yes, they did," he said. "They came in towards the end of—"

He froze, realising he'd been caught out. The *they* had given him away.

"Oh. My. God! You're from the future?" I said.

Wrenching his arm back, he threw me off balance and sprinted away. I followed but couldn't keep up, eventually losing him in the sea of sprawling students.

My head reeled with the implications as I walked back to Brodie's. I thought I was the first time traveller. But if Baxter was here, I couldn't be? Could I? Then again, this was time travel. Baxter might have come here from any point further in the future.

But why was he here? And did that mean he knew how this episode in my life would turn out? He knew how it would end?

I had to find him. I had to know.

Making my way through the crowd, it occurred to me that anyone could be a time traveller from any point in the future. That guy with the curly hair and McEnroe-style headband looking my way. Could he be a future spy? And there, the fiery-haired lecturer on the path who just looked around. Was she keeping tabs on me? Suddenly, it seemed like everyone was watching me, their focus glancing off as I met theirs. Were they all time travellers?

I felt my heart slipping through my ribcage, my organs twisting like a double helix, my legs turning to cooked spaghetti that would no longer hold me upright.

I was so freaked out, I almost stepped right on Vaughan and Nicky lying on the grass behind me. She had her head on his lap as he stroked her hair, like he used to stroke mine when I had a headache. I goggled openly at the pair, so wrapped up in each other, they hadn't even noticed me.

From behind, someone grabbed my arm. And spun me around. Hard.

"Where did you go to?" It was Brodie, arms folded, pouting.

"Nowhere."

My eyes ricocheted back to Vaughan and Nicky, who at that moment looked so much like him and me. At some point, I would reach up and take his hand, to let him know he'd done enough. And Nicky did too, brushing her lips across his fingertips in thanks.

"I saw you chasing that guy." Brodie's voice was a touch shrill. "Did he steal something from you?"

And the look Vaughan gave Nicky. I couldn't put a name to it. I wouldn't. To name it was to acknowledge it was real. But it couldn't be. He was destined to be with *me*. Not *Nicky*.

"Is the guy an old boyfriend of yours?" Brodie persisted, not reading the signs.

"What?"

"That guy you were chasing. Did you date him?"

I grabbed Brodie's hand and led him into an empty corridor in a nearby building. And began pacing. What was going on here? Could I make it all go away if I jumped back in time?

I glanced over at Brodie, watching me intently as if trying to bore into my brain to get answers. *Why does everything have to happen at once?*

First things first.

"Listen, Brodie," I began, "the time we've had together has been fun. Really fun." *Not a good start*. If only I'd had more time to prepare, more ability to think clearly. But my head was filled with Vaughan and Nicky and *that* look.

"But I don't think we should see each other anymore because we need to focus on our studies," I blurted out. OMG. It sounded lame even to my ears.

A storm of emotion crossed Brodie's face, a muscle on his jaw clenched, his shapely shoulders rippled beneath his shirt. "Are you breaking up with me?"

"It's no reflection on you, Brodie," I said. "You've been great." *Great? Seriously?*

"So that's it?" he said. "You've had me for a week. Now, it's time to try someone else?"

Uh-oh. I didn't like where this was going.

"Stupid me, I thought we had something going on," he said. "Something real. But you were just getting your cheap thrills. You filthy slut!"

There it was—the favourite term of the time for sexually active women. *Slut.* There was no equivalent for men. Stud came closest in meaning, though nowhere near in judgement. Young Me burned to answer that but Older Me didn't want to say anything I'd regret. Besides, I did feel sad that things were ending like this and guilty about hurting him after such a sweet week.

"Brodie, this week's been lovely," I said, more sincerely.

"What did I do wrong?" His eyes pinked up at the edges; his eyeballs had a watery glaze. This was turning into a horror show.

"It's not you, it's me," I said. *Lame and lamer. What can I say that he might understand?* "It's just…I'm in love with someone else."

Which was true, I now realised. And *about time,* I could hear the temporal chorus chant. *But is it already too late?*

Brodie eyed me with a mix of anger and pain.

"Who?" he asked.

"I'd rather not say."

His mouth curled in disgust. "You're unnatural."

I lurked behind a pillar, watching Vaughan and Nicky smiling goofily as they said their goodbyes. When she turned to leave, he pulled her back and kissed her forehead ever so softly and she went off with this stupid, smug smile. (I wanted to slap her.)

Vaughan went the other way. So, I followed him. Across the expanse of green, through the half-empty car park. As he started up some stairs towards the science building, I shouted, "Excuse me, Vaughan! Can I have a word?"

Turning to see me, confusion wrinkled his brow in that way he had. "What about?" He could have been at home, asking what the dinner arrangements were, or what Ryan had done to get himself on detention.

"I know this will sound strange, but, err, I was wondering, would you go out with me tonight?"

"Sorry, what?"

"Can we have a drink? Or dinner? There's something I really need to discuss with you."

He stood there, flummoxed for a moment. "Well, I'm kind of with someone just now." And then continued up the stairs.

That winded me, like a punch to the gut. *Those words*, to me from *my* husband. I must have panicked then.

I caught up with him. "I know this sounds strange, but if you'd just let me kiss you, things might become clearer?" He backed away, putting an arm out as a barrier.

"And you are...?"

Oh no. He doesn't know who I am.

"Cassidy," I said. "I'm Nicky's friend."

"Cassidy," he repeated, licking his lips and looking as awkward as I'd ever seen him. "Well, err—" he cleared his throat "—I'm flattered. But..." He looked around, as if searching for a hidden camera—or a helicopter to airlift him out of here. "I have to go to a lecture."

He took off along the path, fast. I had to run to get ahead of him. I skipped backwards as I continued talking.

"You think you don't know me, but you do," I said, trying to meet his eye. I sounded desperate, I knew, because I was. He looked over and away superfast. "And I know you. You're Vaughan O'Neill."

He seemed a little weirded out and sped up. I chased him. *This is not going well!* What could I say to catch his attention and make him believe I wasn't a nutjob? "You like grapefruit, without sugar. You choose dark chocolate over milk. You like a good head on your beer, but it has to be cold.

And you prefer a cool shower after you've been running, which is where you do some of your best thinking."

"What?" He looked right at me now, but his nostrils flared like he found my outburst distasteful.

"It's hard to explain," I said. "But if you'd just let me kiss you, things might be a bit clearer."

I charged forward, wrapped my arms around him and laid one on him, putting the love of twenty-five years behind it. The first was a wash-out so I warmed up and tried again, more sensually. And a third time.

I might as well have been kissing a pillar. No stirrings, no memories, just revulsion tinged with pity.

I gasped as I staggered back. Because I knew.

He doesn't love me anymore.

By now, a few people had gathered round to watch—the guy with the McEnroe headband was one, Baxter was another. Nicky and Jasmina.

"Nicky!" Vaughan said when he noticed her. He hurried over to her. "She kissed me. I didn't kiss back. She said she was your friend, but I've never seen her before."

Never seen me? His words were like knives plunged into my soul.

And Nicky turned to me with an intense dislike I'd never seen on her face in thirty years of friendship. "Sick of your love marathon with Brodie, are you? Feel like a change of rider?"

Harsh.

"Keep your hands off my guy!" she screamed.

Seizing Vaughan's arm, she strode off, with him whispering in her ear and casting disgusted looks back at me, probably explaining what had gone in this *grotesque* scene.

Jasmina hung back, watching me, a feline pleasure in the curl of her lips.

"Well," she began, "this is awkward. And I have a feeling it's going to get a lot worse."

Flashing me a victory smile, she ran to catch up with her friends.

What did she mean, it was going to get worse?

Does she know something?

Oh, how bitterly did I regret that booze-fuelled striking of the launch key now?

But this wasn't right. What about destiny? Fate? Or was there no such thing? I had Vaughan last time. This time Nicky had him. Next time, who knew who would end up with my husband? Was it really that random? Were we all just masses of atoms hurtling through space colliding with others, with no plan whatsoever?

Digging around in my pockets, I pulled out my key ring for a reassuring glimpse of my family. Their picture was gone. Instead, the cold gaze of a ginger cat stared back at me.

"Nooo!" I looked upwards at the plump clouds scudding across the sky, half expecting someone from the lab to be gazing down upon us.

And then I remembered…*the lab!* All was not lost. I could return to the future the same night I left! Only this time I wouldn't hit the launch key so none of this would ever happen. The whole misguided week could be erased from history. Just a glitch in time. And things would go back to normal.

With shaky hands, I took out the time machine, inputted the date 2 *April, 2018*, the time—*8pm*, and location—*CSIRO, Future Tech division*.

"For Vaughan, and the kids!" I whispered.

And pressed *enter*.

Chapter Six

I was back in the tube, which was a huge relief despite the clamour of voices and faces in the mist—Nicky's look of hate. Brodie's misty-eyed anger. Jasmina's twisted enjoyment. Vaughan's confusion.

And then…I was back in the lab, holding a champagne glass. Jasmina was there, though she had a different dress on—one with flowers on it. *She doesn't usually wear flowers!* And, wait! Was that Marcus? The beard was gone and the glasses. He looked more toned on his arms and had no problem meeting my eye.

"Another glass, Cassidy?" he asked. "Or shall I call you a cab?"

I'd made it. We were still toasting my anniversary. Thank God. All the gods, but especially the God of Time Travellers.

"Twenty-five years is not long enough!" I laughed as if it was the best joke ever. Everything had worked out okay in the end.

"Twenty-five years?" Jasmina said. "You were only away…eight days and twenty-two hours."

A white-haired man in a lab coat entered and took a champagne glass. "Congratulations! To many happy returns," he said. It took a moment for me to recognise my old lecturer, Aaron Palmer.

"How do you feel?" he said. "I need all your observations, as soon as your head's back in this time zone."

"You know about my trip?"

"Of course," said Aaron. "Marcus, get Cassidy a laptop so she can make notes of her findings."

I chugged the rest of the champagne and stood up. "I'll do that later. I need to organise a few things for the anniversary." I wobbled as I stood and would have fallen if Marcus hadn't caught me.

"What anniversary?" Aaron asked.

"My wedding anniversary."

"You mean Nicky and Vaughan's anniversary," Jasmina said. "You're not going to that, are you?"

"Nicky's and Vaughan's?" The muscles in my hand stopped working and the glass smashed onto the lab floor.

"How's your head?" Aaron squinted into my eyes.

"Spinning."

"Not surprising. You've passed through multiple dimensions of time and space."

An image invaded my mind, of bricks and white lace. In the background was a voice, deep and muffled, like someone talking underwater. And a scent too. Sickly sweet. As the image gained clarity, I saw the white was a bridal dress Nicky wore. The bricks were the inner walls of a church, with buckets of yellow honeysuckle alongside them. And the words…were Vaughan's. "I take you, Nicolette McGuinness, to be my lawful wedded wife."

It came with a stab of pain in the left temple, so strong I cried out.

"Time's realigning in her mind," Aaron said. "Help me here." I felt Marcus's arms supporting me, before another image bombarded my mind—a hospital room, a baby crying, the sinus-clearing scent of disinfectant. A nurse carried a baby swaddled in pink blankets and placed it on Nicky's chest. I watched through a rectangular frame—a window—as she cried tears of joy, her wet hair stuck to her sweaty head. Vaughan, beside her, pushed back the strands and they shared that new-parent smile. Their baby bliss morphed to anger as they saw me. And a doctor, with a shiny head and white mask slung under his chin, emerged from the room to jostle me away.

When I regained consciousness, I was on the lab floor, broken glass stuck in my knees.

"We need to restrain her." It was Jasmina's voice.

"But what about Matilda and Ryan? Where are they?" I asked.

Consciousness came and went as I lay in a hospital bed in a glary all-white room, leads attached to my chest and forehead, monitors beeping by my side. Dream-like images swarmed through my brain.

Of Nicky telling me: "Go away!"

A police officer with a missing tooth forcing a paper in my hand headed: *Restraining Order.*

Of days working in the lab under Aaron's direction.

Of Jasmina and Brodie—older Brodie—laughing together.

I woke up to find Jasmina sitting beside me, sipping a cappuccino from a takeaway cup.

"Feeling better?"

I will never feel better again.

"I can only stay half an hour," she said. "Brodie and I have to go to Nicky and Vaughan's tonight. Twenty-five years together, hey? Quite an achievement." There was a cruel twist to her smile.

"You already know what happened on my trip, don't you?" I said. "You were there. It was you—this you—in that young skin."

Jasmina slurped her drink. "You mean when you locked my husband in a room and screwed him senseless for a week? Yes, I was there. And I didn't like it."

She took a mirror and lipstick out of her bag to refresh the scarlet shade.

And then I had a thought! "Did you know I'd press blast off that night at the lab? Is that why you called Marcus away, to give me a chance..." *to dig my own grave?*

Her eyes fluttered my way. "We needed someone to take that first trip. You were wringing your hands over a lost career and having had only one boyfriend in your life. Boo-hoo. I knew you were the kind of person who likes things to be perfect. And usually gets what they want."

"You did this to me." I tried to get up but found I was handcuffed to the bed.

"No, Cassidy. You did it to yourself." Jasmina smacked her lips together and put the makeup away. The scraping sound as she pushed her chair back was like a saw through my brain. I cried out. Jasmina fiddled with the drip and the pain eased. "There, that should feel better. Though, I suppose I should thank you. Brodie Mark II is a vastly improved model. Not as arrogant. You sapped some of that over-confidence out of him early on."

"Glad it worked out well for you."

"There were other positive outcomes too. Aaron Palmer didn't commit suicide this time. The world of time travel is glad to have him."

"And what about Christian Parker? Do you know if he was in the Bali explosion?"

"Yeah, he was there," she said. "But something made him stay away from Kuta on that trip. Do you know anything about that? He lived on, to produce another child, who in turn may have a child and so on and so on. Who knows what impact any of them will have on the world in future, good or bad."

"And Gail Bryant? Did she end up with Martin Phelan?" *The abuser and drug addict.*

"No, Gail did not marry Martin this time, which was good for her. Not so for the child from that original union—Melanie Phelan—who was never born second time round. First time through, motivated by her mother's sad history with drugs, she became a social worker who saved many addicts from dying in the streets. The blood of those she couldn't save this time is on your hands."

I lay back on the pillow and squeezed my eyes shut. My head was rock heavy with the burden of my actions. Should I have left them both alone, let them blunder into disaster? I had no idea. What was clear, though, was that time travel was dangerous. No-one could see the end to all things.

"What about my children, Ryan and Matilda? Where are they?" It was the question I most feared to ask. I knew what the logical answer was. But when it came to Matilda and Ryan, I had no logic. They were so solid, so good, they had to exist somewhere.

Jasmina took my hand, all smugness gone. "I'm sorry," she said.

Images of them scrolled through my head. As babies with big smiles, small kids in bright blue uniforms. Teenage Ryan going round in circles, trying to pull off a "Kick Me" sign on his back. Matilda so beautiful in her burgundy formal dress, it made her father cry.

A world without them was not one I wanted to be in.

"We shouldn't let people time travel." I sort of shouted it as I tried to contain a tsunami of emotion. "It's too dangerous. There's too much to lose."

"Too much to gain not to, you mean," said Jasmina. "What some people are prepared to pay, you wouldn't believe! Everyone wants to take a trip through time. To experience the good old days once more."

To place bets on sure-fire winners, or wipe out adversaries before they are even born? To chop and change history, messing up many timelines for the sake of their own.

As I'd done.

"Time-travellers are accompanied by guides now and are only permitted to observe," Jasmina said. "They return before the merge of selves occurs. Unless they pay *really* big bucks."

They'd fixed some "glitches" since my trip, she told me. Now, as travellers re-entered the original time zone, memories attached to the old past were overwritten by those from the consequences of the time adjustments. "This allows them to forget what they've lost. They don't suffer like you."

"I don't want to forget. I want to remember my kids, my love for Vaughan."

Vaughan. The first person I went to when things were right or very wrong in my life. We'd had happy times, like our family holidays, moving into our new home. Some beautiful personal moments—too many to count. As well as arguments—dreadful ones, some of which could never be resolved. It was not a perfect relationship, but we'd got the kids through school. This was supposed to be our time to reconnect.

As Jasmina went to leave, I pulled at my restraints. "Please, can't I go back and put this right?" *This nightmare of my own making.*

"Aaron has developed a way to sequester individual time lines, so people who undergo journeys with poor outcomes can separate and roll back the individual strands of cause and effect," Jasmina said.

"That's great!"

"But I'm afraid it's not possible in your case," she said, barely containing her pleasure. "Your old and young timelines fused together. I have to say, it didn't work out that well for young Cassidy. She didn't fit with her contemporaries anymore. She knew too much. Turns out it's true what they say: you can never go back."

I leaned back on my pillow, closed my eyes, and wished I could time travel once more, back to a time before my birth, when I didn't exist anymore.

"Anyway," Jasmina continued, "best to leave things alone. How do you know you'd do any better second time round? Wasn't that why you travelled in the first place? Because things weren't perfect enough for you? Look how that turned out."

In a distant room, I saw Baxter walk by. And a couple of people I thought I recognised from university.

"You've met Baxter, our time consultant?"

I nodded. "Were they there to watch me?"

"People pay big bucks to observe the first trip through time. Where it all went wrong."

I leaned out and grabbed her hand. "But my children? Please, I have to get them back."

"I'm sorry. To bring your kids back, we'd have to erase Nicky's. Which wouldn't be fair. You do see that, don't you? You're a scientist, after all—third highest in this lab. And a legend in the field of time travel. Be content with that."

She smoothed back her hair and smiled sweetly-not-sweetly at me. "I'd better go. Nicky and Vaughan are expecting us. I'll pass on your regards, shall I?"

With a flutter of her fingers, she waved my hopes goodbye as Aaron came in to do some observations.

On the dark suburban street where I used to live, a black BMW pulls into the curb. Jasmina and Brodie get out. Arm in arm, they walk up to an elegant white brick house—my old home.

I stand across the road, behind a bottlebrush tree, watching all the happy couples arrive for the anniversary dinner. Nicky, blonde and lovely in a full-figured way, waits on the porch to greet them.

At some point, she spots me. I smile and wave, and a drop of blood trickles down my arm. I wipe it away quickly. I had to struggle with Aaron back in the lab when I wanted to get out of bed and take the time machine. The only weapon to hand was a drinking glass. Last I saw, he was unconscious, blood gushing from his neck mingling with the spilt water making a rose pink stream on the floor. If he died—which was a possibility—I'd fix it with another trip through time. But first, I needed to put my own life right and get my children back.

The time machine feels cool against my chest. In my pocket is a note I wrote for my younger self for when she meets Vaughan. "If you do this, without deviating, your future will be perfect."

I take it out and look at it. Aaron's blood has smudged some of the letters. There's no time to fix it. I will give it to my young self at the party and scarper. Or perhaps I'll wait. See what happens. Make any adjustments necessary to keep things on track.

Or have I already done this once before? The party images are all mixed up in my mind.

It doesn't help that memories of my life from age eighteen to now, on the new timeline I forged, keep downloading in my head at random times.

A candlelit dinner for one.

A cat silhouetted on a fence.

Me, sitting at a desk, trying to sketch my children's faces but not being able to recall the details.

Young Vaughan shouting at me to give him some space, that I'm smothering him.

And one persistent memory of a hospital room with no windows and someone screaming. In my voice.

Everyone looks so happy arriving for the party. I can picture the tables out the back, the crystal glasses alive with moonlight, the smell of the herbs sweet in the autumn warmth.

Nicky watches me from across the road. When Vaughan appears at her shoulder, in his blue shirt—looking so handsome—she whispers to him and points my way. And he looks over at me with such an expression of disgust, it makes bile, hot and sour, surge up in my throat. After pumping hands with a couple coming in, he storms across the road.

But when he gets there, he'll find no-one behind the bottlebrush. I've already gone, blasted out of the time.

I am on my way to fix things in the past. For us, and our children. I'll put things right. We'll all be together and happier than ever—though I won't be inviting Nicky anywhere near him in future.

This time, I'll get it right.

This time, everything will be perfect.

Acknowledgements

None of this would have been possible without the support of my partner, Andy Cohen. Or my daughters, Alex and Tash, who so often helped me brainstorm ideas for the NYC Midnight competitions.

I'd also like to thank my online writing group for their encouragement and beta-ing on the stories.

And NYC Midnight without whose competitions, there would have been no torture, nor stories arising from the ashes of my meltdowns! Rock on, guys!

About the author

Paulene Turner is the author of the six-book YA series, The Time Travel Chronicles. A former journalist, she also writes short stories and novellas—some of which have appeared in anthologies and magazines in the UK, US and Australia. As well as writing short plays, she directs them for Short and Sweet, Sydney.

She lives in Sydney with her husband, twin daughters and twin pugs.

You can read more of her short stories on her website at:

www.pauleneturnerwrites.com

Or subscribe to her mailing list to keep up with news on new projects at www.pauleneturnerwrites.com

If you'd like to enter any of the NYC Midnight challenges yourself, www.nycmidnight.com

Paulene's social media contacts:

https://x.com/PauleneTurner

https://www.instagram.com/pauleneturnertimetraveller/

https://www.tiktok.com/@pauleneturnertimetravels

https://www.facebook.com/pauleneturnertimetraveller

https://www.bookbub.com/authors/paulene-turner